THE WORLD'S GREATEST DETECTIVE STORIES

THE WORLD'S GREATEST DETECTIVE STORIES

EMBASSY BOOKS
www.embassybooks.in

The World's Greatest Detective Stories

First Edition 2020

Published in India by:
Embassy Book Distributors
120, Great Western Building,
Maharashtra Chamber of Commerce Lane,
Fort, Mumbai 400 023, India
Tel: (+9122) -30967415, 22819546
Email: info@embassybooks.in
www.embassybooks.in

ISBN 978-93-89995-45-9

Layout and typesetting by Manoranjan Kumar

Printed & Bound in India by Repro India Ltd., Navi Mumbai

Contents

Agatha Christie

DAME AGATHA CHRISTIE (1890-1976) WAS AN ENGLISH AUTHOR and playwright dubbed the "Queen of Crime" for her masterful grasp on storytelling, suspense, and characterization. She wrote sixty-six novels and fourteen short story collections and is the best-selling fiction writer of all time, having sold over two billion copies of her novels.

Her most well-known character is Hercule Poirot, an eccentric Belgian detective who is incredibly astute, precise to a fault, and a remarkable judge of character, solving crimes with the use of his *"little grey cells"*, as he calls them. Poirot is often found in the company of Captain Arthur Hastings, his close friend and the chronicler of his adventures.

1

THE CHOCOLATE BOX

Agatha Christie

It was a wild night. Outside, the wind howled malevolently, and the rain beat against the windows in great gusts.

Poirot and I sat facing the hearth, our legs stretched out to the cheerful blaze. Between us was a small table. On my side of it stood some carefully brewed hot toddy; on Poirot's was a cup of thick, rich chocolate which I would not have drunk for a hundred pounds! Poirot sipped the thick brown mess in the pink china cup, and sighed with contentment.

"*Quelle belle vie*!" he murmured.

"Yes, it's a good old world," I agreed. "Here am I with a job, and a good job too! And here are you, famous—"

"Oh, *mon ami*!" protested Poirot.

"But you are. And rightly so! When I think back on your long line of successes, I am positively amazed. I don't believe you know what failure is!"

"He would be a droll kind of original who could say that!"

"No, but seriously, have you ever failed?"

"Innumerable times, my friend. What would you? *La bonne chance*, it cannot always be on your side. I have been called in too late. Very often another, working towards the same goal, has arrived there first. Twice have I been stricken down with illness just as I was on the point of success. One must take the downs with the ups, my friend."

"I didn't quite mean that," I said. "I meant, had you ever been completely down and out over a case through your own fault?"

"Ah, I comprehend! You ask if I have ever made the complete prize ass of myself, as you say over here? Once, my friend—" A slow, reflective smile hovered over his face. "Yes, once I made a fool of myself."

He sat up suddenly in his chair.

"See here, my friend, you have, I know, kept a record of my little successes. You shall add one more story to the collection, the story of a failure!"

He leaned forward and placed a log on the fire. Then, after carefully wiping his hands on a little duster that hung on a nail by the fireplace, he leaned back and commenced his story.

That of which I tell you (said M. Poirot) took place in Belgium many years ago. It was at the time of the terrible struggle in France between church and state. M. Paul Déroulard was a French deputy of note. It was an open secret that the portfolio of a Minister awaited him. He was among the bitterest of the anti-Catholic party, and it was certain that on his accession to power, he would have to face violent enmity. He was in many ways a peculiar man. Though he neither drank nor smoked, he was nevertheless not so scrupulous in other ways. You comprehend, Hastings, *c'était des femmes—toujours des femmes*!

He had married some years earlier a young lady from Brussels who had brought him a substantial dot. Undoubtedly the money was useful to him in his career, as his family was not rich, though on the other hand he was entitled to call himself M. le Baron if he chose. There were no children of the marriage, and his wife died after two years—the result of a fall downstairs. Among the property which she bequeathed to him was a house on the Avenue Louise in Brussels.

It was in this house that his sudden death took place, the event coinciding with the resignation of the Minister whose portfolio he was to inherit. All the papers printed long notices of his career. His death, which had taken place quite suddenly in the evening after dinner, was attributed to heart-failure.

At that time, *mon ami,* I was, as you know, a member of the Belgian detective force. The death of M. Paul Déroulard was not particularly interesting to me. I am, as you also know, bon catholique, and his demise seemed to me fortunate.

It was some three days afterwards, when my vacation had just begun, that I received a visitor at my own apartments—a lady, heavily veiled, but evidently quite young; and I perceived at once that she was a *jeune fille tout à fait comme il faut.*

"You are Monsieur Hercule Poirot?" she asked in a low sweet voice.

I bowed.

"Of the detective service?"

Again I bowed. "Be seated, I pray of you, mademoiselle," I said.

She accepted a chair and drew aside her veil. Her face was charming, though marred with tears, and haunted as though with some poignant anxiety.

"Monsieur," she said, "I understand that you are now taking a vacation. Therefore you will be free to take up a private case. You understand that I do not wish to call in the police."

I shook my head. "I fear what you ask is impossible, mademoiselle. Even though on vacation, I am still of the police."

She leaned forward. "*Écoutez,* monsieur. All that I ask of you is to investigate. The result of your investigations you are at perfect liberty to report to the police. If what I believe to be true is true, we shall need all the machinery of the law."

That placed a somewhat different complexion on the matter, and I placed myself at her service without more ado.

A slight colour rose in her cheeks. "I thank you, monsieur. It is the death of M. Paul Déroulard that I ask you to investigate."

"*Comment?*" I exclaimed, surprised.

"Monsieur, I have nothing to go upon—nothing but my woman's instinct, but I am convinced—convinced, I tell you—

that M. Déroulard did not die a natural death!"

"But surely the doctors—"

"Doctors may be mistaken. He was so robust, so strong. Ah, Monsieur Poirot, I beseech of you to help me—"

The poor child was almost beside herself. She would have knelt to me. I soothed her as best I could.

"I will help you, mademoiselle. I feel almost sure that your fears are unfounded, but we will see. First, I will ask you to describe to me the inmates of the house."

"There are the domestics, of course, Jeanette, Félicie, and Denise the cook. She has been there many years; the others are simple country girls. Also there is François, but he too is an old servant. Then there is Monsieur Déroulard's mother who lived with him, and myself. My name is Virginie Mesnard. I am a poor cousin of the late Madame Déroulard, M. Paul's wife, and I have been a member of their ménage for over three years. I have now described to you the household. There were also two guests staying in the house."

"And they were?"

"M. de Saint Alard, a neighbour of M. Déroulard's in France. Also an English friend, Mr. John Wilson."

"Are they still with you?"

"Mr. Wilson, yes, but M. de Saint Alard departed yesterday."

"And what is your plan, Mademoiselle Mesnard?"

"If you will present yourself at the house in half an hour's time, I will have arranged some story to account for your presence. I had better represent you to be connected with journalism in some way. I shall say you have come from Paris, and that you have brought a card of introduction from M. de Saint Alard. Madame Déroulard is very feeble in health, and will pay little attention to details."

On mademoiselle's ingenious pretext I was admitted to the house, and after a brief interview with the dead deputy's mother, who was a wonderfully imposing and aristocratic figure though obviously in failing health, I was made free of the premises.

I wonder, my friend (continued Poirot), whether you can

possibly figure to yourself the difficulties of my task? Here was a man whose death had taken place three days previously. If there had been foul play, only one possibility was admittable—poison! And I had had no chance of seeing the body, and there was no possibility of examining, or analysing, any medium in which the poison could have been administered. There were no clues, false or otherwise, to consider. Had the man been poisoned? Had he died a natural death? I, Hercule Poirot, with nothing to help me, had to decide.

First, I interviewed the domestics, and with their aid, I recapitulated the evening. I paid especial notice to the food at dinner, and the method of serving it. The soup had been served by M. Déroulard himself from a tureen. Next a dish of cutlets, then a chicken. Finally a compote of fruits. And all placed on the table, and served by Monsieur himself. The coffee was brought in a big pot to the dinner-table. Nothing there, mon ami—impossible to poison one without poisoning all!

After dinner Madame Déroulard had retired to her own apartments and Mademoiselle Virginie had accompanied her. The three men had adjourned to M. Déroulard's study. Here they had chatted amicably for some time, when suddenly, without any warning, the deputy had fallen heavily to the ground. M. de Saint Alard had rushed out and told François to fetch a doctor immediately. He said it was without doubt an apoplexy, explained the man. But when the doctor arrived, the patient was past help.

Mr. John Wilson, to whom I was presented by Mademoiselle Virginie, was what was known in those days as a regular John Bull Englishman, middle-aged and burly. His account, delivered in very British French, was substantially the same.

"Déroulard went very red in the face, and down he fell."

There was nothing further to be found out there. Next I went to the scene of the tragedy, the study, and was left alone there at my own request. So far there was nothing to support Mademoiselle Mesnard's theory. I could not but believe that it was a delusion on her part. Evidently she had entertained a romantic passion for the dead man which had not permitted her to take a normal view of the case. Nevertheless, I searched the study with meticulous care. It was just possible that a hypodermic needle might have been introduced into the dead man's chair in such a way as to allow of a fatal injection. The minute puncture it would cause was likely to remain unnoticed. But I could discover no sign to support that theory. I flung myself down in the chair with a gesture of despair.

"Enfin, I abandon it!" I said aloud. "There is not a clue anywhere! Everything is perfectly normal."

As I said the words, my eyes fell on a large box of chocolates standing on a table near by, and my heart gave a leap. It might not be a clue to M. Déroulard's death, but here at least was something that was not normal. I lifted the lid. The box was full, untouched; not a chocolate was missing—but that only made the peculiarity that had caught my eye more striking. For, see you, Hastings, while the box itself was pink, the lid was blue. Now, one often sees a blue ribbon on a pink box, and vice versa, but a box of one colour, and a lid of another—no; decidedly—*ça ne se voit jamais*!

I did not as yet see that this little incident was of any use to me, yet I determined to investigate it as being out of the ordinary. I rang the bell for François, and asked him if his late master had been fond of sweets. A faint melancholy smile came to his lips.

"Passionately fond of them, monsieur. He would always have a box of chocolates in the house. He did not drink wine of any kind, you see."

"Yet this box has not been touched?" I lifted the lid to show him.

"*Pardon,* monsieur, but that was a new box purchased on the day of his death, the other being nearly finished."

"Then the other box was finished on the day of his death," I said slowly.

"Yes, monsieur, I found it empty in the morning and threw it away."

"Did M. Déroulard eat sweets at all hours of the day?"

"Usually after dinner, monsieur."

I began to see light.

"François," I said, "you can be discreet?"

"If there is need, monsieur."

"*Bon*! Know, then, that I am of the police. Can you find me that other box?"

"Without doubt, monsieur. It will be in the dustbin."

He departed, and returned in a few minutes with a dust-covered object. It was the duplicate of the box I held, save for the fact that this time the box was blue and the lid was pink. I thanked François, recommended him once more to be discreet, and left the house in the Avenue Louise without more ado.

Next day I called upon the doctor who had attended M. Déroulard. With him I had a difficult task. He entrenched himself prettily behind a wall of learned phraseology, but I fancied that he was not quite as sure about the case as he would like to be.

"There have been many curious occurrences of the kind," he observed, when I had managed to disarm him somewhat. "A sudden fit of anger, a violent emotion—after a heavy dinner, *c'est entendu*—then, with an access of rage, the blood flies to the head, and pst!—there you are!"

"But M. Déroulard had had no violent emotion."

"No? I made sure that he had been having a stormy altercation with M. de Saint Alard."

"Why should he?"

"*C'est évident*!" The doctor shrugged his shoulders. "Was not M. de Saint Alard a Catholic of the most fanatical? Their friendship was being ruined by this question of church and state. Not a day passed without discussions. To M. de Saint Alard, Déroulard appeared almost as Antichrist."

This was unexpected, and gave me food for thought.

"One more question, Doctor: would it be possible to introduce a fatal dose of poison into a chocolate?"

"It would be possible, I suppose," said the doctor slowly. "Pure prussic acid would meet the case if there were no chance of evaporation, and a tiny globule of anything might be swallowed unnoticed—but it does not seem a very likely supposition. A chocolate full of morphine or strychnine—" He made a wry face. "You comprehend, M. Poirot—one bite would be enough! The unwary one would not stand upon ceremony."

"Thank you, M. le Docteur."

I withdrew. Next I made inquiries of the chemists, especially those in the neighbourhood of the Avenue Louise. It is good to be of the police. I got the information I wanted without any trouble. Only in one case could I hear of any poison having been supplied to the house in question. This was some eye drops of atropine sulphate for Madame Déroulard. Atropine is a potent poison, and for the moment I was elated, but the symptoms of atropine poisoning are closely allied to those of ptomaine, and bear no resemblance to those I was studying. Besides, the prescription was an old one. Madame Déroulard had suffered from cataract in both eyes for many years.

I was turning away discouraged when the chemist's voice called me back.

"*Un moment,* M. Poirot. I remember, the girl who brought that prescription, she said something about having to go on to the English chemist. You might try there."

I did. Once more enforcing my official status, I got the information I wanted. On the day before M. Déroulard's death they had made up a prescription for Mr. John Wilson. Not that there was any making up about it. They were simply little tablets of trinitrine. I asked if I might see some. He showed me them, and my heart beat faster—for the tiny tablets were of chocolate.

"It is a poison?" I asked.

"No, monsieur."

"Can you describe to me its effect?"

"It lowers the blood-pressure. It is given for some forms of heart trouble—angina pectoris for instance. It relieves the arterial tension. In arteriosclerosis—"

I interrupted him. "*Ma foi*! This rigmarole says nothing to me. Does it cause the face to flush?"

"Certainly it does."

"And supposing I ate ten—twenty of your little tablets, what then?"

"I should not advise you to attempt it," he replied drily.

"And yet you say it is not poison?"

"There are many things not called poison which can kill a man," he replied as before.

I left the shop elated. At last, things had begun to march!

I now knew that John Wilson held the means for the crime—but what about the motive? He had come to Belgium on business, and had asked M. Déroulard, whom he knew slightly, to put him up. There was apparently no way in which Déroulard's death could benefit him. Moreover, I discovered by inquiries in England that he had suffered for some years from that painful form of heart disease known as angina. Therefore he had a genuine right to have those tablets in his possession. Nevertheless, I was convinced that someone had gone to the chocolate box, opening the full one first by mistake, and had abstracted the contents of the last chocolate, cramming in instead as many little trinitrine tablets as it would hold. The chocolates were large ones. Between twenty or thirty tablets, I felt sure, could have been inserted. But who had done this?

There were two guests in the house. John Wilson had the means. Saint Alard had the motive. Remember, he was a fanatic, and there is no fanatic like a religious fanatic. Could he, by any means, have got hold of John Wilson's trinitrine?

Another little idea came to me. Ah! You smile at my little ideas! Why had Wilson run out of trinitrine? Surely he would bring an adequate supply from England. I called once more at the house in the Avenue Louise. Wilson was out, but I saw the girl who did his room, Félicie. I demanded of her immediately whether it was not true that M. Wilson had lost a bottle from his washstand some little time ago. The girl responded eagerly. It was quite true. She, Félicie, had been blamed for it. The English gentleman had evidently thought that she had broken it, and did not like to say so. Whereas she had never even touched it. Without doubt it was Jeannette—always nosing round where she had no business to be—

I calmed the flow of words, and took my leave. I knew now all that I wanted to know. It remained for me to prove my case. That, I felt, would not be easy. I might be sure that Saint Alard had removed the bottle of trinitrine from John Wilson's washstand, but to convince others, I would have to produce evidence. And I had none to produce!

Never mind. I knew—that was the great thing. You remember our difficulty in the Styles case, Hastings? There again, I knew but it took me a long time to find the last link which made my chain of evidence against the murderer complete.

I asked for an interview with Mademoiselle Mesnard. She came at once. I demanded of her the address of M. de Saint Alard. A look of trouble came over her face.

"Why do you want it, monsieur?"

"Mademoiselle, it is necessary."

She seemed doubtful—troubled.

"He can tell you nothing. He is a man whose thoughts are not in this world. He hardly notices what goes on around him."

"Possibly, mademoiselle. Nevertheless, he was an old friend of M. Déroulard's. There may be things he can tell me—things of the past—old grudges—old love-affairs."

The girl flushed and bit her lip. "As you please—but—but—I feel sure now that I have been mistaken. It was good of you to accede to my demand, but I was upset—almost distraught at the time. I see now that there is no mystery to solve. Leave it, I beg of you, monsieur."

I eyed her closely.

"Mademoiselle," I said, "it is sometimes difficult for a dog to find a scent, but once he has found it, nothing on earth will make him leave it! That is if he is a good dog! And I, mademoiselle, I, Hercule Poirot, am a very good dog."

Without a word she turned away. A few minutes later she returned with the address written on a sheet of paper. I left the house. François was waiting for me outside. He looked at me anxiously.

"There is no news, monsieur?"

"None as yet, my friend."

"Ah! *Pauvre* Monsieur Déroulard!" he sighed. "I too was of his way of thinking. I do not care for priests. Not that I would say so in the house. The women are all devout—a good thing perhaps. *Madame est très pieuse—et* Mademoiselle Virginie *aussi.*"

Mademoiselle Virginie? Was she *"très pieuse?"* Thinking of the tear-stained passionate face I had seen that first day, I wondered.

Having obtained the address of M. de Saint Alard, I wasted no time. I arrived in the neighbourhood of his *château* in the Ardennes but it was some days before I could find a pretext for gaining admission to the house. In the end I did—how do you think—as a plumber, mon ami! It was the affair of a moment to arrange a neat little gas leak in his bedroom. I departed for my tools, and took care to return with them at an hour when I knew I should have the field pretty well to myself. What I was searching for, I hardly knew. The one thing needful, I could not believe there was any chance of finding. He would never have run the risk of keeping it.

Still when I found a little cupboard above the washstand locked, I could not resist the temptation of seeing what was inside it. The lock was quite a simple one to pick. The door swung open. It was full of old bottles. I took them up one by one with a trembling hand. Suddenly, I uttered a cry. Figure to yourself, my friend, I held in my hand a little phial with an English chemist's label. On it were the words: "Trinitrine Tablets. One to be taken when required. Mr. John Wilson."

I controlled my emotion, closed the little cupboard, slipped the bottle into my pocket, and continued to repair the gas leak! One must be methodical. Then I left the *château,* and took train for my own country as soon as possible. I arrived in Brussels late that night. I was writing out a report for the préfet in the morning, when a note was brought to me. It was from old Madame Déroulard, and it summoned me to the house in the Avenue Louise without delay.

François opened the door to me.

"Madame la Baronne is awaiting you."

He conducted me to her apartments. She sat in state in a large armchair. There was no sign of Mademoiselle Virginie.

"M. Poirot," said the old lady. "I have just learned that you are not what you pretend to be. You are a police officer."

"That is so, madame."

"You came here to inquire into the circumstances of my son's death?"

Again I replied: "That is so, madame."

"I should be glad if you would tell me what progress you have made."

I hesitated.

"First I would like to know how you have learned all this, madame."

"From one who is no longer of this world."

Her words, and the brooding way she uttered them, sent a chill to my heart. I was incapable of speech.

"Wherefore, monsieur, I would beg of you most urgently to tell me exactly what progress you have made in your investigation."

"Madame, my investigation is finished."

"My son?"

"Was killed deliberately."

"You know by whom?"

"Yes, madame."

"Who, then?"

"M. de Saint Alard."

The old lady shook her head.

"You are wrong. M. de Saint Alard is incapable of such a crime."

"The proofs are in my hands."

"I beg of you once more to tell me all."

This time I obeyed, going over each step that had led me to the discovery of the truth. She listened attentively. At the end she nodded her head.

"Yes, yes, it is all as you say, all but one thing. It was not M. de Saint Alard who killed my son. It was I, his mother."

I stared at her. She continued to nod her head gently.

"It is well that I sent for you. It is the providence of the good God that Virginie told me before she departed for the convent, what she had done. Listen, M. Poirot! My son was an evil man. He persecuted the church. He led a life of mortal sin. He dragged down other souls beside his own. But there was worse than that. As I came out of my room in this house one morning, I saw my daughter-in-law standing at the head of the stairs. She was reading a letter. I saw my son steal up behind her. One swift push, and she fell, striking her head on the marble steps. When they picked her up she was dead. My son was a murderer, and only I, his mother, knew it."

She closed her eyes for a moment. "You cannot conceive, monsieur, of my agony, my despair. What was I to do? Denounce him to the police? I could not bring myself to do it. It was my duty, but my flesh was weak. Besides, would they believe me? My eyesight had been failing for some time—they would say I was mistaken. I kept silence. But my conscience gave me no peace. By keeping silence I too was a murderer. My son inherited his wife's money. He flourished as the green bay tree. And now he was to have a Minister's portfolio. His persecution of the church would be redoubled. And there was Virginie. She, poor child, beautiful, naturally pious, was fascinated by him. He had a strange and terrible power over women. I saw it coming. I was powerless to prevent it. He had no intention of marrying her. The time came when she was ready to yield everything to him.

"Then I saw my path clear. He was my son. I had given him life. I was responsible for him. He had killed one woman's body, now he would kill another's soul! I went to Mr. Wilson's room, and took the bottle of tablets. He had once said laughingly that there were enough in it to kill a man! I went into the study and opened the big box of chocolates that always stood on the table. I opened a new box by mistake. The other was on the table also. There was just one chocolate left in it. That simplified things.

No one ate chocolates except my son and Virginie. I would keep her with me that night. All went as I had planned—"

She paused, closing her eyes a minute then opened them again.

"M. Poirot, I am in your hands. They tell me I have not many days to live. I am willing to answer for my action before the good God. Must I answer for it on earth also?"

I hesitated. "But the empty bottle, madame," I said to gain time. "How came that into M. de Saint Alard's possession?"

"When he came to say goodbye to me, monsieur, I slipped it into his pocket. I did not know how to get rid of it. I am so infirm that I cannot move about much without help, and finding it empty in my rooms might have caused suspicion. You understand, monsieur -" she drew herself up to her full height—"it was with no idea of casting suspicion on M. de Saint Alard! I never dreamed of such a thing. I thought his valet would find an empty bottle and throw it away without question."

I bowed my head. "I comprehend, madame," I said.

"And your decision, monsieur?"

Her voice was firm and unfaltering, her head held as high as ever. I rose to my feet.

"Madame," I said, "I have the honour to wish you good day. I have made my investigations—and failed! The matter is closed."

He was silent for a moment, then said quietly: "She died just a week later. Mademoiselle Virginie passed through her novitiate, and duly took the veil. That, my friend, is the story. I must admit that I do not make a fine figure in it."

"But that was hardly a failure," I expostulated. "What else could you have thought under the circumstances?"

"Ah, *sacré, mon ami,*" cried Poirot, becoming suddenly animated. "Is it that you do not see? But I was thirty-six times an idiot! My grey cells, they functioned not at all. The whole time I had the true clue in my hands."

"What clue?"

"The chocolate box! Do you not see? Would anyone in possession of their full eyesight make such a mistake? I knew

Madame Déroulard had cataract—the atropine drops told me that. There was only one person in the household whose eyesight was such that she could not see which lid to replace. It was the chocolate box that started me on the track, and yet up to the end I failed consistently to perceive its real significance!

"Also my psychology was at fault. Had M. de Saint Alard been the criminal, he would never have kept an incriminating bottle. Finding it was a proof of his innocence. I had learned already from Mademoiselle Virginie that he was absent-minded. Altogether it was a miserable affair that I have recounted to you there! Only to you have I told the story. You comprehend, I do not figure well in it! An old lady commits a crime in such a simple and clever fashion that I, Hercule Poirot, am completely deceived. *Sapristi*! It does not bear thinking of! Forget it. Or no—remember it, and if you think at any time that I am growing conceited—it is not likely, but it might arise."

I concealed a smile.

"Eh bien, my friend, you shall say to me, 'Chocolate box'. Is it agreed?"

"It's a bargain!"

"After all," said Poirot reflectively, "it was an experience! I, who have undoubtedly the finest brain in Europe at present, can afford to be magnanimous!"

"Chocolate box," I murmured gently.

"*Pardon, mon ami?*"

I looked at Poirot's innocent face, as he bent forward inquiringly, and my heart smote me. I had suffered often at his hands, but I, too, though not possessing the finest brain in Europe, could afford to be magnanimous!

"Nothing," I lied, and lit another pipe, smiling to myself.

Anna Katherine Green

ANNA KATHERINE GREEN (1846-1935) WAS AN AMERICAN author and poet who was one of the first writers of detective fiction. In 1878, she wrote her first novel, *The Leavenworth Case,* which was an iconic murder mystery. The book was critically acclaimed and became an instant bestseller, allowing her to pursue writing as a career and write over 40 novels during her life.

She invented the trope of the "girl detective" with her female amateur sleuth Violet Strange, a high-society debutante hired by Joshua Burke, head of a leading detective firm, who spots her investigative talents and gives her a chance to prove herself.

2

THE SECOND BULLET

Anna Katherine Green

"YOU MUST SEE HER."

"No. No."

"She's a most unhappy woman. Husband and child both taken from her in a moment; and now, all means of living as well, unless some happy thought of yours—some inspiration of your genius—shows us a way of re-establishing her claims to the policy voided by this cry of suicide."

But the small wise head of Violet Strange continued its slow shake of decided refusal.

"I'm sorry," she protested, "but it's quite out of my province. I'm too young to meddle with so serious a matter."

"Not when you can save a bereaved woman the only possible compensation left her by untoward fate?"

"Let the police try their hand at that."

"They have had no success with the case."

"Or you?"

"Nor I either."

"And you expect—"

"Yes, Miss Strange. I expect you to find the missing bullet which will settle the fact that murder and not suicide ended George Hammond's life. If you cannot, then a long litigation awaits this poor widow, ending, as such litigation usually does, in favour of the stronger party. There's the alternative. If you once saw her—"

"But that's what I'm not willing to do. If I once saw her I should yield to her importunities and attempt the seemingly impossible. My instincts bid me say no. Give me something easier."

"Easier things are not so remunerative. There's money in this affair, if the insurance company is forced to pay up. I can offer you—"

"What?"

There was eagerness in the tone despite her effort at nonchalance. The other smiled imperceptibly, and briefly named the sum.

It was larger than she had expected. This her visitor saw by the way her eyelids fell and the peculiar stillness which, for an instant, held her vivacity in check.

"And you think I can earn that?"

Her eyes were fixed on his in an eagerness as honest as it was unrestrained.

He could hardly conceal his amazement, her desire was so evident and the cause of it so difficult to understand. He knew she wanted money—that was her avowed reason for entering into this uncongenial work. But to want it so much! He glanced at her person; it was simply clad but very expensively—how expensively it was his business to know. Then he took in the room in which they sat. Simplicity again, but the simplicity of high art—the drawing-room of one rich enough to indulge in the final luxury of a highly cultivated taste, viz.: unostentatious elegance and the subjection of each carefully chosen ornament to the general effect.

What did this favoured child of fortune lack that she could be reached by such a plea, when her whole being revolted from the nature of the task he offered her? It was a question not new to him; but one he had never heard answered and was not likely to hear answered now. But the fact remained that the consent he had thought dependent upon sympathetic interest could be reached much more readily by the promise of large emolument, and he owned to a feeling of secret disappointment even while he recognized the value of the discovery.

But his satisfaction in the latter, if satisfaction it were, was of very short duration. Almost immediately he observed a change in her. The sparkle which had shone in the eye whose depths he had never been able to penetrate, had dissipated itself in something like a tear and she spoke up in that vigorous tone no one but himself had ever heard, as she said:

"No. The sum is a good one and I could use it; but I will not waste my energy on a case I do not believe in. The man shot himself. He was a speculator, and probably had good reason for his act. Even his wife acknowledges that he has lately had more losses than gains."

"See her. She has something to tell you which never got into the papers."

"You say that? You know that?"

"On my honour, Miss Strange."

Violet pondered; then suddenly succumbed.

"Let her come, then. Prompt to the hour. I will receive her at three. Later I have a tea and two party calls to make."

Her visitor rose to leave. He had been able to subdue all evidence of his extreme gratification, and now took on a formal air. In dismissing a guest, Miss Strange was invariably the society belle and that only. This he had come to recognize.

The case (well known at the time) was, in the fewest possible words, as follows:

On a sultry night in September, a young couple living in one of the large apartment houses in the extreme upper portion of Manhattan were so annoyed by the incessant crying of a child in the adjoining suite, that they got up, he to smoke, and she to sit in the window for a possible breath of cool air. They were congratulating themselves upon the wisdom they had shown in thus giving up all thought of sleep—for the child's crying had not ceased—when (it may have been two o'clock and it may have been a little later) there came from somewhere near, the sharp and somewhat peculiar detonation of a pistol-shot.

He thought it came from above; she, from the rear, and they were staring at each other in the helpless wonder of the moment, when they were struck by the silence. The baby had ceased to cry. All was as still in the adjoining apartment as in their own—too still—much too still. Their mutual stare turned to one of horror. "It came from there!" whispered the wife. "Some accident has occurred to Mr. or Mrs. Hammond—we ought to go—"

Her words—very tremulous ones—were broken by a shout from below. They were standing in their window and had evidently been seen by a passing policeman. "Anything wrong up there?" they heard him cry. Mr. Saunders immediately looked out. "Nothing wrong here," he called down. (They were but two stories from the pavement.) "But I'm not so sure about the rear apartment. We thought we heard a shot. Hadn't you better come up, officer? My wife is nervous about it. I'll meet you at the stair-head and show you the way."

The officer nodded and stepped in. The young couple hastily donned some wraps, and, by the time he appeared on their floor, they were ready to accompany him.

Meanwhile, no disturbance was apparent anywhere else in the house, until the policeman rang the bell of the Hammond apartment. Then, voices began to be heard, and doors to open above and below, but not the one before which the policeman stood.

Another ring, and this time an insistent one;—and still no response. The officer's hand was rising for the third time when there came a sound of fluttering from behind the panels against which he had laid his ear, and finally a choked voice uttering unintelligible words. Then a hand began to struggle with the lock, and the door, slowly opening, disclosed a woman clad in a hastily donned wrapper and giving every evidence of extreme fright.

"Oh!" she exclaimed, seeing only the compassionate faces of her neighbours. "You heard it, too! a pistol-shot from there—

there—my husband's room. I have not dared to go—I—I—O, have mercy and see if anything is wrong! It is so still—so still, and only a moment ago the baby was crying. Mrs. Saunders, Mrs. Saunders, why is it so still?"

She had fallen into her neighbour's arms. The hand with which she had pointed out a certain door had sunk to her side and she appeared to be on the verge of collapse.

The officer eyed her sternly, while noting her appearance, which was that of a woman hastily risen from bed.

"Where were you?" he asked. "Not with your husband and child, or you would know what had happened there."

"I was sleeping down the hall," she managed to gasp out. "I'm not well—I—Oh, why do you all stand still and do nothing? My baby's in there. Go! go!" and, with sudden energy, she sprang upright, her eyes wide open and burning, her small well featured face white as the linen she sought to hide.

The officer demurred no longer. In another instant he was trying the door at which she was again pointing.

It was locked.

Glancing back at the woman, now cowering almost to the floor, he pounded at the door and asked the man inside to open.

No answer came back.

With a sharp turn he glanced again at the wife.

"You say that your husband is in this room?"

She nodded, gasping faintly, "And the child!"

He turned back, listened, then beckoned to Mr. Saunders. "We shall have to break our way in," said he. "Put your shoulder well to the door. Now!"

The hinges of the door creaked; the lock gave way (this special officer weighed two hundred and seventy-five, as he found out, next day), and a prolonged and sweeping crash told the rest.

Mrs. Hammond gave a low cry; and, straining forward from where she crouched in terror on the floor, searched the faces of the two men for some hint of what they saw in the dimly-lighted space beyond. Something dreadful, something which made Mr.

Saunders come rushing back with a shout:

"Take her away! Take her to our apartment, Jennie. She must not see—"

Not see! He realized the futility of his words as his gaze fell on the young woman who had risen up at his approach and now stood gazing at him without speech, without movement, but with a glare of terror in her eyes, which gave him his first realization of human misery.

His own glance fell before it. If he had followed his instinct he would have fled the house rather than answer the question of her look and the attitude of her whole frozen body.

Perhaps in mercy to his speechless terror, perhaps in mercy to herself, she was the one who at last found the word which voiced their mutual anguish.

"Dead?"

No answer. None was needed.

"And my baby?"

O, that cry! It curdled the hearts of all who heard it. It shook the souls of men and women both inside and outside the apartment; then all was forgotten in the wild rush she made. The wife and mother had flung herself upon the scene, and, side by side with the not unmoved policeman, stood looking down upon the desolation made in one fatal instant in her home and heart.

They lay there together, both past help, both quite dead. The child had simply been strangled by the weight of his father's arm which lay directly across the upturned little throat. But the father was a victim of the shot they had heard. There was blood on his breast, and a pistol in his hand.

Suicide! The horrible truth was patent. No wonder they wanted to hold the young widow back. Her neighbour, Mrs. Saunders, crept in on tiptoe and put her arms about the swaying, fainting woman; but there was nothing to say—absolutely nothing.

At least, they thought not. But when they saw her throw herself down, not by her husband, but by the child, and drag it out from under that strangling arm and hug and kiss it and call out wildly for a doctor, the officer endeavoured to interfere and yet could not find the heart to do so, though he knew the child was dead and should not, according to all the rules of the coroner's office, be moved before that official arrived. Yet because no mother could be convinced of a fact like this, he let her sit with it on the floor and try all her little arts to revive it, while he gave orders to the janitor and waited himself for the arrival of doctor and coroner.

She was still sitting there in wide-eyed misery, alternately fondling the little body and drawing back to consult its small set features for some sign of life, when the doctor came, and, after one look at the child, drew it softly from her arms and laid it quietly in the crib from which its father had evidently lifted it but a short time before. Then he turned back to her, and found her on her feet, upheld by her two friends. She had understood his action, and without a groan had accepted her fate. Indeed, she seemed incapable of any further speech or action. She was staring down at her husband's body, which she, for the first time, seemed fully to see. Was her look one of grief or of resentment for the part he had played so unintentionally in her child's death? It was hard to tell; and when, with slowly rising finger, she pointed to the pistol so tightly clutched in the other outstretched hand, no one there—and by this time the room was full—could foretell what her words would be when her tongue regained its usage and she could speak.

What she did say was this:

"Is there a bullet gone? Did he fire off that pistol?" A question so manifestly one of delirium that no one answered it, which seemed to surprise her, though she said nothing till her glance had passed all around the walls of the room to where a window stood open to the night, its lower sash being entirely raised. "There! look there!" she cried, with a commanding accent, and, throwing up her hands, sank a dead weight into the arms of those supporting her.

No one understood; but naturally more than one rushed to

the window. An open space was before them. Here lay the fields not yet parcelled out into lots and built upon; but it was not upon these they looked, but upon the strong trellis which they found there, which, if it supported no vine, formed a veritable ladder between this window and the ground.

Could she have meant to call attention to this fact; and were her words expressive of another idea than the obvious one of suicide?

If so, to what lengths a woman's imagination can go! Or so their combined looks seemed to proclaim, when to their utter astonishment they saw the officer, who had presented a calm appearance up till now, shift his position and with a surprised grunt direct their eyes to a portion of the wall just visible beyond the half-drawn curtains of the bed. The mirror hanging there showed a star-shaped breakage, such as follows the sharp impact of a bullet or a fiercely projected stone.

"He fired two shots. One went wild; the other straight home."

It was the officer delivering his opinion.

Mr. Saunders, returning from the distant room where he had assisted in carrying Mrs. Hammond, cast a look at the shattered glass, and remarked forcibly:

"I heard but one; and I was sitting up, disturbed by that poor infant. Jennie, did you hear more than one shot?" he asked, turning toward his wife.

"No," she answered, but not with the readiness he had evidently expected. "I heard only one, but that was not quite usual in its tone. I'm used to guns," she explained, turning to the officer. "My father was an army man, and he taught me very early to load and fire a pistol. There was a prolonged sound to this shot; something like an echo of itself, following close upon the first ping. Didn't you notice that, Warren?"

"I remember something of the kind," her husband allowed.

"He shot twice and quickly," interposed the policeman, sententiously. "We shall find a spent bullet back of that mirror."

But when, upon the arrival of the coroner, an investigation

was made of the mirror and the wall behind, no bullet was found either there or any where else in the room, save in the dead man's breast. Nor had more than one been shot from his pistol, as five full chambers testified. The case which seemed so simple had its mysteries, but the assertion made by Mrs. Saunders no longer carried weight, nor was the evidence offered by the broken mirror considered as indubitably establishing the fact that a second shot had been fired in the room.

Yet it was equally evident that the charge which had entered the dead speculator's breast had not been delivered at the close range of the pistol found clutched in his hand. There were no powder-marks to be discerned on his pajama-jacket, or on the flesh beneath. Thus anomaly confronted anomaly, leaving open but one other theory: that the bullet found in Mr. Hammond's breast came from the window and the one he shot went out of it. But this would necessitate his having shot his pistol from a point far removed from where he was found; and his wound was such as made it difficult to believe that he would stagger far, if at all, after its infliction.

Yet, because the coroner was both conscientious and alert, he caused a most rigorous search to be made of the ground overlooked by the above mentioned window; a search in which the police joined, but which was without any result save that of rousing the attention of people in the neighbourhood and leading to a story being circulated of a man seen some time the night before crossing the fields in a great hurry. But as no further particulars were forthcoming, and not even a description of the man to be had, no emphasis would have been laid upon this story had it not transpired that the moment a report of it had come to Mrs. Hammond's ears (why is there always some one to carry these reports?) she roused from the torpor into which she had fallen, and in wild fashion exclaimed:

"I knew it! I expected it! He was shot through the window and by that wretch. He never shot himself." Violent declarations which trailed off into the one continuous wail, "O, my baby! my poor baby!"

Such words, even though the fruit of delirium, merited some sort of attention, or so this good coroner thought, and as soon as opportunity offered and she was sufficiently sane and quiet to respond to his questions, he asked her whom she had meant by that wretch, and what reason she had, or thought she had, of attributing her husband's death to any other agency than his own disgust with life.

And then it was that his sympathies, although greatly roused in her favour began to wane. She met the question with a cold stare followed by a few ambiguous words out of which he could make nothing. Had she said wretch? She did not remember. They must not be influenced by anything she might have uttered in her first grief. She was well-nigh insane at the time. But of one thing they might be sure: her husband had not shot himself; he was too much afraid of death for such an act. Besides, he was too happy. Whatever folks might say he was too fond of his family to wish to leave it.

Nor did the coroner or any other official succeed in eliciting anything further from her. Even when she was asked, with cruel insistence, how she explained the fact that the baby was found lying on the floor instead of in its crib, her only answer was: "His father was trying to soothe it. The child was crying dreadfully, as you have heard from those who were kept awake by him that night, and my husband was carrying him about when the shot came which caused George to fall and overlay the baby in his struggles."

"Carrying a baby about with a loaded pistol in his hand?" came back in stern retort.

She had no answer for this. She admitted when informed that the bullet extracted from her husband's body had been found to correspond exactly with those remaining in the five chambers of the pistol taken from his hand, that he was not only the owner of this pistol but was in the habit of sleeping with it under his pillow; but, beyond that, nothing; and this reticence, as well as her manner which was cold and repellent, told against her.

A verdict of suicide was rendered by the coroner's jury,

and the life-insurance company, in which Mr. Hammond had but lately insured himself for a large sum, taking advantage of the suicide clause embodied in the policy, announced its determination of not paying the same.

Such was the situation, as known to Violet Strange and the general public, on the day she was asked to see Mrs. Hammond and learn what might alter her opinion as to the justice of this verdict and the stand taken by the Shuler Life Insurance Company.

The clock on the mantel in Miss Strange's rose-coloured boudoir had struck three, and Violet was gazing in some impatience at the door, when there came a gentle knock upon it, and the maid (one of the elderly, not youthful, kind) ushered in her expected visitor.

"You are Mrs. Hammond?" she asked, in natural awe of the too black figure outlined so sharply against the deep pink of the sea-shell room.

The answer was a slow lifting of the veil which shadowed the features she knew only from the cuts she had seen in newspapers.

"You are—Miss Strange?" stammered her visitor; "the young lady who—"

"I am," chimed in a voice as ringing as it was sweet. "I am the person you have come here to see. And this is my home. But that does not make me less interested in the unhappy, or less desirous of serving them. Certainly you have met with the two greatest losses which can come to a woman—I know your story well enough to say that—; but what have you to tell me in proof that you should not lose your anticipated income as well? Something vital, I hope, else I cannot help you; something which you should have told the coroner's jury—and did not."

The flush which was the sole answer these words called forth did not take from the refinement of the young widow's expression, but rather added to it; Violet watched it in its ebb and flow and, seriously affected by it (why, she did not know, for Mrs. Hammond had made no other appeal either by look or gesture), pushed forward a chair and begged her visitor to be seated.

"We can converse in perfect safety here," she said. "When you feel quite equal to it, let me hear what you have to communicate. It will never go any further. I could not do the work I do if I felt it necessary to have a confidant."

"But you are so young and so—so—"

"So inexperienced you would say and so evidently a member of what New Yorkers call 'society.' Do not let that trouble you. My inexperience is not likely to last long and my social pleasures are more apt to add to my efficiency than to detract from it."

With this Violet's face broke into a smile. It was not the brilliant one so often seen upon her lips, but there was something in its quality which carried encouragement to the widow and led her to say with obvious eagerness:

"You know the facts?"

"I have read all the papers."

"I was not believed on the stand."

"It was your manner—"

"I could not help my manner. I was keeping something back, and, being unused to deceit, I could not act quite naturally."

"Why did you keep something back? When you saw the unfavourable impression made by your reticence, why did you not speak up and frankly tell your story?"

"Because I was ashamed. Because I thought it would hurt me more to speak than to keep silent. I do not think so now; but I did then—and so made my great mistake. You must remember not only the awful shock of my double loss, but the sense of guilt accompanying it; for my husband and I had quarreled that night, quarreled bitterly—that was why I had run away into another room and not because I was feeling ill and impatient of the baby's fretful cries."

"So people have thought." In saying this, Miss Strange was perhaps cruelly emphatic. "You wish to explain that quarrel? You think it will be doing any good to your cause to go into that matter with me now?"

"I cannot say; but I must first clear my conscience and then try to convince you that quarrel or no quarrel, he never took his own life. He was not that kind. He had an abnormal fear of death. I do not like to say it but he was a physical coward. I have seen him turn pale at the least hint of danger. He could no more have turned that muzzle upon his own breast than he could have turned it upon his baby. Some other hand shot him, Miss Strange. Remember the open window, the shattered mirror; and I think I know that hand."

Her head had fallen forward on her breast. The emotion she showed was not so eloquent of grief as of deep personal shame.

"You think you know the man?" In saying this, Violet's voice sunk to a whisper. It was an accusation of murder she had just heard.

"To my great distress, yes. When Mr. Hammond and I were married," the widow now proceeded in a more determined tone, "there was another man—a very violent one—who vowed even at the church door that George and I should never live out two full years together. We have not. Our second anniversary would have been in November."

"But—"

"Let me say this: the quarrel of which I speak was not serious enough to occasion any such act of despair on his part. A man would be mad to end his life on account of so slight a disagreement. It was not even on account of the person of whom I've just spoken, though that person had been mentioned between us earlier in the evening, Mr. Hammond having come across him face to face that very afternoon in the subway. Up to this time neither of us had seen or heard of him since our wedding-day."

"And you think this person whom you barely mentioned, so mindful of his old grudge that he sought out your domicile, and, with the intention of murder, climbed the trellis leading to your room and turned his pistol upon the shadowy figure which was all he could see in the semi-obscurity of a much lowered gas-jet?"

"A man in the dark does not need a bright light to see his

enemy when he is intent upon revenge."

Miss Strange altered her tone.

"And your husband? You must acknowledge that he shot off his pistol whether the other did or not."

"It was in self-defence. He would shoot to save his own life—or the baby's."

"Then he must have heard or seen—"

"A man at the window."

"And would have shot there?"

"Or tried to."

"Tried to?"

"Yes; the other shot first—oh, I've thought it all out—causing my husband's bullet to go wild. It was his which broke the mirror."

Violet's eyes, bright as stars, suddenly narrowed.

"And what happened then?" she asked. "Why cannot they find the bullet?"

"Because it went out of the window;—glanced off and went out of the window."

Mrs. Hammond's tone was triumphant; her look spirited and intense.

Violet eyed her compassionately.

"Would a bullet glancing off from a mirror, however hung, be apt to reach a window so far on the opposite side?"

"I don't know; I only know that it did," was the contradictory, almost absurd, reply.

"What was the cause of the quarrel you speak of between your husband and yourself? You see, I must know the exact truth and all the truth to be of any assistance to you."

"It was—it was about the care I gave, or didn't give, the baby. I feel awfully to have to say it, but George did not think I did my full duty by the child. He said there was no need of its crying so; that if I gave it the proper attention it would not keep the neighbours and himself awake half the night. And I—I got angry and insisted that I did the best I could; that the child was naturally fretful and that if he wasn't satisfied with my way of looking after it, he might try his. All of which was very wrong and unreasonable on my part, as witness the awful punishment which followed."

"And what made you get up and leave him?"

"The growl he gave me in reply. When I heard that, I bounded out of bed and said I was going to the spare room to sleep; and if the baby cried he might just try what he could do himself to stop it."

"And he answered?"

"This, just this—I shall never forget his words as long as I live—'If you go, you need not expect me to let you in again no matter what happens.'"

"He said that?"

"And locked the door after me. You see I could not tell all that."

"It might have been better if you had. It was such a natural quarrel and so unprovocative of actual tragedy."

Mrs. Hammond was silent. It was not difficult to see that she had no very keen regrets for her husband personally. But then he was not a very estimable man nor in any respect her equal.

"You were not happy with him," Violet ventured to remark.

"I was not a fully contented woman. But for all that he had no cause to complain of me except for the reason I have mentioned. I was not a very intelligent mother. But if the baby were living now—O, if he were living now—with what devotion I should care for him."

She was on her feet, her arms were raised, her face impassioned with feeling. Violet, gazing at her, heaved a little sigh. It was perhaps in keeping with the situation, perhaps extraneous to it, but whatever its source, it marked a change in her manner. With no further check upon her sympathy, she said very softly:

"It is well with the child."

The mother stiffened, swayed, and then burst into wild weeping.

"But not with me," she cried, "not with me. I am desolate and bereft. I have not even a home in which to hide my grief and no prospect of one."

"But," interposed Violet, "surely your husband left you something? You cannot be quite penniless?"

"My husband left nothing," was the answer, uttered without bitterness, but with all the hardness of fact. "He had debts. I shall pay those debts. When these and other necessary expenses are liquidated, there will be but little left. He made no secret of the fact that he lived close up to his means. That is why he was induced to take on a life insurance. Not a friend of his but knows his improvidence. I—I have not even jewels. I have only my determination and an absolute conviction as to the real nature of my husband's death."

"What is the name of the man you secretly believe to have shot your husband from the trellis?"

Mrs. Hammond told her.

It was a new one to Violet. She said so and then asked:

"What else can you tell me about him?"

"Nothing, but that he is a very dark man and has a club-foot."

"Oh, what a mistake you've made."

"Mistake? Yes, I acknowledge that."

"I mean in not giving this last bit of information at once to the police. A man can be identified by such a defect. Even his footsteps can be traced. He might have been found that very day. Now, what have we to go upon?"

"You are right, but not expecting to have any difficulty about the insurance money I thought it would be generous in me to keep still. Besides, this is only surmise on my part. I feel certain that my husband was shot by another hand than his own, but I know of no way of proving it. Do you?"

Then Violet talked seriously with her, explaining how their only hope lay in the discovery of a second bullet in the room which had already been ransacked for this very purpose and without the shadow of a result.

A tea, a musicale, and an evening dance kept Violet Strange in a whirl for the remainder of the day. No brighter eye nor more contagious wit lent brilliance to these occasions, but with the passing of the midnight hour no one who had seen her in the blaze of electric lights would have recognized this favoured child of fortune in the earnest figure sitting in the obscurity of an up-town apartment, studying the walls, the ceilings, and the floors by the dim light of a lowered gas-jet. Violet Strange in society was a very different person from Violet Strange under the tension of her secret and peculiar work.

She had told them at home that she was going to spend the night with a friend; but only her old coachman knew who that friend was. Therefore a very natural sense of guilt mingled with her emotions at finding herself alone on a scene whose gruesome mystery she could solve only by identifying herself with the place and the man who had perished there.

Dismissing from her mind all thought of self, she strove to think as he thought, and act as he acted on the night when he found himself (a man of but little courage) left in this room with an ailing child.

At odds with himself, his wife, and possibly with the child screaming away in its crib, what would he be apt to do in his present emergency? Nothing at first, but as the screaming continued he would remember the old tales of fathers walking the floor at night with crying babies, and hasten to follow suit. Violet, in her anxiety to reach his inmost thought, crossed to where the crib had stood, and, taking that as a start, began pacing the room in search of the spot from which a bullet, if shot, would glance aside from the mirror in the direction of the window. (Not that she was ready to accept this theory of Mrs. Hammond, but that she did not wish to entirely dismiss it without putting it to the test.)

She found it in an unexpected quarter of the room and much nearer the bed-head than where his body was found. This, which might seem to confuse matters, served, on the contrary to remove from the case one of its most serious difficulties.

Standing here, he was within reach of the pillow under which his pistol lay hidden, and if startled, as his wife believed him to have been by a noise at the other end of the room, had but to crouch and reach behind him in order to find himself armed and ready for a possible intruder.

Imitating his action in this as in other things, she had herself crouched low at the bedside and was on the point of withdrawing her hand from under the pillow, when a new surprise checked her movement and held her fixed in her position, with eyes staring straight at the adjoining wall. She had seen there what he must have seen in making this same turn—the dark bars of the opposite window-frame outlined in the mirror—and understood at once what had happened. In the nervousness and terror of the moment, George Hammond had mistaken this reflection of the window for the window itself, and shot impulsively at the man he undoubtedly saw covering him from the trellis without. But while this explained the shattering of the mirror, how about the other and still more vital question, of where the bullet went afterward? Was the angle at which it had been fired acute enough to send it out of a window diagonally opposed? No; even if the pistol had been held closer to the man firing it than she had reason to believe, the angle still would be oblique enough to carry it on to the further wall.

But no sign of any such impact had been discovered on this wall. Consequently, the force of the bullet had been expended before reaching it, and when it fell—

Here, her glance, slowly traveling along the floor, impetuously paused. It had reached the spot where the two bodies had been found, and unconsciously her eyes rested there, conjuring up the picture of the bleeding father and the strangled child. How piteous and how dreadful it all was. If she could only understand—Suddenly she rose straight up, staring and immovable in the dim light. Had the idea—the explanation—the only possible explanation covering the whole phenomena come to her at last?

It would seem so, for as she so stood, a look of conviction

settled over her features, and with this look, evidences of a horror which for all her fast accumulating knowledge of life and its possibilities made her appear very small and very helpless.

A half-hour later, when Mrs. Hammond, in her anxiety at hearing nothing more from Miss Strange, opened the door of her room, it was to find, lying on the edge of the sill, the little detective's card with these words hastily written across it:

I do not feel as well as I could wish, and so have telephoned to my own coachman to come and take me home. I will either see or write you within a few days. But do not allow yourself to hope. I pray you do not allow yourself the least hope; the outcome is still very problematical.

When Violet's employer entered his office the next morning it was to find a veiled figure awaiting him which he at once recognized as that of his little deputy. She was slow in lifting her veil and when it finally came free he felt a momentary doubt as to his wisdom in giving her just such a matter as this to investigate. He was quite sure of his mistake when he saw her face, it was so drawn and pitiful.

"You have failed," said he.

"Of that you must judge," she answered; and drawing near she whispered in his ear.

"No!" he cried in his amazement.

"Think," she murmured, "think. Only so can all the facts be accounted for."

"I will look into it; I will certainly look into it," was his earnest reply. "If you are right—But never mind that. Go home and take a horseback ride in the Park. When I have news in regard to this I will let you know. Till then forget it all. Hear me, I charge you to forget everything but your balls and your parties."

And Violet obeyed him.

Some few days after this, the following statement appeared in all the papers:

"Owing to some remarkable work done by the firm of — & —, the well-known private detective agency, the claim made by Mrs. George Hammond against the Shuler Life Insurance Company is likely to be allowed without further litigation. As our readers will remember, the contestant has insisted from the first that the bullet causing her husband's death came from another pistol than the one found clutched in his own hand. But while reasons were not lacking to substantiate this assertion, the failure to discover more than the disputed track of a second bullet led to a verdict of suicide, and a refusal of the company to pay.

"But now that bullet has been found. And where? In the most startling place in the world, viz.: in the larynx of the child found lying dead upon the floor beside his father, strangled as was supposed by the weight of that father's arm. The theory is, and there seems to be none other, that the father, hearing a suspicious noise at the window, set down the child he was endeavouring to soothe and made for the bed and his own pistol, and, mistaking a reflection of the assassin for the assassin himself, sent his shot sidewise at a mirror just as the other let go the trigger which drove a similar bullet into his breast. The course of the one was straight and fatal and that of the other deflected. Striking the mirror at an oblique angle, the bullet fell to the floor where it was picked up by the crawling child, and, as was most natural, thrust at once into his mouth. Perhaps it felt hot to the little tongue; perhaps the child was simply frightened by some convulsive movement of the father who evidently spent his last moment in an endeavour to reach the child, but, whatever the cause, in the quick gasp it gave, the bullet was drawn into the larynx, strangling him.

"That the father's arm, in his last struggle, should have fallen directly across the little throat is one of those anomalies which confounds reason and misleads justice by stopping

investigation at the very point where truth lies and mystery disappears.

"Mrs. Hammond is to be congratulated that there are detectives who do not give too much credence to outward appearances."

We expect soon to hear of the capture of the man who sped home the death-dealing bullet.

G. K. Chesterton

G. K. CHESTERTON (1874-1936) WAS AN ENGLISH WRITER, philosopher, and literary critic. He produced a vast amount of work during his lifetime — over 4,000 essays, 200 short stories, and 80 books.

His contributions to the detective fiction genre took the form of Father Brown, a Roman Catholic priest-detective who appeared in over 50 of Chesterton's short stories. Father Brown is rational, witty, and an uncannily good judge of character; preferring to solve crimes using his intuition rather than Holmesian deductive reasoning.

3

THE HAMMER OF GOD

G. K. Chesterton

THE LITTLE VILLAGE OF BOHUN BEACON WAS PERCHED ON A HILL so steep that the tall spire of its church seemed only like the peak of a small mountain. At the foot of the church stood a smithy, generally red with fires and always littered with hammers and scraps of iron; opposite to this, over a rude cross of cobbled paths, was "The Blue Boar," the only inn of the place. It was upon this crossway, in the lifting of a leaden and silver daybreak, that two brothers met in the street and spoke; though one was beginning the day and the other finishing it. The Rev. and Hon. Wilfred Bohun was very devout, and was making his way to some austere exercises of prayer or contemplation at dawn. Colonel the Hon. Norman Bohun, his elder brother, was by no means devout, and was sitting in evening dress on the bench outside "The Blue Boar," drinking what the philosophic observer was free to regard either as his last glass on Tuesday or his first on Wednesday. The colonel was not particular.

The Bohuns were one of the very few aristocratic families really dating from the Middle Ages, and their pennon had actually seen Palestine. But it is a great mistake to suppose that such houses stand high in chivalric tradition. Few except the poor preserve traditions. Aristocrats live not in traditions but in fashions. The Bohuns had been Mohocks under Queen Anne and Mashers under Queen Victoria. But like more than one of the really ancient houses, they had rotted in the last two centuries into mere drunkards and dandy degenerates, till there had even come a whisper of insanity. Certainly there was something hardly human about the colonel's wolfish pursuit of pleasure, and his chronic resolution not to go home till morning had a touch of the hideous clarity of insomnia. He was a tall, fine animal, elderly, but with hair still startlingly yellow. He would have looked merely blonde and leonine, but his blue eyes were sunk so deep in his face that they looked black. They were a little too close together. He had very long yellow moustaches; on each side of them a fold or furrow from nostril to jaw, so that a sneer seemed cut into his face. Over his evening clothes he wore a curious pale yellow coat that looked more like a very light dressing gown than an overcoat, and on the back of his head was stuck an extraordinary broad-brimmed hat of a bright green colour, evidently some oriental curiosity caught up at random. He was proud of appearing in such incongruous attires—proud of the fact that he always made them look congruous.

His brother the curate had also the yellow hair and the elegance, but he was buttoned up to the chin in black, and his face was clean-shaven, cultivated, and a little nervous. He seemed to live for nothing but his religion; but there were some who said (notably the blacksmith, who was a Presbyterian) that it was a love of Gothic architecture rather than of God, and that his haunting of the church like a ghost was only another and purer turn of the almost morbid thirst for beauty which sent his brother raging after women and wine. This charge was doubtful, while the man's practical piety was indubitable. Indeed, the charge was mostly an ignorant misunderstanding of the love of solitude and secret prayer, and was founded on his being often found kneeling, not before the altar, but in peculiar places, in the crypts or gallery, or even in the belfry. He was at the moment about to enter the church through the yard of the smithy, but stopped and frowned a little as he saw his brother's cavernous eyes staring in the same direction. On the hypothesis that the colonel was interested in the church he did not waste any speculations. There only remained the blacksmith's shop, and though the blacksmith was a Puritan and none of his people, Wilfred Bohun had heard some scandals about a beautiful and rather celebrated wife. He flung a suspicious look across the shed, and the colonel stood up laughing to speak to him.

"Good morning, Wilfred," he said. "Like a good landlord I am watching sleeplessly over my people. I am going to call on the blacksmith."

Wilfred looked at the ground, and said: "The blacksmith is out. He is over at Greenford."

"I know," answered the other with silent laughter; "that is why I am calling on him."

"Norman," said the cleric, with his eye on a pebble in the road, "are you ever afraid of thunderbolts?"

"What do you mean?" asked the colonel. "Is your hobby meteorology?"

"I mean," said Wilfred, without looking up, "do you ever think that God might strike you in the street?"

"I beg your pardon," said the colonel; "I see your hobby is folk-lore."

"I know your hobby is blasphemy," retorted the religious man, stung in the one live place of his nature. "But if you do not fear God, you have good reason to fear man."

The elder raised his eyebrows politely. "Fear man?" he said.

"Barnes the blacksmith is the biggest and strongest man for forty miles round," said the clergyman sternly. "I know you are no coward or weakling, but he could throw you over the wall."

This struck home, being true, and the lowering line by mouth and nostril darkened and deepened. For a moment he stood with the heavy sneer on his face. But in an instant Colonel Bohun had recovered his own cruel good humour and laughed, showing two dog-like front teeth under his yellow moustache. "In that case, my dear Wilfred," he said quite carelessly, "it was wise for the last of the Bohuns to come out partially in armour."

And he took off the queer round hat covered with green, showing that it was lined within with steel. Wilfred recognised it indeed as a light Japanese or Chinese helmet torn down from a trophy that hung in the old family hall.

"It was the first hat to hand," explained his brother airily; "always the nearest hat—and the nearest woman."

"The blacksmith is away at Greenford," said Wilfred quietly; "the time of his return is unsettled."

And with that he turned and went into the church with bowed head, crossing himself like one who wishes to be quit of an unclean spirit. He was anxious to forget such grossness in the cool twilight of his tall Gothic cloisters; but on that morning it was fated that his still round of religious exercises should be everywhere arrested by small shocks. As he entered the church, hitherto always empty at that hour, a kneeling figure rose hastily to its feet and came towards the full daylight of the doorway. When the curate saw it he stood still with surprise. For the early worshipper was none other than the village idiot, a nephew of the blacksmith, one who neither would nor could care for the church or for anything else. He was always called "Mad Joe," and seemed to have no other name; he was a dark, strong, slouching lad, with a heavy white face, dark straight hair, and a mouth always open. As he passed the priest, his moon-calf countenance gave no hint of what he had been doing or thinking of. He had never been known to pray before. What sort of prayers was he saying now? Extraordinary prayers surely.

Wilfred Bohun stood rooted to the spot long enough to see the idiot go out into the sunshine, and even to see his dissolute brother hail him with a sort of avuncular jocularity. The last thing he saw was the colonel throwing pennies at the open mouth of Joe, with the serious appearance of trying to hit it.

This ugly sunlit picture of the stupidity and cruelty of the earth sent the ascetic finally to his prayers for purification and new thoughts. He went up to a pew in the gallery, which brought him under a coloured window which he loved and always quieted his spirit; a blue window with an angel carrying lilies. There he began to think less about the half-wit, with his livid face and mouth like a fish. He began to think less of his evil brother, pacing like a lean lion in his horrible hunger. He sank deeper and deeper into those cold and sweet colours of silver blossoms and sapphire sky.

In this place half an hour afterwards he was found by Gibbs, the village cobbler, who had been sent for him in some haste. He got to his feet with promptitude, for he knew that no small matter would have brought Gibbs into such a place at all. The cobbler was, as in many villages, an atheist, and his appearance in church was a shade more extraordinary than Mad Joe's. It was a morning of theological enigmas.

"What is it?" asked Wilfred Bohun rather stiffly, but putting out a trembling hand for his hat.

The atheist spoke in a tone that, coming from him, was quite startlingly respectful, and even, as it were, huskily sympathetic.

"You must excuse me, sir," he said in a hoarse whisper, "but we didn't think it right not to let you know at once. I'm afraid a rather dreadful thing has happened, sir. I'm afraid your brother—"

Wilfred clenched his frail hands. "What devilry has he done now?" he cried in voluntary passion.

"Why, sir," said the cobbler, coughing, "I'm afraid he's done nothing, and won't do anything. I'm afraid he's done for. You had really better come down, sir."

The curate followed the cobbler down a short winding stair which brought them out at an entrance rather higher than the street. Bohun saw the tragedy in one glance, flat underneath him like a plan. In the yard of the smithy were standing five or six men mostly in black, one in an inspector's uniform. They included the doctor, the Presbyterian minister, and the priest from the Roman Catholic chapel, to which the blacksmith's wife belonged. The latter was speaking to her, indeed, very rapidly, in an undertone, as she, a magnificent woman with red-gold hair, was sobbing blindly on a bench. Between these two groups, and just clear of the main heap of hammers, lay a man in evening dress, spread-eagled and flat on his face. From the height above Wilfred could have sworn to every item of his costume and appearance, down to the Bohun rings upon his fingers; but the skull was only a hideous splash, like a star of blackness and blood.

Wilfred Bohun gave but one glance, and ran down the steps into the yard. The doctor, who was the family physician, saluted him, but he scarcely took any notice. He could only stammer out: "My brother is dead. What does it mean? What is this horrible mystery?" There was an unhappy silence; and then the cobbler, the most outspoken man present, answered: "Plenty of horror, sir," he said; "but not much mystery."

"What do you mean?" asked Wilfred, with a white face.

"It's plain enough," answered Gibbs. "There is only one man for forty miles round that could have struck such a blow as that, and he's the man that had most reason to."

"We must not prejudge anything," put in the doctor, a tall, black-bearded man, rather nervously; "but it is competent for me to corroborate what Mr. Gibbs says about the nature of the blow, sir; it is an incredible blow. Mr. Gibbs says that only one man in this district could have done it. I should have said myself that nobody could have done it."

A shudder of superstition went through the slight figure of the curate. "I can hardly understand," he said.

"Mr. Bohun," said the doctor in a low voice, "metaphors literally fail me. It is inadequate to say that the skull was smashed to bits like an eggshell. Fragments of bone were driven into the body and the ground like bullets into a mud wall. It was the hand of a giant."

He was silent a moment, looking grimly through his glasses; then he added: "The thing has one advantage—that it clears most people of suspicion at one stroke. If you or I or any normally made man in the country were accused of this crime, we should be acquitted as an infant would be acquitted of stealing the Nelson column."

"That's what I say," repeated the cobbler obstinately; "there's only one man that could have done it, and he's the man that would have done it. Where's Simeon Barnes, the blacksmith?"

"He's over at Greenford," faltered the curate.

"More likely over in France," muttered the cobbler.

"No; he is in neither of those places," said a small and colourless voice, which came from the little Roman priest who had joined the group. "As a matter of fact, he is coming up the road at this moment."

The little priest was not an interesting man to look at, having stubbly brown hair and a round and stolid face. But if he had been as splendid as Apollo no one would have looked at him at that moment. Everyone turned round and peered at the pathway which wound across the plain below, along which was indeed walking, at his own huge stride and with a hammer on his shoulder, Simeon the smith. He was a bony and gigantic man, with deep, dark, sinister eyes and a dark chin beard. He was walking and talking quietly with two other men; and though he was never specially cheerful, he seemed quite at his ease.

"My God!" cried the atheistic cobbler, "and there's the hammer he did it with."

"No," said the inspector, a sensible-looking man with a sandy moustache, speaking for the first time. "There's the hammer he did it with over there by the church wall. We have left it and the body exactly as they are."

All glanced round and the short priest went across and looked down in silence at the tool where it lay. It was one of the smallest and the lightest of the hammers, and would not have caught the eye among the rest; but on the iron edge of it were blood and yellow hair.

After a silence the short priest spoke without looking up, and there was a new note in his dull voice. "Mr. Gibbs was hardly right," he said, "in saying that there is no mystery. There is at least the mystery of why so big a man should attempt so big a blow with so little a hammer."

"Oh, never mind that," cried Gibbs, in a fever. "What are we to do with Simeon Barnes?"

"Leave him alone," said the priest quietly. "He is coming

here of himself. I know those two men with him. They are very good fellows from Greenford, and they have come over about the Presbyterian chapel."

Even as he spoke the tall smith swung round the corner of the church, and strode into his own yard. Then he stood there quite still, and the hammer fell from his hand. The inspector, who had preserved impenetrable propriety, immediately went up to him.

"I won't ask you, Mr. Barnes," he said, "whether you know anything about what has happened here. You are not bound to say. I hope you don't know, and that you will be able to prove it. But I must go through the form of arresting you in the King's name for the murder of Colonel Norman Bohun."

"You are not bound to say anything," said the cobbler in officious excitement. "They've got to prove everything. They haven't proved yet that it is Colonel Bohun, with the head all smashed up like that."

"That won't wash," said the doctor aside to the priest. "That's out of the detective stories. I was the colonel's medical man, and I knew his body better than he did. He had very fine hands, but quite peculiar ones. The second and third fingers were the same length. Oh, that's the colonel right enough."

As he glanced at the brained corpse upon the ground the iron eyes of the motionless blacksmith followed them and rested there also.

"Is Colonel Bohun dead?" said the smith quite calmly. "Then he's damned."

"Don't say anything! Oh, don't say anything," cried the atheist cobbler, dancing about in an ecstasy of admiration of the English legal system. For no man is such a legalist as the good Secularist.

The blacksmith turned on him over his shoulder the august face of a fanatic.

"It's well for you infidels to dodge like foxes because the world's law favours you," he said; "but God guards His own in His pocket, as you shall see this day."

Then he pointed to the colonel and said: "When did this dog die in his sins?"

"Moderate your language," said the doctor.

"Moderate the Bible's language, and I'll moderate mine. When did he die?"

"I saw him alive at six o'clock this morning," stammered Wilfred Bohun.

"God is good," said the smith. "Mr. Inspector, I have not the slightest objection to being arrested. It is you who may object to arresting me. I don't mind leaving the court without a stain on my character. You do mind perhaps leaving the court with a bad set-back in your career."

The solid inspector for the first time looked at the blacksmith with a lively eye; as did everybody else, except the short, strange priest, who was still looking down at the little hammer that had dealt the dreadful blow.

"There are two men standing outside this shop," went on the blacksmith with ponderous lucidity, "good tradesmen in Greenford whom you all know, who will swear that they saw me from before midnight till daybreak and long after in the committee room of our Revival Mission, which sits all night, we save souls so fast. In Greenford itself twenty people could swear to me for all that time. If I were a heathen, Mr. Inspector, I would let you walk on to your downfall. But as a Christian man I feel bound to give you your chance, and ask you whether you will hear my alibi now or in court."

The inspector seemed for the first time disturbed, and said, "Of course I should be glad to clear you altogether now."

The smith walked out of his yard with the same long and easy stride, and returned to his two friends from Greenford, who were indeed friends of nearly everyone present. Each of them said a few words which no one ever thought of disbelieving. When they had spoken, the innocence of Simeon stood up as solid as the great church above them.

One of those silences struck the group which are more strange and insufferable than any speech. Madly, in order to make conversation, the curate said to the Catholic priest:

"You seem very much interested in that hammer, Father Brown."

"Yes, I am," said Father Brown; "why is it such a small hammer?"

The doctor swung round on him.

"By George, that's true," he cried; "who would use a little hammer with ten larger hammers lying about?"

Then he lowered his voice in the curate's ear and said: "Only the kind of person that can't lift a large hammer. It is not a question of force or courage between the sexes. It's a question of lifting power in the shoulders. A bold woman could commit ten murders with a light hammer and never turn a hair. She could not kill a beetle with a heavy one."

Wilfred Bohun was staring at him with a sort of hypnotised horror, while Father Brown listened with his head a little on one side, really interested and attentive. The doctor went on with more hissing emphasis:

"Why do these idiots always assume that the only person who hates the wife's lover is the wife's husband? Nine times out of ten the person who most hates the wife's lover is the wife. Who knows what insolence or treachery he had shown her—look there!"

He made a momentary gesture towards the red-haired woman on the bench. She had lifted her head at last and the tears were drying on her splendid face. But the eyes were fixed on the corpse with an electric glare that had in it something of idiocy.

The Rev. Wilfred Bohun made a limp gesture as if waving away all desire to know; but Father Brown, dusting off his sleeve some ashes blown from the furnace, spoke in his indifferent way.

"You are like so many doctors," he said; "your mental science is really suggestive. It is your physical science that is utterly impossible. I agree that the woman wants to kill the co-respondent much more than the petitioner does. And I agree that a woman will always pick up a small hammer instead of a big one. But the difficulty is one of physical impossibility. No woman ever born could have smashed a man's skull out flat like that." Then he added reflectively, after a pause: "These people haven't grasped the whole of it. The man was actually wearing an iron helmet, and the blow scattered it like broken glass. Look at that woman. Look at her arms."

Silence held them all up again, and then the doctor said rather sulkily: "Well, I may be wrong; there are objections to everything. But I stick to the main point. No man but an idiot would pick up that little hammer if he could use a big hammer."

With that the lean and quivering hands of Wilfred Bohun went up to his head and seemed to clutch his scanty yellow hair. After an instant they dropped, and he cried: "That was the word I wanted; you have said the word."

Then he continued, mastering his discomposure: "The words you said were, 'No man but an idiot would pick up the small hammer.'"

"Yes," said the doctor. "Well?"

"Well," said the curate, "no man but an idiot did." The rest stared at him with eyes arrested and riveted, and he went on in a febrile and feminine agitation.

"I am a priest," he cried unsteadily, "and a priest should be no shedder of blood. I—I mean that he should bring no one to the gallows. And I thank God that I see the criminal clearly now—because he is a criminal who cannot be brought to the gallows."

"You will not denounce him?" inquired the doctor.

"He would not be hanged if I did denounce him," answered Wilfred with a wild but curiously happy smile. "When I went into the church this morning I found a madman praying there—that poor Joe, who has been wrong all his life. God knows what he prayed; but with such strange folk it is not incredible to suppose that their prayers are all upside down. Very likely a lunatic would pray before killing a man. When I last saw poor Joe he was with my brother. My brother was mocking him."

"By Jove!" cried the doctor, "this is talking at last. But how do you explain—"

The Rev. Wilfred was almost trembling with the excitement

of his own glimpse of the truth. "Don't you see; don't you see," he cried feverishly; "that is the only theory that covers both the queer things, that answers both the riddles. The two riddles are the little hammer and the big blow. The smith might have struck the big blow, but would not have chosen the little hammer. His wife would have chosen the little hammer, but she could not have struck the big blow. But the madman might have done both. As for the little hammer—why, he was mad and might have picked up anything. And for the big blow, have you never heard, doctor, that a maniac in his paroxysm may have the strength of ten men?"

The doctor drew a deep breath and then said, "By golly, I believe you've got it."

Father Brown had fixed his eyes on the speaker so long and steadily as to prove that his large grey, ox-like eyes were not quite so insignificant as the rest of his face. When silence had fallen he said with marked respect: "Mr. Bohun, yours is the only theory yet propounded which holds water every way and is essentially unassailable. I think, therefore, that you deserve to be told, on my positive knowledge, that it is not the true one." And with that the old little man walked away and stared again at the hammer.

"That fellow seems to know more than he ought to," whispered the doctor peevishly to Wilfred. "Those popish priests are deucedly sly."

"No, no," said Bohun, with a sort of wild fatigue. "It was the lunatic. It was the lunatic."

The group of the two clerics and the doctor had fallen away from the more official group containing the inspector and the man he had arrested. Now, however, that their own party had broken up, they heard voices from the others. The priest looked up quietly and then looked down again as he heard the blacksmith say in a loud voice:

"I hope I've convinced you, Mr. Inspector. I'm a strong man, as you say, but I couldn't have flung my hammer bang here from Greenford. My hammer hasn't got wings that it should come flying half a mile over hedges and fields."

The inspector laughed amicably and said: "No, I think you can be considered out of it, though it's one of the rummiest coincidences I ever saw. I can only ask you to give us all the assistance you can in finding a man as big and strong as yourself. By George! you might be useful, if only to hold him! I suppose you yourself have no guess at the man?"

"I may have a guess," said the pale smith, "but it is not at a man." Then, seeing the scared eyes turn towards his wife on the bench, he put his huge hand on her shoulder and said: "Nor a woman either."

"What do you mean?" asked the inspector jocularly. "You don't think cows use hammers, do you?"

"I think no thing of flesh held that hammer," said the blacksmith in a stifled voice; "mortally speaking, I think the man died alone."

Wilfred made a sudden forward movement and peered at him with burning eyes.

"Do you mean to say, Barnes," came the sharp voice of the cobbler, "that the hammer jumped up of itself and knocked the man down?"

"Oh, you gentlemen may stare and snigger," cried Simeon; "you clergymen who tell us on Sunday in what a stillness the Lord smote Sennacherib. I believe that One who walks invisible in every house defended the honour of mine, and laid the defiler dead before the door of it. I believe the force in that blow was just the force there is in earthquakes, and no force less."

Wilfred said, with a voice utterly undescribable: "I told Norman myself to beware of the thunderbolt."

"That agent is outside my jurisdiction," said the inspector with a slight smile.

"You are not outside His," answered the smith; "see you to it," and, turning his broad back, he went into the house.

The shaken Wilfred was led away by Father Brown, who had an easy and friendly way with him. "Let us get out of this horrid place, Mr. Bohun," he said. "May I look inside your church? I hear it's one of the oldest in England. We take some interest, you know," he added with a comical grimace, "in old English churches."

Wilfred Bohun did not smile, for humour was never his strong point. But he nodded rather eagerly, being only too ready to explain the Gothic splendours to someone more likely to be sympathetic than the Presbyterian blacksmith or the atheist cobbler.

"By all means," he said; "let us go in at this side." And he led the way into the high side entrance at the top of the flight of steps. Father Brown was mounting the first step to follow him when he felt a hand on his shoulder, and turned to behold the dark, thin figure of the doctor, his face darker yet with suspicion.

"Sir," said the physician harshly, "you appear to know some secrets in this black business. May I ask if you are going to keep them to yourself?"

"Why, doctor," answered the priest, smiling quite pleasantly, "there is one very good reason why a man of my trade should keep things to himself when he is not sure of them, and that is that it is so constantly his duty to keep them to himself when he is sure of them. But if you think I have been discourteously reticent with you or anyone, I will go to the extreme limit of my custom. I will give you two very large hints."

"Well, sir?" said the doctor gloomily.

"First," said Father Brown quietly, "the thing is quite in your own province. It is a matter of physical science. The blacksmith is mistaken, not perhaps in saying that the blow was divine, but certainly in saying that it came by a miracle. It was no miracle, doctor, except in so far as man is himself a miracle, with his strange and wicked and yet half-heroic heart. The force that smashed that skull was a force well known to scientists—one of the most frequently debated of the laws of nature."

The doctor, who was looking at him with frowning intentness, only said: "And the other hint?"

"The other hint is this," said the priest. "Do you remember the blacksmith, though he believes in miracles, talking scornfully of the impossible fairy tale that his hammer had wings and flew half a mile across country?"

"Yes," said the doctor, "I remember that."

"Well," added Father Brown, with a broad smile, "that fairy tale was the nearest thing to the real truth that has been said today." And with that he turned his back and stumped up the steps after the curate.

The Reverend Wilfred, who had been waiting for him, pale and impatient, as if this little delay were the last straw for his nerves, led him immediately to his favourite corner of the church, that part of the gallery closest to the carved roof and lit by the wonderful window with the angel. The little Latin priest explored and admired everything exhaustively, talking cheerfully but in a low voice all the time. When in the course of his investigation he found the side exit and the winding stair down which Wilfred had rushed to find his brother dead, Father Brown ran not down but up, with the agility of a monkey, and his clear voice came from an outer platform above.

"Come up here, Mr. Bohun," he called. "The air will do you good."

Bohun followed him, and came out on a kind of stone gallery or balcony outside the building, from which one could see the illimitable plain in which their small hill stood, wooded away to the purple horizon and dotted with villages and farms. Clear and square, but quite small beneath them, was the blacksmith's yard, where the inspector still stood taking notes and the corpse still lay like a smashed fly.

"Might be the map of the world, mightn't it?" said Father Brown.

"Yes," said Bohun very gravely, and nodded his head.

Immediately beneath and about them the lines of the Gothic building plunged outwards into the void with a sickening swiftness akin to suicide. There is that element of Titan energy in the architecture of the Middle Ages that, from whatever aspect it be seen, it always seems to be rushing away, like the strong back of some maddened horse. This church was hewn out of ancient and silent stone, bearded with old fungoids and stained with the nests of birds. And yet, when they saw it from below, it sprang like a fountain at the stars; and when they saw it, as now, from above, it poured like a cataract into a voiceless pit. For these two men on the tower were left alone with the most terrible aspect of Gothic; the monstrous foreshortening and disproportion, the dizzy perspectives, the glimpses of great things small and small things great; a topsy-turvydom of stone in the mid-air. Details of stone, enormous by their proximity, were relieved against a pattern of fields and farms, pygmy in their distance. A carved bird or beast at a corner seemed like some vast walking or flying dragon wasting the pastures and villages below. The whole atmosphere was dizzy and dangerous, as if men were upheld in air amid the gyrating wings of colossal genii; and the whole of that old church, as tall and rich as a cathedral, seemed to sit upon the sunlit country like a cloudburst.

"I think there is something rather dangerous about standing on these high places even to pray," said Father Brown. "Heights were made to be looked at, not to be looked from."

"Do you mean that one may fall over," asked Wilfred.

"I mean that one's soul may fall if one's body doesn't," said the other priest.

"I scarcely understand you," remarked Bohun indistinctly.

"Look at that blacksmith, for instance," went on Father Brown calmly; "a good man, but not a Christian—hard, imperious, unforgiving. Well, his Scotch religion was made up by men who prayed on hills and high crags, and learnt to look down on the world more than to look up at heaven. Humility is the mother of giants. One sees great things from the valley; only small things from the peak."

"But he—he didn't do it," said Bohun tremulously.

"No," said the other in an odd voice; "we know he didn't do it."

After a moment he resumed, looking tranquilly out over the plain with his pale grey eyes. "I knew a man," he said, "who began by worshipping with others before the altar, but who grew fond of high and lonely places to pray from, corners or niches in the belfry or the spire. And once in one of those dizzy places, where the whole world seemed to turn under him like a wheel, his brain turned also, and he fancied he was God. So that, though he was a good man, he committed a great crime."

Wilfred's face was turned away, but his bony hands turned blue and white as they tightened on the parapet of stone.

"He thought it was given to him to judge the world and strike down the sinner. He would never have had such a thought if he had been kneeling with other men upon a floor. But he saw all men walking about like insects. He saw one especially strutting just below him, insolent and evident by a bright green hat—a poisonous insect."

Rooks cawed round the corners of the belfry; but there was no other sound till Father Brown went on.

"This also tempted him, that he had in his hand one of the most awful engines of nature; I mean gravitation, that mad and quickening rush by which all earth's creatures fly back to her heart when released. See, the inspector is strutting just below us in the smithy. If I were to toss a pebble over this parapet it would be something like a bullet by the time it struck him. If I were to drop a hammer—even a small hammer—"

Wilfred Bohun threw one leg over the parapet, and Father Brown had him in a minute by the collar.

"Not by that door," he said quite gently; "that door leads to hell."

Bohun staggered back against the wall, and stared at him with frightful eyes.

"How do you know all this?" he cried. "Are you a devil?"

"I am a man," answered Father Brown gravely; "and therefore have all devils in my heart. Listen to me," he said after a short pause. "I know what you did—at least, I can guess the great part of it. When you left your brother you were racked with no unrighteous rage, to the extent even that you snatched up a small hammer, half inclined to kill him with his foulness on his mouth. Recoiling, you thrust it under your buttoned coat instead, and rushed into the church. You pray wildly in many places, under the angel window, upon the platform above, and a higher platform still, from which you could see the colonel's Eastern hat like the back of a green beetle crawling about. Then something snapped in your soul, and you let God's thunderbolt fall."

Wilfred put a weak hand to his head, and asked in a low voice: "How did you know that his hat looked like a green beetle?"

"Oh, that," said the other with the shadow of a smile, "that was common sense. But hear me further. I say I know all this; but no one else shall know it. The next step is for you; I shall take no more steps; I will seal this with the seal of confession. If you ask me why, there are many reasons, and only one that concerns you. I leave things to you because you have not yet gone very far wrong, as assassins go. You did not help to fix the crime on the smith when it was easy; or on his wife, when that was easy. You tried to fix it on the imbecile because you knew that he could not suffer. That was one of the gleams that it is my business to find in assassins. And now come down into the village, and go your own way as free as the wind; for I have said my last word."

They went down the winding stairs in utter silence, and came out into the sunlight by the smithy. Wilfred Bohun carefully unlatched the wooden gate of the yard, and going up to the inspector, said: "I wish to give myself up; I have killed my brother."

Ernest Bramah

ERNEST BRAMAH (1868-1942) WAS A NOTORIOUSLY RECLUSIVE English author whose work spanned various genres, including detective fiction, political fiction, and the supernatural. His most famous creation was Kai Lung, an educated Chinese storyteller who chronicled the series of misadventures he often found himself in.

Bramah's other famous creation was Max Carrados, a wealthy, refined blind detective and numismatist who specializes in forgeries. The Carrados stories were written alongside Doyle's Sherlock Holmes stories in the *Strand* magazine.

4

THE COIN OF DIONYSIUS

Ernest Bramah

IT WAS EIGHT O'CLOCK AT NIGHT AND RAINING, SCARCELY A TIME when a business so limited in its clientele as that of a coin dealer could hope to attract any customer, but a light was still showing in the small shop that bore over its window the name of Baxter, and in the even smaller office at the back the proprietor himself sat reading the latest *Pall Mall.* His enterprise seemed to be justified, for presently the door bell gave its announcement, and throwing down his paper Mr. Baxter went forward.

As a matter of fact the dealer had been expecting someone and his manner as he passed into the shop was unmistakably suggestive of a caller of importance. But at the first glance towards his visitor the excess of deference melted out of his bearing, leaving the urbane, self-possessed shopman in the presence of the casual customer.

"Mr. Baxter, I think?" said the latter. He had laid aside his dripping umbrella and was unbuttoning overcoat and coat to reach an inner pocket. "You hardly remember me, I suppose? Mr. Carlyle—two years ago I took up a case for you—"

"To be sure. Mr. Carlyle, the private detective—"

"Inquiry agent," corrected Mr. Carlyle precisely.

"Well," smiled Mr. Baxter, "for that matter I am a coin dealer and not an antiquarian or a numismatist. Is there anything in that way that I can do for you?"

"Yes," replied his visitor; "it is my turn to consult you." He had taken a small wash-leather bag from the inner pocket and now turned something carefully out upon the counter. "What can you tell me about that?"

The dealer gave the coin a moment's scrutiny.

"There is no question about this," he replied. "It is a Sicilian tetradrachm of Dionysius."

"Yes, I know that—I have it on the label out of the cabinet. I can tell you further that it's supposed to be one that Lord Seastoke gave two hundred and fifty pounds for at the Brice sale in '94."

"It seems to me that you can tell me more about it than I can tell you," remarked Mr. Baxter. "What is it that you really want to know?"

"I want to know," replied Mr. Carlyle, "whether it is genuine or not."

"Has any doubt been cast upon it?"

"Certain circumstances raised a suspicion—that is all."

The dealer took another look at the tetradrachm through his magnifying glass, holding it by the edge with the careful touch of an expert. Then he shook his head slowly in a confession of ignorance.

"Of course I could make a guess—"

"No, don't," interrupted Mr. Carlyle hastily. "An arrest hangs on it and nothing short of certainty is any good to me."

"Is that so, Mr. Carlyle?" said Mr. Baxter, with increased interest. "Well, to be quite candid, the thing is out of my line. Now if it was a rare Saxon penny or a doubtful noble I'd stake my reputation on my opinion, but I do very little in the classical series."

Mr. Carlyle did not attempt to conceal his disappointment as he returned the coin to the bag and replaced the bag in the inner pocket.

"I had been relying on you," he grumbled reproachfully. "Where on earth am I to go now?"

"There is always the British Museum."

"Ah, to be sure, thanks. But will anyone who can tell me be there now?"

"Now? No fear!" replied Mr. Baxter. "Go round in the morning—"

"But I must know to-night," explained the visitor, reduced to despair again. "To-morrow will be too late for the purpose."

Mr. Baxter did not hold out much encouragement in the circumstances.

"You can scarcely expect to find anyone at business now," he remarked. "I should have been gone these two hours myself only I happened to have an appointment with an American millionaire who fixed his own time." Something indistinguishable from a wink slid off Mr. Baxter's right eye. "Offmunson he's called, and a bright young pedigree-hunter has traced his descent from Offa, King of Mercia. So he—quite naturally—wants a set of Offas as a sort of collateral proof."

"Very interesting," murmured Mr. Carlyle, fidgeting with his watch. "I should love an hour's chat with you about your millionaire customers—some other time. Just now—look here, Baxter, can't you give me a line of introduction to some dealer in this sort of thing who happens to live in town? You must know dozens of experts."

"Why, bless my soul, Mr. Carlyle, I don't know a man of them away from his business," said Mr. Baxter, staring. "They may live in Park Lane or they may live in Petticoat Lane for all I know. Besides, there aren't so many experts as you seem to imagine. And the two best will very likely quarrel over it. You've had to do with 'expert witnesses,' I suppose?"

"I don't want a witness; there will be no need to give evidence. All I want is an absolutely authoritative pronouncement that I can act on. Is there no one who can really say whether the thing is genuine or not?"

Mr. Baxter's meaning silence became cynical in its implication as he continued to look at his visitor across the counter. Then he relaxed.

"Stay a bit; there is a man—an amateur—I remember hearing wonderful things about some time ago. They say he really does know."

"There you are," explained Mr. Carlyle, much relieved. "There always is someone. Who is he?"

"Funny name," replied Baxter. "Something Wynn or Wynn something." He craned his neck to catch sight of an important motor-car that was drawing to the kerb before his window. "Wynn Carrados! You'll excuse me now, Mr. Carlyle, won't you? This looks like Mr. Offmunson."

Mr. Carlyle hastily scribbled the name down on his cuff.

"Wynn Carrados, right. Where does he live?"

"Haven't the remotest idea," replied Baxter, referring the arrangement of his tie to the judgment of the wall mirror. "I have never seen the man myself. Now, Mr. Carlyle, I'm sorry I can't do any more for you. You won't mind, will you?"

Mr. Carlyle could not pretend to misunderstand. He enjoyed the distinction of holding open the door for the transatlantic representative of the line of Offa as he went out, and then made his way through the muddy streets back to his office. There was only one way of tracing a private individual at such short notice—through the pages of the directories, and the gentleman did not flatter himself by a very high estimate of his chances.

Fortune favoured him, however. He very soon discovered a Wynn Carrados living at Richmond, and, better still, further search failed to unearth another. There was, apparently, only one householder at all events of that name in the neighbourhood of London. He jotted down the address and set out for Richmond.

The house was some distance from the station, Mr. Carlyle learned. He took a taxicab and drove, dismissing the vehicle at the gate. He prided himself on his power of observation and the accuracy of his deductions which resulted from it—a detail of his business. "It's nothing more than using one's eyes and putting two and two together," he would modestly declare, when he wished to be deprecatory rather than impressive. By the time he had reached the front door of "The Turrets" he had formed some opinion of the position and tastes of the people who lived there.

A man-servant admitted Mr. Carlyle and took his card—his private card, with the bare request for an interview that would not detain Mr. Carrados for ten minutes. Luck still favoured him; Mr. Carrados was at home and would see him at once. The servant, the hall through which they passed, and the room into which he was shown, all contributed something to the deductions which the quietly observant gentleman was half unconsciously recording.

"Mr. Carlyle," announced the servant.

The room was a library or study. The only occupant, a man of about Carlyle's own age, had been using a typewriter up to the moment of his visitor's entrance. He now turned and stood up with an expression of formal courtesy.

"It's very good of you to see me at this hour," apologised Mr. Carlyle.

The conventional expression of Mr. Carrados's face changed a little.

"Surely my man has got your name wrong?" he explained. "Isn't it Louis Calling?"

Mr. Carlyle stopped short and his agreeable smile gave place to a sudden flash of anger or annoyance.

"No sir," he replied stiffly. "My name is on the card which you have before you."

"I beg your pardon," said Mr. Carrados, with perfect good-humour. "I hadn't seen it. But I used to know a Calling some years ago—at St. Michael's."

"St. Michael's!" Mr. Carlyle's features underwent another change, no less instant and sweeping than before. "St. Michael's! Wynn Carrados? Good heavens! it isn't Max Wynn—old 'Winning' Wynn"?

"A little older and a little fatter—yes," replied Carrados. "I have changed my name you see."

"Extraordinary thing meeting like this," said his visitor, dropping into a chair and staring hard at Mr. Carrados. "I have changed more than my name. How did you recognize me?"

"The voice," replied Carrados. "It took me back to that little smoke-dried attic den of yours where we—"

"My God!" exclaimed Carlyle bitterly, "don't remind me of what we were going to do in those days." He looked round the well-furnished, handsome room and recalled the other signs of wealth that he had noticed. "At all events, you seem fairly comfortable, Wynn."

"I am alternately envied and pitied," replied Carrados, with a placid tolerance of circumstance that seemed characteristic of him. "Still, as you say, I am fairly comfortable."

"Envied, I can understand. But why are you pitied?"

"Because I am blind," was the tranquil reply.

"Blind!" exclaimed Mr. Carlyle, using his own eyes superlatively. "Do you mean—literally blind?"

"Literally.... I was riding along a bridle-path through a wood about a dozen years ago with a friend. He was in front. At one point a twig sprang back—you know how easily a thing like that happens. It just flicked my eye—nothing to think twice about."

"And that blinded you?"

"Yes, ultimately. It's called amaurosis."

"I can scarcely believe it. You seem so sure and self-reliant. Your eyes are full of expression—only a little quieter than they used to be. I believe you were typing when I came....Aren't you having me?"

"You miss the dog and the stick?" smiled Carrados. "No; it's a fact."

"What an awful affliction for you, Max. You were always such an impulsive, reckless sort of fellow—never quiet. You must miss such a fearful lot."

"Has anyone else recognized you?" asked Carrados quietly.

"Ah, that was the voice, you said," replied Carlyle.

"Yes; but other people heard the voice as well. Only I had no blundering, self-confident eyes to be hoodwinked."

"That's a rum way of putting it," said Carlyle. "Are your ears never hoodwinked, may I ask?"

"Not now. Nor my fingers. Nor any of my other senses that

have to look out for themselves."

"Well, well," murmured Mr. Carlyle, cut short in his sympathetic emotions. "I'm glad you take it so well. Of course, if you find it an advantage to be blind, old man—" He stopped and reddened. "I beg your pardon," he concluded stiffly.

"Not an advantage perhaps," replied the other thoughtfully. "Still it has compensations that one might not think of. A new world to explore, new experiences, new powers awakening; strange new perceptions; life in the fourth dimension. But why do you beg my pardon, Louis?"

"I am an ex-solicitor, struck off in connexion with the falsifying of a trust account, Mr. Carrados," replied Carlyle, rising.

"Sit down, Louis," said Carrados suavely. His face, even his incredibly living eyes, beamed placid good-nature. "The chair on which you will sit, the roof above you, all the comfortable surroundings to which you have so amiably alluded, are the direct result of falsifying a trust account. But do I call you 'Mr. Carlyle' in consequence? Certainly not, Louis."

"I did not falsify the account," cried Carlyle hotly. He sat down however, and added more quietly: "But why do I tell you all this? I have never spoken of it before."

"Blindness invites confidence," replied Carrados. "We are out of the running—human rivalry ceases to exist. Besides, why shouldn't you? In my case the account *was* falsified."

"Of course that's all bunkum, Max" commented Carlyle. "Still, I appreciate your motive."

"Practically everything I possess was left to me by an American cousin, on the condition that I took the name of Carrados. He made his fortune by an ingenious conspiracy of doctoring the crop reports and unloading favourably in consequence. And I need hardly remind you that the receiver is equally guilty with the thief."

"But twice as safe. I know something of that, Max ... Have you any idea what my business is?"

"You shall tell me," replied Carrados.

"I run a private inquiry agency. When I lost my profession I had to do something for a living. This occurred. I dropped my name, changed my appearance and opened an office. I knew the legal side down to the ground and I got a retired Scotland Yard man to organize the outside work."

"Excellent!" cried Carrados. "Do you unearth many murders?"

"No," admitted Mr. Carlyle; "our business lies mostly on the conventional lines among divorce and defalcation."

"That's a pity," remarked Carrados. "Do you know, Louis, I always had a secret ambition to be a detective myself. I have even thought lately that I might still be able to do something at it if the chance came my way. That makes you smile?"

"Well, certainly, the idea—"

"Yes, the idea of a blind detective—the blind tracking the alert—"

"Of course, as you say, certain facilities are no doubt quickened," Mr. Carlyle hastened to add considerately, "but, seriously, with the exception of an artist, I don't suppose there is any man who is more utterly dependent on his eyes."

Whatever opinion Carrados might have held privately, his genial exterior did not betray a shadow of dissent. For a full minute he continued to smoke as though he derived an actual visual enjoyment from the blue sprays that travelled and dispersed across the room. He had already placed before his visitor a box containing cigars of a brand which that gentleman keenly appreciated but generally regarded as unattainable, and the matter-of-fact ease and certainty with which the blind man had brought the box and put it before him had sent a questioning flicker through Carlyle's mind.

"You used to be rather fond of art yourself, Louis," he remarked presently. "Give me your opinion of my latest purchase—the bronze lion on the cabinet there." Then, as Carlyle's gaze went about the room, he added quickly: "No, not that cabinet—the one on your left."

Carlyle shot a sharp glance at his host as he got up, but

Carrados's expression was merely benignly complacent. Then he strolled across to the figure.

"Very nice," he admitted. "Late Flemish, isn't it?"

"No, It is a copy of Vidal's 'Roaring Lion.'"

"Vidal?"

"A French artist." The voice became indescribably flat. "He, also, had the misfortune to be blind, by the way."

"You old humbug, Max!" shrieked Carlyle, "you've been thinking that out for the last five minutes." Then the unfortunate man bit his lip and turned his back towards his host.

"Do you remember how we used to pile it up on that obtuse ass Sanders, and then roast him?" asked Carrados, ignoring the half-smothered exclamation with which the other man had recalled himself.

"Yes," replied Carlyle quietly. "This is very good," he continued, addressing himself to the bronze again. "How ever did he do it?"

"With his hands."

"Naturally. But, I mean, how did he study his model?"

"Also with his hands. He called it 'seeing near.'"

"Even with a lion—handled it?"

"In such cases he required the services of a keeper, who brought the animal to bay while Vidal exercised his own particular gifts ... You don't feel inclined to put me on the track of a mystery, Louis?"

Unable to regard this request as anything but one of old Max's unquenchable pleasantries, Mr. Carlyle was on the point of making a suitable reply when a sudden thought caused him to smile knowingly. Up to that point, he had, indeed, completely forgotten the object of his visit. Now that he remembered the doubtful Dionysius and Baxter's recommendation he immediately assumed that some mistake had been made. Either Max was not the Wynn Carrados he had been seeking or else the dealer had been misinformed; for although his host was wonderfully expert in the face of his misfortune, it was inconceivable that he could decide the genuineness of a coin without seeing it. The opportunity seemed a good one of getting even with Carrados by taking him at his word.

"Yes," he accordingly replied, with crisp deliberation, as he re-crossed the room; "yes, I will, Max. Here is the clue to what seems to be a rather remarkable fraud." He put the tetradrachm into his host's hand. "What do you make of it?"

For a few seconds Carrados handled the piece with the delicate manipulation of his finger-tips while Carlyle looked on with a self-appreciative grin. Then with equal gravity the blind man weighed the coin in the balance of his hand. Finally he touched it with his tongue.

"Well?" demanded the other.

"Of course I have not much to go on, and if I was more fully in your confidence I might come to another conclusion—"

"Yes, yes," interposed Carlyle, with amused encouragement.

"Then I should advise you to arrest the parlourmaid, Nina Brun, communicate with the police authorities of Padua for particulars of the career of Helene Brunesi, and suggest to Lord Seastoke that he should return to London to see what further depredations have been made in his cabinet."

Mr. Carlyle's groping hand sought and found a chair, on to which he dropped blankly. His eyes were unable to detach themselves for a single moment from the very ordinary spectacle of Mr. Carrados's mildly benevolent face, while the sterilized ghost of his now forgotten amusement still lingered about his features.

"Good heavens!" he managed to articulate, "how do you know?"

"Isn't that what you wanted of me?" asked Carrados suavely.

"Don't humbug, Max," said Carlyle severely. "This is no joke." An undefined mistrust of his own powers suddenly possessed him in the presence of this mystery. "How do you come to know of Nina Brun and Lord Seastoke?"

"You are a detective, Louis," replied Carrados. "How does one know these things? By using one's eyes and putting two and two together."

Carlyle groaned and flung out an arm petulantly.

"Is it all bunkum, Max? Do you really see all the time—though that doesn't go very far towards explaining it."

"Like Vidal, I see very well—at close quarters," replied Carrados, lightly running a forefinger along the inscription on the tetradrachm. "For longer range I keep another pair of eyes. Would you like to test them?"

Mr. Carlyle's assent was not very gracious; it was, in fact, faintly sulky. He was suffering the annoyance of feeling distinctly unimpressive in his own department; but he was also curious.

"The bell is just behind you, if you don't mind," said his host. "Parkinson will appear. You might take note of him while he is in."

The man who had admitted Mr. Carlyle proved to be Parkinson.

"This gentleman is Mr. Carlyle, Parkinson," explained Carrados the moment the man entered. "You will remember him for the future?"

Parkinson's apologetic eye swept the visitor from head to foot, but so lightly and swiftly that it conveyed to that gentleman the comparison of being very deftly dusted.

"I will endeavour to do so, sir," replied Parkinson, turning again to his master.

"I shall be at home to Mr. Carlyle whenever he calls. That is all."

"Very well, sir."

"Now, Louis," remarked Mr. Carrados briskly, when the door had closed again, "you have had a good opportunity of studying Parkinson. What is he like?"

"In what way?"

"I mean as a matter of description. I am a blind man—I haven't seen my servant for twelve years—what idea can you give me of him? I asked you to notice."

"I know you did, but your Parkinson is the sort of man who has very little about him to describe. He is the embodiment of the ordinary. His height is about average—"

"Five feet nine," murmured Carrados. "Slightly above the mean."

"Scarcely noticeably so. Clean-shaven. Medium brown hair. No particularly marked features. Dark eyes. Good teeth."

"False," interposed Carrados. "The teeth—not the statement."

"Possibly," admitted Mr. Carlyle. "I am not a dental expert and I had no opportunity of examining Mr. Parkinson's mouth in detail. But what is the drift of all this?"

"His clothes?"

"Oh, just the ordinary evening dress of a valet. There is not much room for variety in that."

"You noticed, in fact, nothing special by which Parkinson could be identified?"

"Well, he wore an unusually broad gold ring on the little finger of the left hand."

"But that is removable. And yet Parkinson has an ineradicable mole—a small one, I admit—on his chin. And you a human sleuth-hound. Oh, Louis!"

"At all events," retorted Carlyle, writhing a little under this good-humoured satire, although it was easy enough to see in it Carrados's affectionate intention—"at all events, I dare say I can give as good a description of Parkinson as he can give of me."

"That is what we are going to test. Ring the bell again."

"Seriously?"

"Quite. I am trying my eyes against yours. If I can't give you fifty out of a hundred I'll renounce my private detectorial ambition for ever."

"It isn't quite the same," objected Carlyle, but he rang the bell.

"Come in and close the door, Parkinson," said Carrados when the man appeared. "Don't look at Mr. Carlyle again—in fact, you had better stand with your back towards him, he won't mind. Now describe to me his appearance as you observed it."

Parkinson tendered his respectful apologies to Mr. Carlyle for the liberty he was compelled to take, by the deferential quality of his voice.

"Mr. Carlyle, sir, wears patent leather boots of about size seven and very little used. There are five buttons, but on the left boot one button—the third up—is missing, leaving loose threads and not the more usual metal fastener. Mr. Carlyle's trousers, sir, are of a dark material, a dark grey line of about a quarter of an inch width on a darker ground. The bottoms are turned permanently up and are, just now, a little muddy, if I may say so."

"Very muddy," interposed Mr. Carlyle generously. "It is a wet night, Parkinson."

"Yes, sir; very unpleasant weather. If you will allow me, sir, I will brush you in the hall. The mud is dry now, I notice. Then, sir," continued Parkinson, reverting to the business in hand, "there are dark green cashmere hose. A curb-pattern key-chain passes into the left-hand trouser pocket."

From the visitor's nether garments the photographic-eyed Parkinson proceeded to higher ground, and with increasing wonder Mr. Carlyle listened to the faithful catalogue of his possessions. His fetter-and-link albert of gold and platinum was minutely described. His spotted blue ascot, with its gentlemanly pearl scarfpin, was set forth, and the fact that the buttonhole in the left lapel of his morning coat showed signs of use was duly noted. What Parkinson saw he recorded, but he made no deductions. A handkerchief carried in the cuff of the right sleeve was simply that to him and not an indication that Mr. Carlyle was, indeed, left-handed.

But a more delicate part of Parkinson's undertaking remained. He approached it with a double cough.

"As regards Mr. Carlyle's personal appearance, sir—"

"No, enough!" cried the gentleman concerned hastily. "I am more than satisfied. You are a keen observer, Parkinson."

"I have trained myself to suit my master's requirements, sir," replied the man. He looked towards Mr. Carrados, received a nod and withdrew.

Mr. Carlyle was the first to speak.

"That man of yours would be worth five pounds a week to me, Max," he remarked thoughtfully. "But, of course—"

"I don't think that he would take it," replied Carrados, in a voice of equally detached speculation. "He suits me very well. But you have the chance of using his services—indirectly."

"You still mean that—seriously?"

"I notice in you a chronic disinclination to take me seriously, Louis. It is really—to an Englishman—almost painful. Is there something inherently comic about me or the atmosphere of The Turrets?"

"No, my friend," replied Mr. Carlyle, "but there is something essentially prosperous. That is what points to the improbable. Now what is it?"

"It might be merely a whim, but it is more than that," replied Carrados. "It is, well, partly vanity, partly *ennui*, partly"—certainly there was something more nearly tragic in his voice than comic now—"partly hope."

Mr. Carlyle was too tactful to pursue the subject.

"Those are three tolerable motives," he acquiesced. "I'll do anything you want, Max, on one condition."

"Agreed. And it is?"

"That you tell me how you knew so much of this affair." He tapped the silver coin which lay on the table near them. "I am not easily flabbergasted," he added.

"You won't believe that there is nothing to explain—that it was purely second-sight?"

"No," replied Carlyle tersely: "I won't."

"You are quite right. And yet the thing is very simple."

"They always are—when you know," soliloquised the other. "That's what makes them so confoundedly difficult when you don't."

"Here is this one then. In Padua, which seems to be regaining its old reputation as the birthplace of spurious antiques, by the way, there lives an ingenious craftsman named Pietro Stelli. This simple soul, who possesses a talent not inferior to that of Cavino at his best, has for many years turned his hand to the not unprofitable occupation of forging rare Greek and Roman coins. As a collector and student of certain Greek colonials and a specialist in forgeries I have been familiar with Stelli's workmanship for years. Latterly he seems to have come under the influence of an international crook called—at the moment—Dompierre, who soon saw a way of utilizing Stelli's genius on a royal scale. Helene Brunesi, who in private life is—and really is, I believe—Madame Dompierre, readily lent her services to the enterprise."

"Quite so," nodded Mr. Carlyle, as his host paused.

"You see the whole sequence, of course?"

"Not exactly—not in detail," confessed Mr. Carlyle.

"Dompierre's idea was to gain access to some of the most celebrated cabinets of Europe and substitute Stelli's fabrications for the genuine coins. The princely collection of rarities that he would thus amass might be difficult to dispose of safely, but I have no doubt that he had matured his plans. Helene, in the person of Nina Brun, an Anglicised French parlourmaid—a part which she fills to perfection—was to obtain wax impressions of the most valuable pieces and to make the exchange when the counterfeits reached her. In this way it was obviously hoped that the fraud would not come to light until long after the real coins had been sold, and I gather that she has already done her work successfully in general houses. Then, impressed by her excellent references and capable manner, my housekeeper engaged her, and for a few weeks she went about her duties here. It was fatal to this detail of the scheme, however, that I have the misfortune to be blind. I am told that Helene has so innocently angelic a face as to disarm suspicion, but I was incapable of being impressed and that good material was thrown away. But one morning my material fingers—which, of course, knew nothing of Helene's angelic face—discovered an unfamiliar touch about the surface of my favourite Euclideas, and, although there was doubtless nothing to be seen, my critical sense of smell reported that wax had been recently pressed against it. I began to make discreet inquiries and in the meantime my cabinets went to the local bank for safety. Helene countered by receiving a telegram from Angiers, calling her to the death-bed of her aged mother. The aged mother succumbed; duty compelled Helene to remain at the side of her stricken patriarchal father, and doubtless The Turrets was written off the syndicate's operations as a bad debt."

"Very interesting," admitted Mr. Carlyle; "but at the risk of seeming obtuse"—his manner had become delicately chastened—"I must say that I fail to trace the inevitable connexion between Nina Brun and this particular forgery—assuming that it is a forgery."

"Set your mind at rest about that, Louis," replied Carrados. "It is a forgery, and it is a forgery that none but Pietro Stelli could have achieved. That is the essential connexion. Of course, there are accessories. A private detective coming urgently to see me with a notable tetradrachm in his pocket, which he announces to be the clue to a remarkable fraud—well, really, Louis, one scarcely needs to be blind to see through that."

"And Lord Seastoke? I suppose you happened to discover that Nina Brun had gone there?"

"No, I cannot claim to have discovered that, or I should certainly have warned him at once when I found out—only recently—about the gang. As a matter of fact, the last information I had of Lord Seastoke was a line in yesterday's *Morning Post* to the effect that he was still at Cairo. But many of these pieces—" He brushed his finger almost lovingly across the vivid chariot race that embellished the reverse of the coin, and broke off to remark: "You really ought to take up the subject, Louis. You have no idea how useful it might prove to you some day."

"I really think I must," replied Carlyle grimly. "Two hundred and fifty pounds the original of this cost, I believe."

"Cheap, too; it would make five hundred pounds in New York to-day. As I was saying, many are literally unique. This gem by Kimon is—here is his signature, you see; Peter is particularly good at lettering—and as I handled the genuine tetradrachm about two years ago, when Lord Seastoke exhibited it at a meeting of our society in Albemarle Street, there is nothing at all wonderful in my being able to fix the locale of your mystery. Indeed, I feel that I ought to apologize for it all being so simple."

"I think," remarked Mr. Carlyle, critically examining the loose threads on his left boot, "that the apology on that head would be more appropriate from me."

Arthur Conan Doyle

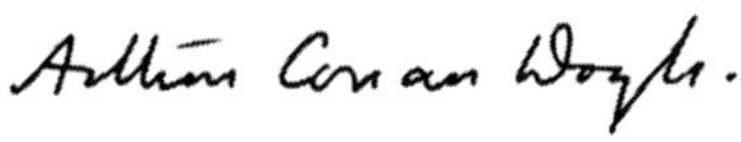

Sir Arthur Conan Doyle (1859-1930) was an English author and doctor best remembered for his creation of Sherlock Holmes. Upon publication of the first novel featuring him, *A Study in Scarlet*, it was immediately well-received and Doyle went on to write four novels and 56 short stories involving Holmes. He is one of, if not the, best-known fictional detectives and has been adapted for the stage and screen countless times.

Holmes is a world-famous private detective renowned for his masterful deductive reasoning skills, intellect, and wit, often one-upping the local police force and Scotland Yard at their jobs. He is often seen with his friend and chronicler John Watson.

5

THE ADVENTURE OF THE SPECKLED BAND

Arthur Conan Doyle

ON GLANCING OVER MY NOTES OF THE SEVENTY ODD CASES IN which I have during the last eight years studied the methods of my friend Sherlock Holmes, I find many tragic, some comic, a large number merely strange, but none commonplace; for, working as he did rather for the love of his art than for the acquirement of wealth, he refused to associate himself with any investigation which did not tend towards the unusual, and even the fantastic. Of all these varied cases, however, I cannot recall any which presented more singular features than that which was associated with the well-known Surrey family of the Roylotts of Stoke Moran. The events in question occurred in the early days of my association with Holmes, when we were sharing rooms as bachelors in Baker Street. It is possible that I might have placed them upon record before, but a promise of secrecy was made at the time, from which I have only been freed during the last month by the untimely death of the lady to whom the pledge was given. It is perhaps as well that the facts should now come to light, for I have reasons to know that there are wide-spread rumors as to the death of Dr. Grimesby Roylott which tend to make the matter even more terrible than the truth.

It was early in April in the year '83 that I woke one morning to find Sherlock Holmes standing, fully dressed, by the side of my bed. He was a late riser as a rule, and as the clock on the mantel-piece showed me that it was only a quarter past seven, I blinked up at him in some surprise, and perhaps just a little resentment, for I was myself regular in my habits.

"Very sorry to knock you up, Watson," said he, "but it's the common lot this morning. Mrs. Hudson has been knocked up, she retorted upon me, and I on you."

"What is it, then—a fire?"

"No; a client. It seems that a young lady has arrived in a considerable state of excitement, who insists upon seeing me. She is waiting now in the sitting-room. Now, when young ladies wander about the metropolis at this hour of the morning, and knock sleepy people up out of their beds, I presume that it is something very pressing which they have to communicate. Should it prove to be an interesting case, you would, I am sure, wish to follow it from the outset. I thought, at any rate, that I should call you and give you the chance."

"My dear fellow, I would not miss it for anything."

I had no keener pleasure than in following Holmes in his professional investigations, and in admiring the rapid deductions, as swift as intuitions, and yet always founded on a logical basis, with which he unravelled the problems which were submitted to him. I rapidly threw on my clothes, and was ready in a few minutes to accompany my friend down to the sitting-room. A lady dressed in black and heavily veiled, who had been sitting in the window, rose as we entered.

"Good-morning, madam," said Holmes, cheerily. "My name is Sherlock Holmes. This is my intimate friend and associate, Dr. Watson, before whom you can speak as freely as before myself. Ha! I am glad to see that Mrs. Hudson has had the good sense to light the fire. Pray draw up to it, and I shall order you a cup of hot coffee, for I observe that you are shivering."

"It is not cold which makes me shiver," said the woman, in a low voice, changing her seat as requested.

"What, then?"

"It is fear, Mr. Holmes. It is terror." She raised her veil as she spoke, and we could see that she was indeed in a pitiable state of agitation, her face all drawn and gray, with restless, frightened eyes, like those of some hunted animal. Her features and figure were those of a woman of thirty, but her hair was shot with premature gray, and her expression was weary and haggard. Sherlock Holmes ran her over with one of his quick, all-comprehensive glances.

"You must not fear," said he, soothingly, bending forward and patting her forearm. "We shall soon set matters right, I have no doubt. You have come in by train this morning, I see."

"You know me, then?"

"No, but I observe the second half of a return ticket in the palm of your left glove. You must have started early, and yet you had a good drive in a dog-cart, along heavy roads, before you reached the station."

The lady gave a violent start, and stared in bewilderment at my companion.

"There is no mystery, my dear madam," said he, smiling. "The left arm of your jacket is spattered with mud in no less than seven places. The marks are perfectly fresh. There is no vehicle save a dog-cart which throws up mud in that way, and then only when you sit on the left-hand side of the driver."

"Whatever your reasons may be, you are perfectly correct," said she. "I started from home before six, reached Leatherhead at twenty past, and came in by the first train to Waterloo. Sir, I can stand this strain no longer; I shall go mad if it continues. I have no one to turn to—none, save only one, who cares for me, and he, poor fellow, can be of little aid. I have heard of you, Mr. Holmes; I have heard of you from Mrs. Farintosh, whom you helped in the hour of her sore need. It was from her that I had your address. Oh, sir, do you not think that you could help me, too, and at least throw a little light through the dense darkness which surrounds me? At present it is out of my power to reward you for your services, but in a month or six weeks I shall be married, with the control of my own income, and then at least you shall not find me ungrateful."

Holmes turned to his desk, and unlocking it, drew out a small case-book, which he consulted.

"Farintosh," said he. "Ah yes, I recall the case; it was concerned with an opal tiara. I think it was before your time, Watson. I can only say, madam, that I shall be happy to devote the same care to your case as I did to that of your friend. As to reward, my profession is its own reward; but you are at liberty to defray whatever expenses I may be put to, at the time which suits you best. And now I beg that you will lay before us everything that may help us in forming an opinion upon the matter."

"Alas!" replied our visitor, "the very horror of my situation lies in the fact that my fears are so vague, and my suspicions depend so entirely upon small points, which might seem trivial to another, that even he to whom of all others I have a right to look for help and advice looks upon all that I tell him about it as the fancies of a nervous woman. He does not say so, but I can read it from his soothing answers and averted eyes. But I have heard, Mr. Holmes, that you can see deeply into the manifold wickedness of the human heart. You may advise me how to walk amid the dangers which encompass me."

"I am all attention, madam."

"My name is Helen Stoner, and I am living with my step-father, who is the last survivor of one of the oldest Saxon families in England, the Roylotts of Stoke Moran, on the western border of Surrey."

Holmes nodded his head. "The name is familiar to me," said he.

"The family was at one time among the richest in England, and the estates extended over the borders into Berkshire in the north, and Hampshire in the west. In the last century, however, four successive heirs were of a dissolute and wasteful disposition, and the family ruin was eventually completed by a gambler in the days of the Regency. Nothing was left save a few acres of ground, and the two-hundred-year-old house, which is itself crushed under a heavy mortgage. The last squire dragged out his existence there, living the horrible life of an aristocratic pauper; but his only son, my step-father, seeing that he must adapt himself to the new conditions, obtained an advance from a relative, which enabled him to take a medical degree, and went out to Calcutta, where, by his professional skill and his force of character, he established a large practice. In a fit of anger, however, caused by some robberies which had been perpetrated in the house, he beat his native butler to death, and narrowly escaped a capital sentence. As it was, he suffered a long term of imprisonment, and afterwards returned to England a morose and disappointed man.

"When Dr. Roylott was in India he married my mother, Mrs. Stoner, the young widow of Major-general Stoner, of the Bengal Artillery. My sister Julia and I were twins, and we were only two years old at the time of my mother's re-marriage. She had a considerable sum of money—not less than £1000 a year—and this she bequeathed to Dr. Roylott entirely while we resided with him, with a provision that a certain annual sum should be allowed to each of us in the event of our marriage. Shortly after our return to England my mother died—she was killed eight years ago in a railway accident near Crewe. Dr. Roylott then abandoned his attempts to establish himself in practice in London, and took us to live with him in the old ancestral house at Stoke Moran. The money which my mother had left was enough for all our wants, and there seemed to be no obstacle to our happiness.

"But a terrible change came over our step-father about this time. Instead of making friends and exchanging visits with our neighbors, who had at first been overjoyed to see a Roylott of Stoke Moran back in the old family seat, he shut himself up in his house, and seldom came out save to indulge in ferocious quarrels with whoever might cross his path. Violence of temper approaching to mania has been hereditary in the men of the family, and in my step-father's case it had, I believe, been intensified by his long residence in the tropics. A series of disgraceful brawls took place, two of which ended in the police-court, until at last he became the terror of the village, and the folks would fly at his approach, for he is a man of immense strength, and absolutely uncontrollable in his anger.

"Last week he hurled the local blacksmith over a parapet into a stream, and it was only by paying over all the money which I could gather together that I was able to avert another public exposure. He had no friends at all save the wandering gypsies, and he would give these vagabonds leave to encamp upon the few acres of bramble-covered land which represent the family estate, and would accept in return the hospitality of their tents, wandering away with them sometimes for weeks on end. He has a passion also for Indian animals, which are sent over to him by a correspondent, and he has at this moment a cheetah and a baboon, which wander freely over his grounds, and are feared by the villagers almost as much as their master.

"You can imagine from what I say that my poor sister Julia and I had no great pleasure in our lives. No servant would stay with us, and for a long time we did all the work of the house. She was but thirty at the time of her death, and yet her hair had already begun to whiten, even as mine has."

"Your sister is dead, then?"

"She died just two years ago, and it is of her death that I wish to speak to you. You can understand that, living the life which I have described, we were little likely to see anyone of our own age and position. We had, however, an aunt, my mother's maiden sister, Miss Honoria Westphail, who lives near Harrow, and we were occasionally allowed to pay short visits at this lady's house. Julia went there at Christmas two years ago, and met there a half-pay major of marines, to whom she became engaged. My step-father learned of the engagement when my sister returned, and offered no objection to the marriage; but within a fortnight of the day which had been fixed for the wedding, the terrible event occurred which has deprived me of my only companion."

Sherlock Holmes had been leaning back in his chair with his

eyes closed and his head sunk in a cushion, but he half opened his lids now and glanced across at his visitor.

"Pray be precise as to details," said he.

"It is easy for me to be so, for every event of that dreadful time is seared into my memory. The manor-house is, as I have already said, very old, and only one wing is now inhabited. The bedrooms in this wing are on the ground floor, the sitting-rooms being in the central block of the buildings. Of these bedrooms the first is Dr. Roylott's, the second my sister's, and the third my own. There is no communication between them, but they all open out into the same corridor. Do I make myself plain?"

"Perfectly so."

"The windows of the three rooms open out upon the lawn. That fatal night Dr. Roylott had gone to his room early, though we knew that he had not retired to rest, for my sister was troubled by the smell of the strong Indian cigars which it was his custom to smoke. She left her room, therefore, and came into mine, where she sat for some time, chatting about her approaching wedding. At eleven o'clock she rose to leave me but she paused at the door and looked back.

"'Tell me, Helen,' said she, 'have you ever heard any one whistle in the dead of the night?'

"'Never,' said I.

"'I suppose that you could not possibly whistle, yourself, in your sleep?'

"'Certainly not. But why?'

"'Because during the last few nights I have always, about three in the morning, heard a low, clear whistle. I am a light sleeper, and it has awakened me. I cannot tell where it came from—perhaps from the next room, perhaps from the lawn. I thought that I would just ask you whether you had heard it.'

"'No, I have not. It must be those wretched gypsies in the plantation.'

"'Very likely. And yet if it were on the lawn, I wonder that you did not hear it also.'

"'Ah, but I sleep more heavily than you.'

"'Well, it is of no great consequence, at any rate.' She smiled back at me, closed my door, and a few moments later I heard her key turn in the lock."

"Indeed," said Holmes. "Was it your custom always to lock yourselves in at night?"

"Always."

"And why?"

"I think that I mentioned to you that the doctor kept a cheetah and a baboon. We had no feeling of security unless our doors were locked."

"Quite so. Pray proceed with your statement."

"I could not sleep that night. A vague feeling of impending misfortune impressed me. My sister and I, you will recollect, were twins, and you know how subtle are the links which bind two souls which are so closely allied. It was a wild night. The wind was howling outside, and the rain was beating and splashing against the windows. Suddenly, amid all the hubbub of the gale, there burst forth the wild scream of a terrified woman. I knew that it was my sister's voice. I sprang from my bed, wrapped a shawl round me, and rushed into the corridor. As I opened my door I seemed to hear a low whistle, such as my sister described, and a few moments later a clanging sound, as if a mass of metal had fallen. As I ran down the passage, my sister's door was unlocked, and revolved slowly upon its hinges. I stared at it horror-stricken, not knowing what was about to issue from it. By the light of the corridor-lamp I saw my sister appear at the opening, her face blanched with terror, her hands groping for help, her whole figure swaying to and fro like that of a drunkard. I ran to her and threw my arms round her, but at that moment her knees seemed to give way and she fell to the ground. She writhed as one who is in terrible pain, and her limbs were dreadfully convulsed. At first I thought that she had not recognized me, but as I bent over her she suddenly shrieked out in a voice which I shall never forget, 'Oh, my God! Helen! It was the band! The speckled band!' There was something else which she would fain have said, and she stabbed with her finger into the air in the direction of the doctor's room, but a fresh convulsion seized her and choked her words. I rushed out, calling loudly for my step-father, and I met him hastening from his room in his dressing-gown. When he reached my sister's side she was unconscious, and though he poured brandy down her throat and sent for medical aid from the village, all efforts were in vain, for she slowly sank and died without having recovered her consciousness. Such was the dreadful end of my beloved sister."

"One moment," said Holmes; "are you sure about this whistle and metallic sound? Could you swear to it?"

"That was what the county coroner asked me at the inquiry. It is my strong impression that I heard it, and yet, among the crash of the gale and the creaking of an old house, I may possibly have been deceived."

"Was your sister dressed?"

"No, she was in her night-dress. In her right hand was found the charred stump of a match, and in her left a matchbox."

"Showing that she had struck a light and looked about her when the alarm took place. That is important. And what conclusions did the coroner come to?"

"He investigated the case with great care, for Dr. Roylott's conduct had long been notorious in the county, but he was unable to find any satisfactory cause of death. My evidence showed that the door had been fastened upon the inner side, and the windows were blocked by old-fashioned shutters with broad iron bars, which were secured every night. The walls were carefully sounded, and were shown to be quite solid all round, and the flooring was also thoroughly examined, with the same result. The chimney is wide, but is barred up by four large staples. It is certain, therefore, that my sister was quite alone when she met her end. Besides, there were no marks of any violence upon her."

"How about poison?"

"The doctors examined her for it, but without success."

"What do you think that this unfortunate lady died of, then?"

"It is my belief that she died of pure fear and nervous shock, though what it was that frightened her I cannot imagine."

"Were there gypsies in the plantation at the time?"

"Yes, there are nearly always some there."

"Ah, and what did you gather from this allusion to a band—a speckled band?"

"Sometimes I have thought that it was merely the wild talk of delirium, sometimes that it may have referred to some band of people, perhaps to these very gypsies in the plantation. I do not know whether the spotted handkerchiefs which so many of them wear over their heads might have suggested the strange adjective which she used."

Holmes shook his head like a man who is far from being satisfied.

"These are very deep waters," said he; "pray go on with your narrative."

"Two years have passed since then, and my life has been until lately lonelier than ever. A month ago, however, a dear friend, whom I have known for many years, has done me the honor to ask my hand in marriage. His name is Armitage—Percy Armitage—the second son of Mr. Armitage, of Crane Water, near Reading. My step-father has offered no opposition to the match, and we are to be married in the course of the spring. Two days ago some repairs were started in the west wing of the building, and my bedroom wall has been pierced, so that I have had to move into the chamber in which my sister died, and to sleep in the very bed in which she slept. Imagine, then, my thrill of terror when last night, as I lay awake, thinking over her terrible fate, I suddenly heard in the silence of the night the low whistle which had been the herald of her own death. I sprang up and lit the lamp, but nothing was to be seen in the room. I was too shaken to go to bed again, however, so I dressed, and as soon as it was daylight I slipped down, got a dog-cart at the 'Crown Inn,' which is opposite, and drove to Leatherhead, from whence I have come on this morning with the one object of seeing you and asking your advice."

"You have done wisely," said my friend. "But have you told

me all?"

"Yes, all."

"Miss Roylott, you have not. You are screening your step-father."

"Why, what do you mean?"

For answer Holmes pushed back the frill of black lace which fringed the hand that lay upon our visitor's knee. Five little livid spots, the marks of four fingers and a thumb, were printed upon the white wrist.

"You have been cruelly used," said Holmes.

The lady colored deeply and covered over her injured wrist. "He is a hard man," she said, "and perhaps he hardly knows his own strength."

There was a long silence, during which Holmes leaned his chin upon his hands and stared into the crackling fire.

"This is a very deep business," he said, at last. "There are a thousand details which I should desire to know before I decide upon our course of action. Yet we have not a moment to lose. If we were to come to Stoke Moran to-day, would it be possible for us to see over these rooms without the knowledge of your step-father?"

"As it happens, he spoke of coming into town to-day upon some most important business. It is probable that he will be away all day, and that there would be nothing to disturb you. We have a house-keeper now, but she is old and foolish, and I could easily get her out of the way."

"Excellent. You are not averse to this trip, Watson?"

"By no means."

"Then we shall both come. What are you going to do yourself?"

"I have one or two things which I would wish to do now that I am in town. But I shall return by the twelve o'clock train, so as to be there in time for your coming."

"And you may expect us early in the afternoon. I have myself some small business matters to attend to. Will you not wait and breakfast?"

"No, I must go. My heart is lightened already since I have confided my trouble to you. I shall look forward to seeing you again this afternoon." She dropped her thick black veil over her face and glided from the room.

"And what do you think of it all, Watson?" asked Sherlock Holmes, leaning back in his chair.

"It seems to me to be a most dark and sinister business."

"Dark enough and sinister enough."

"Yet if the lady is correct in saying that the flooring and walls are sound, and that the door, window, and chimney are impassable, then her sister must have been undoubtedly alone when she met her mysterious end."

"What becomes, then, of these nocturnal whistles, and what of the very peculiar words of the dying woman?"

"I cannot think."

"When you combine the ideas of whistles at night, the presence of a band of gypsies who are on intimate terms with this old doctor, the fact that we have every reason to believe that the doctor has an interest in preventing his step-daughter's marriage, the dying allusion to a band, and, finally, the fact that Miss Helen Stoner heard a metallic clang, which might have been caused by one of those metal bars which secured the shutters falling back into their place, I think that there is good ground to think that the mystery may be cleared along those lines."

"But what, then, did the gypsies do?"

"I cannot imagine."

"I see many objections to any such theory."

"And so do I. It is precisely for that reason that we are going to Stoke Moran this day. I want to see whether the objections are fatal, or if they may be explained away. But what in the name of the devil!"

The ejaculation had been drawn from my companion by the fact that our door had been suddenly dashed open, and that a huge man had framed himself in the aperture. His costume was a peculiar mixture of the professional and of the agricultural, having a black top-hat, a long frock-coat, and a pair of high gaiters, with a hunting-crop swinging in his hand. So tall was he that his hat actually brushed the cross bar of the doorway, and his breadth seemed to span it across from side to side. A large face, seared with a thousand wrinkles, burned yellow with the sun, and marked with every evil passion, was turned from one to the other of us, while his deep-set, bile-shot eyes, and his high, thin, fleshless nose, gave him somewhat the resemblance to a fierce old bird of prey.

"Which of you is Holmes?" asked this apparition.

"My name, sir; but you have the advantage of me," said my companion, quietly.

"I am Dr. Grimesby Roylott, of Stoke Moran."

"Indeed, doctor," said Holmes, blandly. "Pray take a seat."

"I will do nothing of the kind. My step-daughter has been here. I have traced her. What has she been saying to you?"

"It is a little cold for the time of the year," said Holmes.

"What has she been saying to you?" screamed the old man, furiously.

"But I have heard that the crocuses promise well," continued my companion, imperturbably.

"Ha! You put me off, do you?" said our new visitor, taking a step forward and shaking his hunting-crop. "I know you, you scoundrel! I have heard of you before. You are Holmes, the meddler."

My friend smiled.

"Holmes, the busybody!"

His smile broadened.

"Holmes, the Scotland-yard Jack-in-office!"

Holmes chuckled heartily. "Your conversation is most entertaining," said he. "When you go out close the door, for there is a decided draught."

"I will go when I have said my say. Don't you dare to meddle with my affairs. I know that Miss Stoner has been here. I traced her! I am a dangerous man to fall foul of! See here." He stepped swiftly forward, seized the poker, and bent it into a curve with his huge brown hands.

"See that you keep yourself out of my grip," he snarled, and hurling the twisted poker into the fireplace, he strode out of the room.

"He seems a very amiable person," said Holmes, laughing. "I am not quite so bulky, but if he had remained I might have shown him that my grip was not much more feeble than his own." As he spoke he picked up the steel poker, and with a sudden effort straightened it out again.

"Fancy his having the insolence to confound me with the official detective force! This incident gives zest to our investigation, however, and I only trust that our little friend will not suffer from her imprudence in allowing this brute to trace her. And now, Watson, we shall order breakfast, and afterwards I shall walk down to Doctors' Commons, where I hope to get some data which may help us in this matter."

*

It was nearly one o'clock when Sherlock Holmes returned from his excursion. He held in his hand a sheet of blue paper, scrawled over with notes and figures.

"I have seen the will of the deceased wife," said he. "To determine its exact meaning I have been obliged to work out the present prices of the investments with which it is concerned. The total income, which at the time of the wife's death was little short of £1100, is now, through the fall in agricultural prices, not more than £750. Each daughter can claim an income of £250, in case of marriage. It is evident, therefore, that if both girls had married, this beauty would have had a mere pittance, while even one of them would cripple him to a very serious extent. My morning's work has not been wasted, since it has proved that he has the very strongest motives for standing in the way of anything of the sort. And now, Watson, this is too serious for dawdling, especially as the old man is aware that we are interesting ourselves in his affairs; so if you are ready, we shall call a cab and drive to Waterloo. I should be very much obliged if you would slip your revolver into your pocket. An Eley's No. 2 is an excellent argument with gentlemen who can twist steel pokers into knots. That and a tooth-brush are, I think, all that we need."

At Waterloo we were fortunate in catching a train for Leatherhead, where we hired a trap at the station inn, and drove for four or five miles through the lovely Surrey lanes. It was a perfect day, with a bright sun and a few fleecy clouds in the heavens. The trees and way-side hedges were just throwing out their first green shoots, and the air was full of the pleasant smell of the moist earth. To me at least there was a strange contrast between the sweet promise of the spring and this sinister quest upon which we were engaged. My companion sat in the front of the trap, his arms folded, his hat pulled down over his eyes, and his chin sunk upon his breast, buried in the deepest thought. Suddenly, however, he started, tapped me on the shoulder, and pointed over the meadows.

"Look there!" said he.

A heavily-timbered park stretched up in a gentle slope, thickening into a grove at the highest point. From amid the branches there jutted out the gray gables and high roof-tree of a very old mansion.

"Stoke Moran?" said he.

"Yes, sir, that be the house of Dr. Grimesby Roylott," remarked the driver.

"There is some building going on there," said Holmes; "that is where we are going."

"There's the village," said the driver, pointing to a cluster of roofs some distance to the left; "but if you want to get to the house, you'll find it shorter to get over this stile, and so by the foot-path over the fields. There it is, where the lady is walking."

"And the lady, I fancy, is Miss Stoner," observed Holmes, shading his eyes. "Yes, I think we had better do as you suggest."

We got off, paid our fare, and the trap rattled back on its way to Leatherhead.

"I thought it as well," said Holmes, as we climbed the stile, "that this fellow should think we had come here as architects, or on some definite business. It may stop his gossip. Good-afternoon, Miss Stoner. You see that we have been as good as our word."

Our client of the morning had hurried forward to meet us with a face which spoke her joy. "I have been waiting so eagerly for you," she cried, shaking hands with us warmly. "All has turned out splendidly. Dr. Roylott has gone to town, and it is unlikely that he will be back before evening."

"We have had the pleasure of making the doctor's acquaintance," said Holmes, and in a few words he sketched out what had occurred. Miss Stoner turned white to the lips as she listened.

"Good heavens!" she cried, "he has followed me, then."

"So it appears."

"He is so cunning that I never know when I am safe from him. What will he say when he returns?"

"He must guard himself, for he may find that there is some one more cunning than himself upon his track. You must lock yourself up from him to-night. If he is violent, we shall take you away to your aunt's at Harrow. Now, we must make the best use of our time, so kindly take us at once to the rooms which we are to examine."

The building was of gray, lichen-blotched stone, with a high central portion, and two curving wings, like the claws of a crab, thrown out on each side. In one of these wings the windows were broken, and blocked with wooden boards, while the roof was partly caved in, a picture of ruin. The central portion was in little better repair, but the right-hand block was comparatively modern, and the blinds in the windows, with the blue smoke curling up from the chimneys, showed that this was where the family resided. Some scaffolding had been erected against the end wall, and the stone-work had been broken into, but there were no signs of any workmen at the moment of our visit. Holmes walked slowly up and down the ill-trimmed lawn, and examined with deep attention the outsides of the windows.

"This, I take it, belongs to the room in which you used to sleep, the centre one to your sister's, and the one next to the main building to Dr. Roylott's chamber?"

"Exactly so. But I am now sleeping in the middle one."

"Pending the alterations, as I understand. By-the-way, there does not seem to be any very pressing need for repairs at that end wall."

"There were none. I believe that it was an excuse to move me from my room."

"Ah! that is suggestive. Now, on the other side of this narrow wing runs the corridor from which these three rooms open. There are windows in it, of course?"

"Yes, but very small ones. Too narrow for any one to pass through."

"As you both locked your doors at night, your rooms were unapproachable from that side. Now, would you have the kindness to go into your room and bar your shutters."

Miss Stoner did so, and Holmes, after a careful examination through the open window, endeavored in every way to force the shutter open, but without success. There was no slit through which a knife could be passed to raise the bar. Then with his lens he tested the hinges, but they were of solid iron, built firmly into the massive masonry. "Hum!" said he, scratching his chin in some perplexity; "my theory certainly presents some difficulties. No one could pass these shutters if they were bolted. Well, we shall see if the inside throws any light upon the matter."

A small side door led into the whitewashed corridor from which the three bedrooms opened. Holmes refused to examine the third chamber, so we passed at once to the second, that in which Miss Stoner was now sleeping, and in which her sister had met with her fate. It was a homely little room, with a low ceiling and a gaping fireplace, after the fashion of old country-houses. A brown chest of drawers stood in one corner, a narrow white-counterpaned bed in another, and a dressing-table on the left-hand side of the window. These articles, with two small wicker-work chairs, made up all the furniture in the room, save for a square of Wilton carpet in the centre. The boards round and the panelling of the walls were of brown, worm-eaten oak, so old and discolored that it may have dated from the original building of the house. Holmes drew one of the chairs into a corner and sat silent, while his eyes travelled round and round and up and down, taking in every detail of the apartment.

"Where does that bell communicate with?" he asked, at last, pointing to a thick bell-rope which hung down beside the bed, the tassel actually lying upon the pillow.

"It goes to the house-keeper's room."

"It looks newer than the other things?"

"Yes, it was only put there a couple of years ago."

"Your sister asked for it, I suppose?"

"No, I never heard of her using it. We used always to get what we wanted for ourselves."

"Indeed, it seemed unnecessary to put so nice a bell-pull there. You will excuse me for a few minutes while I satisfy myself as to this floor." He threw himself down upon his face with his lens in his hand, and crawled swiftly backward and forward, examining minutely the cracks between the boards. Then he did the same with the wood-work with which the chamber was panelled. Finally he walked over to the bed, and spent some time in staring at it, and in running his eye up and down the wall. Finally he took the bell-rope in his hand and gave it a brisk tug.

"Why, it's a dummy," said he.

"Won't it ring?"

"No, it is not even attached to a wire. This is very interesting. You can see now that it is fastened to a hook just above where the little opening for the ventilator is."

"How very absurd! I never noticed that before."

"Very strange!" muttered Holmes, pulling at the rope. "There are one or two very singular points about this room. For example, what a fool a builder must be to open a ventilator into another room, when, with the same trouble, he might have communicated with the outside air!"

"That is also quite modern," said the lady.

"Done about the same time as the bell-rope?" remarked Holmes.

"Yes, there were several little changes carried out about that time."

"They seem to have been of a most interesting character—dummy bell-ropes, and ventilators which do not ventilate. With your permission, Miss Stoner, we shall now carry our researches into the inner apartment."

Dr. Grimesby Roylott's chamber was larger than that of his step-daughter, but was as plainly furnished. A camp-bed, a small wooden shelf full of books, mostly of a technical character, an arm-chair beside the bed, a plain wooden chair against the wall, a round table, and a large iron safe were the principal things which met the eye. Holmes walked slowly round and examined each and all of them with the keenest interest.

"What's in here?" he asked, tapping the safe.

"My step-father's business papers."

"Oh! you have seen inside, then?"

"Only once, some years ago. I remember that it was full of papers."

"There isn't a cat in it, for example?"

"No. What a strange idea!"

"Well, look at this!" He took up a small saucer of milk which stood on the top of it.

"No; we don't keep a cat. But there is a cheetah and a baboon."

"Ah, yes, of course! Well, a cheetah is just a big cat, and yet a saucer of milk does not go very far in satisfying its wants, I dare say. There is one point which I should wish to determine." He squatted down in front of the wooden chair, and examined the seat of it with the greatest attention.

"Thank you. That is quite settled," said he, rising and putting his lens in his pocket. "Hello! Here is something interesting!"

The object which had caught his eye was a small dog-lash hung on one corner of the bed. The lash, however, was curled upon itself, and tied so as to make a loop of whip-cord.

"What do you make of that, Watson?"

"It's a common enough lash. But I don't know why it should be tied."

"That is not quite so common, is it? Ah, me! it's a wicked world, and when a clever man turns his brains to crime it is the worst of all. I think that I have seen enough now, Miss Stoner, and with your permission we shall walk out upon the lawn."

I had never seen my friend's face so grim or his brow so dark as it was when we turned from the scene of this investigation. We had walked several times up and down the lawn, neither Miss Stoner nor myself liking to break in upon his thoughts before he roused himself from his reverie.

"It is very essential, Miss Stoner," said he, "that you should absolutely follow my advice in every respect."

"I shall most certainly do so."

"The matter is too serious for any hesitation. Your life may depend upon your compliance."

"I assure you that I am in your hands."

"In the first place, both my friend and I must spend the night in your room."

Both Miss Stoner and I gazed at him in astonishment.

"Yes, it must be so. Let me explain. I believe that that is the village inn over there?"

"Yes, that is the 'Crown.'"

"Very good. Your windows would be visible from there?"

"Certainly."

"You must confine yourself to your room, on pretence of a headache, when your step-father comes back. Then when you hear him retire for the night, you must open the shutters of your window, undo the hasp, put your lamp there as a signal to us, and then withdraw quietly with everything which you are likely to want into the room which you used to occupy. I have no doubt that, in spite of the repairs, you could manage there for one night."

"Oh yes, easily."

"The rest you will leave in our hands."

"But what will you do?"

"We shall spend the night in your room, and we shall investigate the cause of this noise which has disturbed you."

"I believe, Mr. Holmes, that you have already made up your mind," said Miss Stoner, laying her hand upon my companion's sleeve.

"Perhaps I have."

"Then for pity's sake tell me what was the cause of my sister's death."

"I should prefer to have clearer proofs before I speak."

"You can at least tell me whether my own thought is correct, and if she died from some sudden fright."

"No, I do not think so. I think that there was probably some more tangible cause. And now, Miss Stoner, we must leave you, for if Dr. Roylott returned and saw us, our journey would be in vain. Good-bye, and be brave, for if you will do what I have told you, you may rest assured that we shall soon drive away the dangers that threaten you."

Sherlock Holmes and I had no difficulty in engaging a bedroom and sitting-room at the "Crown Inn." They were on the upper floor, and from our window we could command a view of the avenue gate, and of the inhabited wing of Stoke Moran Manor House. At dusk we saw Dr. Grimesby Roylott drive past, his huge form looming up beside the little figure of the lad who drove him. The boy had some slight difficulty in undoing the heavy iron gates, and we heard the hoarse roar of the doctor's voice, and saw the fury with which he shook his clinched fists at him. The trap drove on, and a few minutes later we saw a sudden light spring up among the trees as the lamp was lit in one of the sitting-rooms.

"Do you know, Watson," said Holmes, as we sat together in the gathering darkness, "I have really some scruples as to taking you to-night. There is a distinct element of danger."

"Can I be of assistance?"

"Your presence might be invaluable."

"Then I shall certainly come."

"It is very kind of you."

"You speak of danger. You have evidently seen more in these rooms than was visible to me."

"No, but I fancy that I may have deduced a little more. I imagine that you saw all that I did."

"I saw nothing remarkable save the bell-rope, and what purpose that could answer I confess is more than I can imagine."

"You saw the ventilator, too?"

"Yes, but I do not think that it is such a very unusual thing to have a small opening between two rooms. It was so small that a rat could hardly pass through."

"I knew that we should find a ventilator before ever we came to Stoke Moran."

"My dear Holmes!"

"Oh yes, I did. You remember in her statement she said that her sister could smell Dr. Roylott's cigar. Now, of course that suggested at once that there must be a communication between the two rooms. It could only be a small one, or it would have been remarked upon at the coroner's inquiry. I deduced a ventilator."

"But what harm can there be in that?"

"Well, there is at least a curious coincidence of dates. A ventilator is made, a cord is hung, and a lady who sleeps in the bed dies. Does not that strike you?"

"I cannot as yet see any connection."

"Did you observe anything very peculiar about that bed?"

"No."

"It was clamped to the floor. Did you ever see a bed fastened like that before?"

"I cannot say that I have."

"The lady could not move her bed. It must always be in the same relative position to the ventilator and to the rope—for so we may call it, since it was clearly never meant for a bell-pull."

"Holmes," I cried, "I seem to see dimly what you are hinting at. We are only just in time to prevent some subtle and horrible crime."

"Subtle enough and horrible enough. When a doctor does go wrong, he is the first of criminals. He has nerve and he has knowledge. Palmer and Pritchard were among the heads of their profession. This man strikes even deeper, but I think, Watson, that we shall be able to strike deeper still. But we shall have horrors enough before the night is over; for goodness' sake let us have a quiet pipe, and turn our minds for a few hours to something more cheerful."

*

About nine o'clock the light among the trees was extinguished, and all was dark in the direction of the Manor House. Two hours passed slowly away, and then, suddenly, just at the stroke of eleven, a single bright light shone out right in front of us.

"That is our signal," said Holmes, springing to his feet; "it comes from the middle window."

As we passed out he exchanged a few words with the landlord, explaining that we were going on a late visit to an acquaintance, and that it was possible that we might spend the night there. A moment later we were out on the dark road, a chill wind blowing in our faces, and one yellow light twinkling in front of us through the gloom to guide us on our sombre errand.

There was little difficulty in entering the grounds, for unrepaired breaches gaped in the old park wall. Making our way among the trees, we reached the lawn, crossed it, and were about to enter through the window, when out from a clump of laurel bushes there darted what seemed to be a hideous and distorted child, who threw itself upon the grass with writhing limbs, and then ran swiftly across the lawn into the darkness.

"My God!" I whispered; "did you see it?"

Holmes was for the moment as startled as I. His hand closed like a vice upon my wrist in his agitation. Then he broke into a low laugh, and put his lips to my ear.

"It is a nice household," he murmured. "That is the baboon."

I had forgotten the strange pets which the doctor affected. There was a cheetah, too; perhaps we might find it upon our shoulders at any moment. I confess that I felt easier in my

"GOOD-BYE, AND BE BRAVE"

mind when, after following Holmes's example and slipping off my shoes, I found myself inside the bedroom. My companion noiselessly closed the shutters, moved the lamp onto the table, and cast his eyes round the room. All was as we had seen it in the daytime. Then creeping up to me and making a trumpet of his hand, he whispered into my ear again so gently that it was all that I could do to distinguish the words:

"The least sound would be fatal to our plans."

I nodded to show that I had heard.

"We must sit without light. He would see it through the ventilator."

I nodded again.

"Do not go asleep; your very life may depend upon it. Have your pistol ready in case we should need it. I will sit on the side of the bed, and you in that chair."

I took out my revolver and laid it on the corner of the table.

Holmes had brought up a long thin cane, and this he placed upon the bed beside him. By it he laid the box of matches and the stump of a candle. Then he turned down the lamp, and we were left in darkness.

How shall I ever forget that dreadful vigil? I could not hear a sound, not even the drawing of a breath, and yet I knew that my companion sat open-eyed, within a few feet of me, in the same state of nervous tension in which I was myself. The shutters cut off the least ray of light, and we waited in absolute darkness. From outside came the occasional cry of a night-bird, and once at our very window a long drawn cat-like whine, which told us that the cheetah was indeed at liberty. Far away we could hear the deep tones of the parish clock, which boomed out every quarter of an hour. How long they seemed, those quarters! Twelve struck, and one and two and three, and still we sat waiting silently for whatever might befall.

Suddenly there was the momentary gleam of a light up in the direction of the ventilator, which vanished immediately, but was succeeded by a strong smell of burning oil and heated metal. Some one in the next room had lit a dark-lantern. I heard a gentle sound of movement, and then all was silent once more, though the smell grew stronger. For half an hour I sat with straining ears. Then suddenly another sound became audible—a very gentle, soothing sound, like that of a small jet of steam escaping continually from a kettle. The instant that we heard it, Holmes sprang from the bed, struck a match, and lashed furiously with his cane at the bell-pull.

"You see it, Watson?" he yelled. "You see it?"

But I saw nothing. At the moment when Holmes struck the light I heard a low, clear whistle, but the sudden glare flashing into my weary eyes made it impossible for me to tell what it was at which my friend lashed so savagely. I could, however, see that his face was deadly pale, and filled with horror and loathing.

He had ceased to strike, and was gazing up at the ventilator, when suddenly there broke from the silence of the night the most horrible cry to which I have ever listened. It swelled up louder and louder, a hoarse yell of pain and fear and anger all mingled in the one dreadful shriek. They say that away down in the village, and even in the distant parsonage, that cry raised the sleepers from their beds. It struck cold to our hearts, and I stood gazing at Holmes, and he at me, until the last echoes of it had died away into the silence from which it rose.

"What can it mean?" I gasped.

"It means that it is all over," Holmes answered. "And perhaps, after all, it is for the best. Take your pistol, and we will enter Dr. Roylott's room."

With a grave face he lit the lamp and led the way down the corridor. Twice he struck at the chamber door without any reply from within. Then he turned the handle and entered, I at his heels, with the cocked pistol in my hand.

It was a singular sight which met our eyes. On the table stood a dark-lantern with the shutter half open, throwing a brilliant beam of light upon the iron safe, the door of which was ajar. Beside this table, on the wooden chair, sat Dr. Grimesby Roylott, clad in a long gray dressing-gown, his bare ankles protruding beneath, and his feet thrust into red heelless Turkish slippers.

Across his lap lay the short stock with the long lash which we had noticed during the day. His chin was cocked upward and his eyes were fixed in a dreadful, rigid stare at the corner of the ceiling. Round his brow he had a peculiar yellow band, with brownish speckles, which seemed to be bound tightly round his head. As we entered he made neither sound nor motion.

"The band! the speckled band!" whispered Holmes.

I took a step forward. In an instant his strange head-gear began to move, and there reared itself from among his hair the squat diamond-shaped head and puffed neck of a loathsome serpent.

"It is a swamp adder!" cried Holmes; "the deadliest snake in India. He has died within ten seconds of being bitten. Violence does, in truth, recoil upon the violent, and the schemer falls into the pit which he digs for another. Let us thrust this creature back into its den, and we can then remove Miss Stoner to some place of shelter, and let the county police know what has happened."

As he spoke he drew the dog-whip swiftly from the dead man's lap, and throwing the noose round the reptile's neck, he drew it from its horrid perch, and carrying it at arm's length, threw it into the iron safe, which he closed upon it.

*

Such are the true facts of the death of Dr. Grimesby Roylott, of Stoke Moran. It is not necessary that I should prolong a narrative which has already run to too great a length, by telling how we broke the sad news to the terrified girl, how we conveyed her by the morning train to the care of her good aunt at Harrow, of how the slow process of official inquiry came to the conclusion that the doctor met his fate while indiscreetly playing with a dangerous pet. The little which I had yet to learn of the case was told me by Sherlock Holmes as we travelled back next day.

"I had," said he, "come to an entirely erroneous conclusion, which shows, my dear Watson, how dangerous it always is to reason from insufficient data. The presence of the gypsies, and the use of the word 'band,' which was used by the poor girl, no doubt to explain the appearance which she had caught a hurried glimpse of by the light of her match, were sufficient to put me upon an entirely wrong scent. I can only claim the merit that I instantly reconsidered my position when, however, it became clear to me that whatever danger threatened an occupant of the room could not come either from the window or the door. My attention was speedily drawn, as I have already remarked to you, to this ventilator, and to the bell-rope which hung down to the bed. The discovery that this was a dummy, and that the bed was clamped to the floor, instantly gave rise to the suspicion that the rope was there as bridge for something passing through the hole, and coming to the bed. The idea of a snake instantly occurred to me, and when I coupled it with my knowledge that the doctor was furnished with a supply of creatures from India, I felt that I was probably on the right track. The idea of using a form of poison which could not possibly be discovered by any chemical test was just such a one as would occur to a clever and ruthless man who had had an Eastern training. The rapidity with which such a poison would take effect would also, from his point of view, be an advantage. It would be a sharp-eyed coroner, indeed, who could distinguish the two little dark punctures which would show where the poison fangs had done their work. Then I thought of the whistle. Of course he must recall the snake before the morning light revealed it to the victim. He had trained it, probably by the use of the milk which we saw, to return to him when summoned. He would put it through this ventilator at the hour that he thought best, with the certainty that it would crawl down the rope and land on the bed. It might or might not bite the occupant, perhaps she might escape every night for a week, but sooner or later she must fall a victim.

"I had come to these conclusions before ever I had entered his room. An inspection of his chair showed me that he had been in the habit of standing on it, which of course would be necessary in order that he should reach the ventilator. The sight of the safe, the saucer of milk, and the loop of whip-cord were enough to finally dispel any doubts which may have remained. The metallic clang heard by Miss Stoner was obviously caused by her step-father hastily closing the door of his safe upon its terrible occupant. Having once made up my mind, you know the steps which I took in order to put the matter to the proof. I heard the creature hiss, as I have no doubt that you did also, and I instantly lit the light and attacked it."

"With the result of driving it through the ventilator."

"And also with the result of causing it to turn upon its master at the other side. Some of the blows of my cane came home, and roused its snakish temper, so that it flew upon the first person it saw. In this way I am no doubt indirectly responsible for Dr. Grimesby Roylott's death, and I cannot say that it is likely to weigh very heavily upon my conscience."

Wilkie Collins

WILKIE COLLINS (1824-1889) WAS AN ENGLISH AUTHOR AND playwright, and one of the earliest and best writers of detective fiction. His novels *The Moonstone* and *The Woman in White* are among his best and cement him as a master of his craft, with their intricate plots and engaging narrative style. He was a close friend of and mentored by Charles Dickens, with whom he collaborated on several books.

6

THE BITER BIT

Wilkie Collins

Extracted from the Correspondence of the London Police.

FROM CHIEF INSPECTOR THEAKSTONE, OF THE DETECTIVE POLICE, TO SERGEANT BULMER, OF THE SAME FORCE.

London, 4th July, 18—.

SERGEANT BULMER,

This is to inform you that you are wanted to assist in looking up a case of importance, which will require all the attention of an experienced member of the force. The matter of the robbery on which you are now engaged you will please to shift over to the young man who brings you this letter. You will tell him all the circumstances of the case, just as they stand; you will put him up to the progress you have made (if any) toward detecting the person or persons by whom the money has been stolen; and you will leave him to make the best he can of the matter now in your hands. He is to have the whole responsibility of the case, and the whole credit of his success if he brings it to a proper issue.

So much for the orders that I am desired to communicate to you.

A word in your ear, next, about this new man who is to take your place. His name is Matthew Sharpin, and he is to have the chance given him of dashing into our office at one jump—supposing he turns out strong enough to take it. You will naturally ask me how he comes by this privilege. I can only tell you that he has some uncommonly strong interest to back him in certain high quarters, which you and I had better not mention except under our breaths. He has been a lawyer's clerk, and he is wonderfully conceited in his opinion of himself, as well as mean and underhand to look at. According to his own account, he leaves his old trade and joins ours of his own free will and preference. You will no more believe that than I do. My notion is, that he has managed to ferret out some private information in connection with the affairs of one of his master's clients, which makes him rather an awkward customer to keep in the office for the future, and which, at the same time, gives him hold enough over his employer to make it dangerous to drive him into a corner by turning him away. I think the giving him this unheard-of chance among us is, in plain words, pretty much like giving him hush-money to keep him quiet. However that may be, Mr. Matthew Sharpin is to have the case now in your hands, and if he succeeds with it, he pokes his ugly nose into our office as sure as fate. I put you up to this, sergeant, so that you may not stand in your own light by giving the new man any cause to complain of you at headquarters, and remain yours,

FRANCIS THEAKSTONE.

FROM MR. MATTHEW SHARPIN TO CHIEF INSPECTOR THEAKSTONE.

London, 5th July, 18—.

DEAR SIR,

Having now been favoured with the necessary instructions from Sergeant Bulmer, I beg to remind you of certain directions which I have received relating to the report of my future proceedings which I am to prepare for examination at headquarters.

The object of my writing, and of your examining what I have written before you send it to the higher authorities, is, I am informed, to give me, as an untried hand, the benefit of your advice in case I want it (which I venture to think I shall not) at any stage of my proceedings. As the extraordinary circumstances of the case on which I am now engaged make it impossible for me to absent myself from the place where the robbery was committed until I have made some progress toward discovering the thief, I am necessarily precluded from consulting you personally. Hence the necessity of my writing down the various details, which might, perhaps, be better communicated by word of mouth. This, if I am not mistaken, is the position in which we are now placed. I state my own impressions on the subject in writing, in order that we may clearly understand each other at the outset; and have the honour to remain your obedient servant,

MATTHEW SHARPIN.

FROM CHIEF INSPECTOR THEAKSTONE TO MR. MATTHEW SHARPIN.

London, 5th July, 18—.

SIR,

You have begun by wasting time, ink, and paper. We both of us perfectly well knew the position we stood in toward each other when I sent you with my letter to Sergeant Bulmer. There was not the least need to repeat it in writing. Be so good as to employ your pen in future on the business actually in hand.

You have now three separate matters on which to write me. First, you have to draw up a statement of your instructions received from Sergeant Bulmer, in order to show us that nothing has escaped your memory, and that you are thoroughly acquainted with all the circumstances of the case which has been intrusted to you. Secondly, you are to inform me what it is you propose to do. Thirdly, you are to report every inch of your progress (if you make any) from day to day, and, if need be, from hour to hour as well. This is *your* duty. As to what *my* duty may be, when I want you to remind me of it, I will write and tell you so. In the mean time, I remain yours,

FRANCIS THEAKSTONE.

FROM MR. MATTHEW SHARPIN TO CHIEF INSPECTOR THEAKSTONE.

London, 6th July, 18—.

SIR,

You are rather an elderly person, and, as such, naturally inclined to be a little jealous of men like me, who are in the prime of their lives and their faculties. Under these circumstances, it is my duty to be considerate toward you, and not to bear too hardly on your small failings. I decline, therefore, altogether to take offense at the tone of your letter; I give you the full benefit of the natural generosity of my nature; I sponge the very existence of your surly communication out of my memory—in short, Chief Inspector Theakstone, I forgive you, and proceed to business.

My first duty is to draw up a full statement of the instructions I have received from Sergeant Bulmer. Here they are at your service, according to my version of them.

At number Thirteen Rutherford Street, Soho, there is a stationer's shop. It is kept by one Mr. Yatman. He is a married man, but has no family. Besides Mr. and Mrs. Yatman, the other inmates in the house are a lodger, a young single man named Jay, who occupies the front room on the second floor—a shopman, who sleeps in one of the attics, and a servant-of-all-work, whose bed is in the back kitchen. Once a week a charwoman comes to help this servant. These are all the persons who, on ordinary occasions, have means of access to the interior of the house, placed, as a matter of course, at their disposal.

Mr. Yatman has been in business for many years, carrying on his affairs prosperously enough to realize a handsome independence for a person in his position. Unfortunately for himself, he endeavoured to increase the amount of his property by speculating.

He ventured boldly in his investments; luck went against him; and rather less than two years ago he found himself a poor man again. All that was saved out of the wreck of his property was the sum of two hundred pounds.

Although Mr. Yatman did his best to meet his altered circumstances, by giving up many of the luxuries and comforts to which he and his wife had been accustomed, he found it impossible to retrench so far as to allow of putting by any money from the income produced by his shop. The business has been declining of late years, the cheap advertising stationers having done it injury with the public. Consequently, up to the last week, the only surplus property possessed by Mr. Yatman consisted of the two hundred pounds which had been recovered from the wreck of his fortune. This sum was placed as a deposit in a joint-stock bank of the highest possible character.

Eight days ago Mr. Yatman and his lodger, Mr. Jay, held a conversation on the subject of the commercial difficulties which are hampering trade in all directions at the present time. Mr. Jay (who lives by supplying the newspapers with short paragraphs relating to accidents, offenses, and brief records of remarkable occurrences in general—who is, in short, what they call a penny-a-liner) told his landlord that he had been in the city that day and heard unfavourable rumours on the subject of the joint-stock banks. The rumours to which he alluded had already reached the ears of Mr. Yatman from other quarters, and the confirmation of them by his lodger had such an effect on his mind—predisposed as it was to alarm by the experience of his former losses—that he resolved to go at once to the bank and withdraw his deposit. It was then getting on toward the end of the afternoon, and he arrived just in time to receive his money before the bank closed.

He received the deposit in bank-notes of the following amounts: one fifty-pound note, three twenty-pound notes, six ten-pound notes, and six five-pound notes. His object in drawing the money in this form was to have it ready to lay out immediately in trifling loans, on good security, among the small tradespeople of his district, some of whom are sorely pressed for the very means of existence at the present time. Investments of this kind seemed to Mr. Yatman to be the most safe and the most profitable on which he could now venture.

He brought the money back in an envelope placed in his breast pocket, and asked his shopman, on getting home, to look for a small, flat, tin cash-box, which had not been used for years, and which, as Mr. Yatman remembered it, was exactly of the right size to hold the bank-notes. For some time the cash-box was searched for in vain. Mr. Yatman called to his wife to know if she had any idea where it was. The question was overheard by the servant-of-all-work, who was taking up the tea-tray at the time, and by Mr. Jay, who was coming downstairs on his way out to the theatre. Ultimately the cash-box was found by the shopman. Mr. Yatman placed the bank-notes in it, secured them by a padlock, and put the box in his coat pocket. It stuck out of the coat pocket a very little, but enough to be seen. Mr. Yatman remained at home, upstairs, all that evening. No visitors called. At eleven o'clock he went to bed, and put the cash-box under his pillow.

When he and his wife woke the next morning the box was gone. Payment of the notes was immediately stopped at the Bank of England, but no news of the money has been heard of since that time.

So far the circumstances of the case are perfectly clear. They point unmistakably to the conclusion that the robbery must have been committed by some person living in the house. Suspicion falls, therefore, upon the servant-of-all-work, upon the shopman, and upon Mr. Jay. The two first knew that the cash-box was being inquired for by their master, but did not know what it was he wanted to put into it. They would assume, of course, that it was money. They both had opportunities (the servant when she took away the tea, and the shopman when he came, after shutting up, to give the keys of the till to his master) of seeing the cash-box in Mr. Yatman's pocket, and of inferring naturally, from its position there, that he intended to take it into his bedroom with him at night.

Mr. Jay, on the other hand, had been told, during the afternoon's conversation on the subject of joint-stock banks, that his landlord had a deposit of two hundred pounds in one of them. He also knew that Mr. Yatman left him with the intention of drawing that money out; and he heard the inquiry for the cash-box afterward, when he was coming downstairs. He must, therefore, have inferred that the money was in the house, and that the cash-box was the receptacle intended to contain it. That he could have had any idea, however, of the place in which Mr. Yatman intended to keep it for the night is impossible, seeing that he went out before the box was found, and did not return till his landlord was in bed. Consequently, if he committed the robbery, he must have gone into the bedroom purely on speculation.

Speaking of the bedroom reminds me of the necessity of noticing the situation of it in the house, and the means that exist of gaining easy access to it at any hour of the night.

The room in question is the back room on the first floor. In consequence of Mrs. Yatman's constitutional nervousness on the subject of fire, which makes her apprehend being burned alive in her room, in case of accident, by the hampering of the lock if the key is turned in it, her husband has never been accustomed to lock the bedroom door. Both he and his wife are, by their own admission, heavy sleepers; consequently, the risk to be run by any evil-disposed persons wishing to plunder the bedroom was of the most trifling kind. They could enter the room by merely turning the handle of the door; and, if they moved with ordinary caution, there was no fear of their waking the sleepers inside. This fact is of importance. It strengthens our conviction that the money must have been taken by one of the inmates of the house, because it tends to show that the robbery, in this case, might have been committed by persons not possessed of the superior vigilance and running of the experienced thief.

Such are the circumstances, as they were related to Sergeant Bulmer when he was first called in to discover the guilty parties, and, if possible, to recover the lost bank-notes. The strictest inquiry which he could institute failed of producing the smallest fragment of evidence against any of the persons on whom suspicion naturally fell. Their language and behaviour on being informed of the robbery was perfectly consistent with the language and behaviour of innocent people. Sergeant Bulmer felt from the first that this was a case for private inquiry and secret observation. He began by recommending Mr. and Mrs. Yatman to affect a feeling of perfect confidence in the innocence of the persons living under their roof, and he then opened the campaign by employing himself in following the goings and comings, and in discovering the friends, the habits, and the secrets of the maid-of-all-work.

Three days and nights of exertion on his own part, and on that of others who were competent to assist his investigations, were enough to satisfy him that there was no sound cause for suspicion against the girl.

He next practised the same precaution in relation to the shopman. There was more difficulty and uncertainty in privately clearing up this person's character without his knowledge, but the obstacles were at last smoothed away with tolerable success; and, though there is not the same amount of certainty in this case which there was in the case of the girl, there is still fair reason for supposing that the shopman has had nothing to do with the robbery of the cash-box.

As a necessary consequence of these proceedings, the range of suspicion now becomes limited to the lodger, Mr. Jay.

When I presented your letter of introduction to Sergeant Bulmer, he had already made some inquiries on the subject of this young man. The result, so far, has not been at all favourable. Mr. Jay's habits are irregular; he frequents public houses, and seems to be familiarly acquainted with a great many dissolute characters; he is in debt to most of the tradespeople whom he employs; he has not paid his rent to Mr. Yatman for the last month; yesterday evening he came home excited by liquor, and last week he was seen talking to a prizefighter; in short, though Mr. Jay does call himself a journalist, in virtue of his penny-a-line contributions to the newspapers, he is a young man of low taste, vulgar manners, and bad habits. Nothing has yet been discovered in relation to him which redounds to his credit in the smallest degree.

I have now reported, down to the very last details, all the particulars communicated to me by Sergeant Bulmer. I believe you will not find an omission anywhere; and I think you will admit, though you are prejudiced against me, that a clearer statement of facts was never laid before you than the statement I have now made. My next duty is to tell you what I propose to do now that the case is confided to my hands.

In the first place, it is clearly my business to take up the case at the point where Sergeant Bulmer has left it. On his authority, I am justified in assuming that I have no need to trouble myself about the maid-of-all-work and the shopman. Their characters are now to be considered as cleared up. What remains to be privately investigated is the question of the guilt or innocence of Mr. Jay. Before we give up the notes for lost, we must make sure, if we can, that he knows nothing about them.

This is the plan that I have adopted, with the full approval of Mr. and Mrs. Yatman, for discovering whether Mr. Jay is or is not the person who has stolen the cash-box:

I propose to-day to present myself at the house in the character of a young man who is looking for lodgings. The back room on the second floor will be shown to me as the room to let, and I shall establish myself there to-night as a person from the country who has come to London to look for a situation in a respectable shop or office.

By this means I shall be living next to the room occupied by Mr. Jay. The partition between us is mere lath and plaster.

I shall make a small hole in it, near the cornice, through which I can see what Mr. Jay does in his room, and hear every word that is said when any friend happens to call on him. Whenever he is at home, I shall be at my post of observation; whenever he goes out, I shall be after him. By employing these means of watching him, I believe I may look forward to the discovery of his secret—if he knows anything about the lost bank-notes—as to a dead certainty.

What you may think of my plan of observation I can not undertake to say. It appears to me to unite the invaluable merits of boldness and simplicity. Fortified by this conviction, I close the present communication with feelings of the most sanguine description in regard to the future, and remain your obedient servant,

MATTHEW SHARPIN.

FROM THE SAME TO THE SAME.

7th July.

SIR,

As you have not honoured me with any answer to my last communication, I assume that, in spite of your prejudices against me, it has produced the favourable impression on your mind which I ventured to anticipate. Gratified and encouraged beyond measure by the token of approval which your eloquent silence conveys to me, I proceed to report the progress that has been made in the course of the last twenty-four hours.

I am now comfortably established next door to Mr. Jay, and I am delighted to say that I have two holes in the partition instead of one. My natural sense of humour has led me into the pardonable extravagance of giving them both appropriate names. One I call my peep-hole, and the other my pipe-hole. The name of the first explains itself; the name of the second refers to a small tin pipe or tube inserted in the hole, and twisted so that the mouth of it comes close to my ear while I am standing at my post of observation. Thus, while I am looking at Mr. Jay through my peep-hole, I can hear every word that may be spoken in his room through my pipe-hole.

Perfect candour—a virtue which I have possessed from my childhood—compels me to acknowledge, before I go any farther, that the ingenious notion of adding a pipe-hole to my proposed peep-hole originated with Mrs. Yatman. This lady—a most intelligent and accomplished person, simple, and yet distinguished in her manners, has entered into all my little plans with an enthusiasm and intelligence which I can not too highly praise. Mr. Yatman is so cast down by his loss that he is quite incapable of affording me any assistance. Mrs. Yatman, who is evidently most tenderly attached to him, feels her husband's sad condition of mind even more acutely than she feels the loss of the money, and is mainly stimulated to exertion by her desire to assist in raising him from the miserable state of prostration into which he has now fallen.

"The money, Mr. Sharpin," she said to me yesterday evening, with tears in her eyes, "the money may be regained by rigid economy and strict attention to business. It is my husband's wretched state of mind that makes me so anxious for the discovery of the thief. I may be wrong, but I felt hopeful of success as soon as you entered the house; and I believe that, if the wretch who robbed us is to be found, you are the man to discover him." I accepted this gratifying compliment in the spirit in which it was offered, firmly believing that I shall be found, sooner or later, to have thoroughly deserved it.

Let me now return to business—that is to say, to my peep-hole and my pipe-hole.

I have enjoyed some hours of calm observation of Mr. Jay. Though rarely at home, as I understand from Mrs. Yatman, on ordinary occasions, he has been indoors the whole of this day. That is suspicious, to begin with. I have to report, further, that he rose at a late hour this morning (always a bad sign in a young man), and that he lost a great deal of time, after he was up, in yawning and complaining to himself of headache. Like other debauched characters, he ate little or nothing for breakfast. His next proceeding was to smoke a pipe—a dirty clay pipe, which a gentleman would have been ashamed to put between his lips. When he had done smoking he took out pen, ink, and paper, and sat down to write with a groan—whether of remorse for having taken the bank-notes, or of disgust at the task before him, I am unable to say. After writing a few lines (too far away from my peep-hole to give me a chance of reading over his shoulder), he leaned back in his chair, and amused himself by humming the tunes of popular songs. I recognized "My Mary Anne," "Bobbin' Around," and "Old Dog Tray," among other melodies. Whether these do or do not represent secret signals by which he communicates with his accomplices remains to be seen. After he had amused himself for some time by humming, he got up and began to walk about the room, occasionally stopping to add a sentence to the paper on his desk. Before long he went to a locked cupboard and opened it. I strained my eyes eagerly, in expectation of making a discovery. I saw him take something carefully out of the cupboard—he turned round—and it was only a pint bottle of brandy! Having drunk some of the liquor, this extremely indolent reprobate lay down on his bed again, and in five minutes was fast asleep.

After hearing him snoring for at least two hours, I was recalled to my peep-hole by a knock at his door. He jumped up and opened it with suspicious activity.

A very small boy, with a very dirty face, walked in, said, "Please, sir, they're waiting for you," sat down with his legs a long way from the ground, and instantly fell asleep! Mr. Jay swore an oath, tied a wet towel round his head, and, going back to his paper, began to cover it with, writing as fast as his fingers could move the pen. Occasionally getting up to dip the towel in water and tie it on again, he continued at this employment for nearly three hours; then folded up the leaves of writing, woke the boy, and gave them to him, with this remarkable expression: "Now, then, young sleepy-head, quick march! If you see the governor, tell him to have the money ready for me when I call for it." The boy grinned and disappeared. I was sorely tempted to follow "sleepy-head," but, on reflection, considered it safest still to keep my eye on the proceedings of Mr. Jay.

In half an hour's time he put on his hat and walked out. Of course, I put on my hat and walked out also. As I went downstairs I passed Mrs. Yatman going up. The lady has been kind enough to undertake, by previous arrangement between us, to search Mr. Jay's room while he is out of the way, and while I am necessarily engaged in the pleasing duty of following him wherever he goes. On the occasion to which I now refer, he walked straight to the nearest tavern, and ordered a couple of mutton-chops for his dinner. I placed myself in the next box to him, and ordered a couple of mutton-chops for my dinner. Before I had been in the room a minute, a young man of highly suspicious manners and appearance, sitting at a table opposite, took his glass of porter in his hand and joined Mr. Jay. I pretended to be reading the newspaper, and listened, as in duty bound, with all my might.

"Jack has been here inquiring after you," says the young man.

"Did he leave any message?" asks Mr. Jay.

"Yes," says the other. "He told me, if I met with you, to say that he wished very particularly to see you to-night, and that he would give you a look in at Rutherford Street at seven o'clock."

"All right," says Mr. Jay. "I'll get back in time to see him."

Upon this, the suspicious-looking young man finished his porter, and saying that he was rather in a hurry, took leave of his friend (perhaps I should not be wrong if I said his accomplice?), and left the room.

At twenty-five minutes and a half past six—in these serious cases it is important to be particular about time—Mr. Jay finished his chops and paid his bill. At twenty-six minutes and three quarters I finished my chops and paid mine. In ten minutes more I was inside the house in Rutherford Street, and was received by Mrs. Yatman in the passage. That charming woman's face exhibited an expression of melancholy and disappointment which it quite grieved me to see.

"I am afraid, ma'am," says I, "that you have not hit on any little criminating discovery in the lodger's room?"

She shook her head and sighed. It was a soft, languid, fluttering sigh—and, upon my life, it quite upset me. For the moment I forgot business, and burned with envy of Mr. Yatman.

"Don't despair, ma'am," I said, with an insinuating mildness which seemed to touch her. "I have heard a mysterious conversation—I know of a guilty appointment—and I expect great things from my peep-hole and my pipe-hole to-night. Pray don't be alarmed, but I think we are on the brink of a discovery."

Here my enthusiastic devotion to business got the better part of my tender feelings. I looked—winked—nodded—left her.

When I got back to my observatory, I found Mr. Jay digesting his mutton-chops in an arm-chair, with his pipe in his mouth. On his table were two tumblers, a jug of water, and the pint bottle of brandy. It was then close upon seven o'clock. As the hour struck the person described as "Jack" walked in.

He looked agitated—I am happy to say he looked violently agitated. The cheerful glow of anticipated success diffused itself (to use a strong expression) all over me, from head to foot. With breathless interest I looked through my peep-hole, and saw the visitor—the "Jack" of this delightful case—sit down, facing me, at the opposite side of the table to Mr. Jay. Making allowance for the difference in expression which their countenances just now happened to exhibit, these two abandoned villains were so much alike in other respects as to lead at once to the conclusion that they were brothers. Jack was the cleaner man and the better dressed of the two. I admit that, at the outset. It is, perhaps, one of my failings to push justice and impartiality to their utmost limits. I am no Pharisee; and where Vice has its redeeming point, I say, let Vice have its due—yes, yes, by all manner of means, let Vice have its due.

"What's the matter now, Jack?" says Mr. Jay.

"Can't you see it in my face?" says Jack. "My dear fellow, delays are dangerous. Let us have done with suspense, and risk it, the day after to-morrow."

"So soon as that?" cries Mr. Jay, looking very much astonished. "Well, I'm ready, if you are. But, I say, Jack, is somebody else ready too? Are you quite sure of that?"

He smiled as he spoke—a frightful smile—and laid a very strong emphasis on those two words, "Somebody else." There is evidently a third ruffian, a nameless desperado, concerned in the business.

"Meet us to-morrow," says Jack, "and judge for yourself. Be in the Regent's Park at eleven in the morning, and look out for us at the turning that leads to the Avenue Road."

"I'll be there," says Mr. Jay. "Have a drop of brandy and water? What are you getting up for? You're not going already?"

"Yes I am," says Jack. "The fact is, I'm so excited and agitated that I can't sit still anywhere for five minutes together. Ridiculous as it may appear to you, I'm in a perpetual state of nervous flutter. I can't, for the life of me, help fearing that we shall be found out. I fancy that every man who looks twice at me in the street is a spy—"

At these words I thought my legs would have given way under me. Nothing but strength of mind kept me at my peep-hole—nothing else, I give you my word of honour.

"Stuff and nonsense!" cries Mr. Jay, with all the effrontery of a veteran in crime. "We have kept the secret up to this time, and we will manage cleverly to the end. Have a drop of brandy and water, and you will feel as certain about it as I do."

Jack steadily refused the brandy and water, and steadily persisted in taking his leave.

"I must try if I can't walk it off," he said. "Remember to-morrow morning—eleven o'clock, Avenue Road, side of the Regent's Park."

With those words he went out. His hardened relative laughed desperately and resumed the dirty clay pipe.

I sat down on the side of my bed, actually quivering with excitement.

It is clear to me that no attempt has yet been made to change the stolen bank-notes, and I may add that Sergeant Bulmer was of that opinion also when he left the case in my hands. What is the natural conclusion to draw from the conversation which I have just set down? Evidently that the confederates meet to-morrow to take their respective shares in the stolen money, and to decide on the safest means of getting the notes changed the day after. Mr. Jay is, beyond a doubt, the leading criminal in this business, and he will probably run the chief risk—that of changing the fifty-pound note. I shall, therefore, still make it my business to follow him—attending at the Regent's Park to-morrow, and doing my best to hear what is said there. If another appointment is made for the day after, I shall, of course, go to it. In the meantime, I shall want the immediate assistance of two competent persons (supposing the rascals separate after their meeting) to follow the two minor criminals. It is only fair to add that, if the rogues all retire together, I shall probably keep my subordinates in reserve. Being naturally ambitious, I desire, if possible, to have the whole credit of discovering this robbery to myself.

8th July.

I have to acknowledge, with thanks, the speedy arrival of my two subordinates—men of very average abilities, I am afraid; but, fortunately, I shall always be on the spot to direct them.

My first business this morning was necessarily to prevent possible mistakes by accounting to Mr. and Mrs. Yatman for the presence of two strangers on the scene. Mr. Yatman (between ourselves, a poor, feeble man) only shook his head and groaned. Mrs. Yatman (that superior woman) favoured me with a charming look of intelligence.

"Oh, Mr. Sharpin!" she said, "I am so sorry to see those two men! Your sending for their assistance looks as if you were beginning to be doubtful of success."

I privately winked at her (she is very good in allowing me to do so without taking offence), and told her, in my facetious way, that she laboured under a slight mistake.

"It is because I am sure of success, ma'am, that I send for them. I am determined to recover the money, not for my own sake only, but for Mr. Yatman's sake—and for yours."

I laid a considerable amount of stress on those last three words. She said, "Oh, Mr. Sharpin!" again, and blushed of a heavenly red, and looked down at her work. I could go to the world's end with that woman if Mr. Yatman would only die.

I sent off the two subordinates to wait until I wanted them at the Avenue Road gate of the Regent's Park. Half an hour afterward I was following the same direction myself at the heels of Mr. Jay.

The two confederates were punctual to the appointed time. I blush to record it, but it is nevertheless necessary to state that the third rogue—the nameless desperado of my report, or, if you prefer it, the mysterious "somebody else" of the conversation between the two brothers—is—a woman! and, what is worse, a young woman! and, what is more lamentable still, a nice-looking woman! I have long resisted a growing conviction that, wherever there is mischief in this world, an individual of the fair sex is inevitably certain to be mixed up in it. After the experience of this morning, I can struggle against that sad conclusion no longer. I give up the sex—excepting Mrs. Yatman, I give up the sex.

The man named "Jack" offered the woman his arm. Mr. Jay placed himself on the other side of her. The three then walked away slowly among the trees. I followed them at a respectful distance. My two subordinates, at a respectful distance also, followed me.

It was, I deeply regret to say, impossible to get near enough to them to overhear their conversation without running too great a risk of being discovered. I could only infer from their gestures and actions that they were all three talking with extraordinary earnestness on some subject which deeply interested them. After having been engaged in this way a full quarter of an hour, they suddenly turned round to retrace their steps. My presence of mind did not forsake me in this emergency. I signed to the two subordinates to walk on carelessly and pass them, while I myself slipped dexterously behind a tree. As they came by me, I heard "Jack" address these words to Mr. Jay:

"Let us say half past ten to-morrow morning. And mind you come in a cab. We had better not risk taking one in this neighbourhood."

Mr. Jay made some brief reply which I could not overhear. They walked back to the place at which they had met, shaking hands there with an audacious cordiality which it quite sickened me to see. They then separated. I followed Mr. Jay. My subordinates paid the same delicate attention to the other two.

Instead of taking me back to Rutherford Street, Mr. Jay led me to the Strand. He stopped at a dingy, disreputable-looking house, which, according to the inscription over the door, was a newspaper office, but which, in my judgment, had all the external appearance of a place devoted to the reception of stolen goods.

After remaining inside for a few minutes, he came out whistling, with his finger and thumb in his waistcoat pocket. Some men would now have arrested him on the spot. I remembered the necessity of catching the two confederates, and the importance of not interfering with the appointment that had been made for the next morning. Such coolness as this, under trying circumstances, is rarely to be found, I should imagine, in a young beginner, whose reputation as a detective policeman is still to make.

From the house of suspicious appearance Mr. Jay betook himself to a cigar-divan, and read the magazines over a cheroot. From the divan he strolled to the tavern and had his chops. I strolled to the tavern and had my chops. When he had done he went back to his lodging. When I had done I went back to mine. He was overcome with drowsiness early in the evening, and went to bed. As soon as I heard him snoring, I was overcome with drowsiness and went to bed also.

Early in the morning my two subordinates came to make their report.

They had seen the man named "Jack" leave the woman at

the gate of an apparently respectable villa residence not far from the Regent's Park. Left to himself, he took a turning to the right, which led to a sort of suburban street, principally inhabited by shopkeepers. He stopped at the private door of one of the houses, and let himself in with his own key—looking about him as he opened the door, and staring suspiciously at my men as they lounged along on the opposite side of the way. These were all the particulars which the subordinates had to communicate. I kept them in my room to attend on me, if needful, and mounted to my peep-hole to have a look at Mr. Jay.

He was occupied in dressing himself, and was taking extraordinary pains to destroy all traces of the natural slovenliness of his appearance. This was precisely what I expected. A vagabond like Mr. Jay knows the importance of giving himself a respectable look when he is going to run the risk of changing a stolen bank-note. At five minutes past ten o'clock he had given the last brush to his shabby hat and the last scouring with bread-crumb to his dirty gloves. At ten minutes past ten he was in the street, on his way to the nearest cab-stand, and I and my subordinates were close on his heels.

He took a cab, and we took a cab. I had not overheard them appoint a place of meeting when following them in the Park on the previous day, but I soon found that we were proceeding in the old direction of the Avenue Road gate. The cab in which Mr. Jay was riding turned into the Park slowly. We stopped outside, to avoid exciting suspicion. I got out to follow the cab on foot. Just as I did so, I saw it stop, and detected the two confederates approaching it from among the trees. They got in, and the cab was turned about directly. I ran back to my own cab, and told the driver to let them pass him, and then to follow as before.

The man obeyed my directions, but so clumsily as to excite their suspicions. We had been driving after them about three minutes (returning along the road by which we had advanced) when I looked out of the window to see how far they might be ahead of us. As I did this, I saw two hats popped out of the windows of their cab, and two faces looking back at me. I sank into my place in a cold sweat; the expression is coarse, but no other form of words can describe my condition at that trying moment.

"We are found out!" I said, faintly, to my two subordinates. They stared at me in astonishment. My feelings changed instantly from the depth of despair to the height of indignation.

"It is the cabman's fault. Get out, one of you," I said, with dignity—"get out, and punch his head."

Instead of following my directions (I should wish this act of disobedience to be reported at headquarters) they both looked out of the window. Before I could express my just indignation, they both grinned, and said to me, "Please to look out, sir!"

I did look out. Their cab had stopped.

Where?

At a church door!

What effect this discovery might have had upon the ordinary run of men I don't know. Being of a strong religious turn myself, it filled me with horror. I have often read of the unprincipled cunning of criminal persons, but I never before heard of three thieves attempting to double on their pursuers by entering a church! The sacrilegious audacity of that proceeding is, I should think, unparalleled in the annals of crime.

I checked my grinning subordinates by a frown. It was easy to see what was passing in their superficial minds. If I had not been able to look below the surface, I might, on observing two nicely-dressed men and one nicely-dressed woman enter a church before eleven in the morning on a week day, have come to the same hasty conclusion at which my inferiors had evidently arrived. As it was, appearances had no power to impose on *me*. I got out, and, followed by one of my men, entered the church. The other man I sent round to watch the vestry door. You may catch a weasel asleep, but not your humble servant, Matthew Sharpin!

We stole up the gallery stairs, diverged to the organ-loft, and peered through the curtains in front. There they were, all three, sitting in a pew below—yes, incredible as it may appear, sitting in a pew below!

Before I could determine what to do, a clergyman made his appearance in full canonicals from the vestry door, followed by a clerk. My brain whirled and my eyesight grew dim. Dark remembrances of robberies committed in vestries floated through my mind. I trembled for the excellent man in full canonicals—I even trembled for the clerk.

The clergyman placed himself inside the altar rails. The three desperadoes approached him. He opened his book, and began to read. What? you will ask.

I answer, without the slightest hesitation, the first lines of the Marriage Service.

My subordinate had the audacity to look at me, and then to stuff his pocket-handkerchief into his mouth. I scorned to pay any attention to him. After I had discovered that the man "Jack" was the bridegroom, and that the man Jay acted the part of father, and gave away the bride, I left the church, followed by my men, and joined the other subordinate outside the vestry door. Some people in my position would now have felt rather crestfallen, and would have begun to think that they had made a very foolish mistake. Not the faintest misgiving of any kind troubled me. I did not feel in the slightest degree depreciated in my own estimation. And even now, after a lapse of three hours, my mind remains, I am happy to say, in the same calm and hopeful condition.

As soon as I and my subordinates were assembled together outside the church, I intimated my intention of still following the other cab in spite of what had occurred. My reason for deciding on this course will appear presently. The two subordinates appeared to be astonished at my resolution. One of them had the impertinence to say to me,

"If you please, sir, who is it that we are after? A man who has stolen money, or a man who has stolen a wife?"

The other low person encouraged him by laughing. Both have deserved an official reprimand, and both, I sincerely trust, will be sure to get it.

When the marriage ceremony was over, the three got into their cab, and once more our vehicle (neatly hidden round the corner of the church) started to follow theirs.

We traced them to the terminus of the Southwestern Railway. The newly-married couple took tickets for Richmond, paying their fare with a half sovereign, and so depriving me of the pleasure of arresting them, which I should certainly have done if they had offered a banknote. They parted from Mr. Jay, saying, "Remember the address—14 Babylon Terrace. You dine with us to-morrow week." Mr. Jay accepted the invitation, and added, jocosely, that he was going home at once to get off his clean clothes, and to be comfortable and dirty again for the rest of the day. I have to report that I saw him home safely, and that he is comfortable and dirty again (to use his own disgraceful language) at the present moment.

Here the affair rests, having by this time reached what I may call its first stage.

I know very well what persons of hasty judgment will be inclined to say of my proceedings thus far. They will assert that I have been deceiving myself all through in the most absurd way; they will declare that the suspicious conversations which I have reported referred solely to the difficulties and dangers of successfully carrying out a runaway match; and they will appeal to the scene in the church as offering undeniable proof of the correctness of their assertions. So let it be. I dispute nothing up to this point. But I ask a question, out of the depths of my own sagacity as a man of the world, which the bitterest of my enemies will not, I think, find it particularly easy to answer.

Granted the fact of the marriage, what proof does it afford me of the innocence of the three persons concerned in that clandestine transaction? It gives me none. On the contrary, it strengthens my suspicions against Mr. Jay and his confederates, because it suggests a distinct motive for their stealing the money. A gentleman who is going to spend his honeymoon at Richmond wants money; and a gentleman who is in debt to all his tradespeople wants money. Is this an unjustifiable imputation of bad motives? In the name of outraged Morality, I deny it. These men have combined together, and have stolen a woman. Why should they not combine together and steal a cash-box? I take my stand on the logic of rigid Virtue, and I defy all the sophistry of Vice to move me an inch out of my position.

Speaking of virtue, I may add that I have put this view of the case to Mr. and Mrs. Yatman. That accomplished and charming woman found it difficult at first to follow the close chain of my reasoning. I am free to confess that she shook her head, and shed tears, and joined her husband in premature lamentation over the loss of the two hundred pounds. But a little careful explanation on my part, and a little attentive listening on hers, ultimately changed her opinion. She now agrees with me that there is nothing in this unexpected circumstance of the clandestine marriage which absolutely tends to divert suspicion from Mr. Jay, or Mr. "Jack," or the runaway lady. "Audacious hussy" was the term my fair friend used in speaking of her; but let that pass. It is more to the purpose to record that Mrs. Yatman has not lost confidence in me, and that Mr. Yatman promises to follow her example, and do his best to look hopefully for future results.

I have now, in the new turn that circumstances have taken, to await advice from your office. I pause for fresh orders with all the composure of a man who has got two strings to his bow. When I traced the three confederates from the church door to the railway terminus, I had two motives for doing so. First, I followed them as a matter of official business, believing them still to have been guilty of the robbery. Secondly, I followed them as a matter of private speculation, with a view of discovering the place of refuge to which the runaway couple intended to retreat, and of making my information a marketable commodity to offer to the young lady's family and friends. Thus, whatever happens, I may congratulate myself beforehand on not having wasted my time. If the office approves of my conduct, I have my plan ready for further proceedings. If the office blames me, I shall take myself off, with my marketable information, to the genteel villa residence in the neighbourhood of the Regent's Park. Any way, the affair puts money into my pocket, and does credit to my penetration as an uncommonly sharp man.

I have only one word more to add, and it is this: If any individual ventures to assert that Mr. Jay and his confederates are innocent of all share in the stealing of the cash-box, I, in return, defy that individual—though he may even be the Chief Inspector Theakstone himself—to tell me who has committed the robbery at Rutherford Street, Soho.

Strong in that conviction, I have the honour to be your very obedient servant,

MATTHEW SHARPIN.

FROM CHIEF INSPECTOR THEAKSTONE TO SERGEANT BULMER.

Birmingham, July 9th.

SERGEANT BULMER,

That empty-headed puppy, Mr. Matthew Sharpin, has made a mess of the case at Rutherford Street, exactly as I expected he would. Business keeps me in this town, so I write to you to set the matter straight. I inclose with this the pages of feeble scribble-scrabble which the creature Sharpin calls a report. Look them over; and when you have made your way through all the gabble, I think you will agree with me that the conceited booby has looked for the thief in every direction but the right one. You can lay your hand on the guilty person in five minutes, now. Settle the case at once; forward your report to me at this place, and tell Mr. Sharpin that he is suspended till further notice.

Yours,
FRANCIS THEAKSTONE.

FROM SERGEANT BULMER TO CHIEF INSPECTOR THEAKSTONE.

London, July 10th.

INSPECTOR THEAKSTONE,

Your letter and inclosure came safe to hand. Wise men, they say, may always learn something even from a fool. By the time I had got through Sharpin's maundering report of his own folly, I saw my way clear enough to the end of the Rutherford Street case, just as you thought I should. In half an hour's time I was at the house. The first person I saw there was Mr. Sharpin himself.

"Have you come to help me?" says he.

"Not exactly," says I. "I've come to tell you that you are suspended till further notice."

"Very good," says he, not taken down by so much as a single peg in his own estimation. "I thought you would be jealous of me. It's very natural; and I don't blame you. Walk in, pray, and make yourself at home. I'm off to do a little detective business on my own account, in the neighbourhood of the Regent's Park. Ta-ta, sergeant, ta-ta!"

With those words he took himself out of the way, which was exactly what I wanted him to do.

As soon as the maid-servant had shut the door, I told her to inform her master that I wanted to say a word to him in private. She showed me into the parlour behind the shop, and there was Mr. Yatman all alone, reading the newspaper.

"About this matter of the robbery, sir," says I.

He cut me short, peevishly enough, being naturally a poor, weak, womanish sort of man. "Yes, yes, I know," says he. "You have come to tell me that your wonderfully clever man, who has bored holes in my second-floor partition, has made a mistake, and is off the scent of the scoundrel who has stolen my money."

"Yes, sir," says I. "That *is* one of the things I came to tell you. But I have got something else to say besides that."

"Can you tell me who the thief is?" says he more pettish than ever.

"Yes, sir," says I, "I think I can."

He put down the newspaper, and began to look rather anxious and frightened.

"Not my shopman?" says he. "I hope, for the man's own sake, it's not my shopman."

"Guess again, sir," says I.

"That idle slut, the maid?" says he.

"She is idle, sir," says I, "and she is also a slut; my first inquiries about her proved as much as that. But she's not the thief."

"Then, in the name of heaven, who is?" says he.

"Will you please to prepare yourself for a very disagreeable surprise, sir?" says I. "And, in case you lose your temper, will you excuse remarking that I am the stronger man of the two, and that, if you allow yourself to lay hands on me, I may unintentionally hurt you, in pure self-defence."

He turned as pale as ashes, and pushed his chair two or three feet away from me.

"You have asked me to tell you, sir, who has taken your money," I went on. "If you insist on my giving you an answer—"

"I do insist," he said, faintly. "Who has taken it?"

"Your wife has taken it," I said, very quietly, and very positively at the same time.

He jumped out of the chair as if I had put a knife into him, and struck his fist on the table so heavily that the wood cracked again.

"Steady, sir," says I. "Flying into a passion won't help you to the truth."

"It's a lie!" says he, with another smack of his fist on the table—"a base, vile, infamous lie! How dare you—"

He stopped, and fell back into the chair again, looked about him in a bewildered way, and ended by bursting out crying.

"When your better sense comes back to you, sir," says I, "I am sure you will be gentleman enough to make an apology for the language you have just used. In the mean time, please to listen, if you can, to a word of explanation. Mr. Sharpin has sent in a report to our inspector of the most irregular and ridiculous kind, setting down not only all his own foolish doings and sayings, but the doings and sayings of Mrs. Yatman as well. In most cases, such a document would have been fit only for the wastepaper basket; but in this particular case it so happens that Mr. Sharpin's budget of nonsense leads to a certain conclusion, which the simpleton of a writer has been quite innocent of suspecting from the beginning to the end. Of that conclusion I am so sure that I will forfeit my place if it does not turn out that Mrs. Yatman has been practising upon the folly and conceit of this young man, and that she has tried to shield herself from discovery by purposely encouraging him to suspect the wrong persons. I tell you that confidently; and I will even go farther. I will undertake to give a decided opinion as to why Mrs. Yatman took the money, and what she has done with it, or with a part of it. Nobody can look at that lady, sir, without being struck by the great taste and beauty of her dress—"

As I said those last words, the poor man seemed to find his powers of speech again. He cut me short directly as haughtily as if he had been a duke instead of a stationer.

"Try some other means of justifying your vile calumny against my wife," says he. "Her milliner's bill for the past year is on my file of receipted accounts at this moment."

"Excuse me, sir," says I, "but that proves nothing. Milliners, I must tell you, have a certain rascally custom which comes within the daily experience of our office. A married lady who wished it can keep two accounts at her dressmaker's: one is the account which her husband sees and pays; the other is the private account, which contains all the extravagant items, and which the wife pays secretly, by installments, whenever she can. According to our usual experience, these installments are mostly squeezed out of the housekeeping money. In your case, I suspect, no installments have been paid; proceedings have been threatened; Mrs. Yatman, knowing your altered circumstances, has felt herself driven into a corner, and she has paid her private account out of your cash-box."

"I won't believe it," says he. "Every word you speak is an abominable insult to me and to my wife."

"Are you man enough, sir," says I, taking him up short, in order to save time and words, "to get that receipted bill you spoke of just now off the file, and come with me at once to the milliner's shop where Mrs. Yatman deals?"

He turned red in the face at that, got the bill directly, and put on his hat. I took out of my pocketbook the list containing the numbers of the lost notes, and we left the house together immediately.

Arrived at the milliner's (one of the expensive West-end houses, as I expected), I asked for a private interview, on important business, with the mistress of the concern. It was not the first time that she and I had met over the same delicate investigation. The moment she set eyes on me she sent for her husband. I mentioned who Mr. Yatman was, and what we wanted.

"This is strictly private?" inquires the husband. I nodded my head.

"And confidential?" says the wife. I nodded again.

"Do you see any objection, dear, to obliging the sergeant with a sight of the books?" says her husband.

"None in the world, love, if you approve of it," says the wife.

All this while poor Mr. Yatman sat looking the picture of astonishment and distress, quite out of place at our polite conference. The books were brought, and one minute's look at the pages in which Mrs. Yatman's name figured was enough, and more than enough, to prove the truth of every word that I had spoken.

There, in one book, was the husband's account which Mr. Yatman had settled; and there, in the other, was the private account, crossed off also, the date of settlement being the very day after the loss of the cash-box. This said private account amounted to the sum of a hundred and seventy-five pounds, odd shillings, and it extended over a period of three years. Not a single installment had been paid on it. Under the last line was an entry to this effect: "Written to for the third time, June 23d." I pointed to it, and asked the milliner if that meant "last June." Yes, it did mean last June; and she now deeply regretted to say that it had been accompanied by a threat of legal proceedings.

"I thought you gave good customers more than three years' credit?" says I.

The milliner looks at Mr. Yatman, and whispers to me, "Not when a lady's husband gets into difficulties."

She pointed to the account as she spoke. The entries after the time when Mr. Yatman's circumstances became involved were just as extravagant for a person in his wife's situation, as the entries for the year before that period. If the lady had economized in other things, she had certainly not economized in the matter of dress.

There was nothing left now but to examine the cash-book, for form's sake. The money had been paid in notes, the amounts and numbers of which exactly tallied with the figures set down in my list.

After that, I thought it best to get Mr. Yatman out of the house immediately. He was in such a pitiable condition that I called a cab and accompanied him home in it. At first he cried and raved like a child; but I soon quieted him; and I must add, to his credit, that he made me a most handsome apology for his language as the cab drew up at his house door. In return, I tried to give him some advice about how to set matters right for the future with his wife. He paid very little attention to me, and went up stairs muttering to himself about a separation. Whether Mrs. Yatman will come cleverly out of the scrape or not seems doubtful. I should say myself that she would go into screeching hysterics, and so frighten the poor man into forgiving her. But this is no business of ours. So far as we are concerned, the case is now at an end, and the present report may come to a conclusion along with it.

I remain, accordingly, yours to command,

THOMAS BULMER.

P.S.—I have to add that, on leaving Rutherford Street, I met Mr. Matthew Sharpin coming to pack up his things.

"Only think!" says he, rubbing his hands in great spirits, "I've been to the genteel villa residence, and the moment I mentioned my business they kicked me out directly. There were two witnesses of the assault, and it's worth a hundred pounds to me if it's worth a farthing."

"I wish you joy of your luck," says I.

"Thank you," says he. "When may I pay you the same compliment on finding the thief?"

"Whenever you like," says I, "for the thief is found."

"Just what I expected," says he. "I've done all the work, and now you cut in and claim all the credit—Mr. Jay, of course."

"No," says I.

"Who is it then?" says he.

"Ask Mrs. Yatman," says I. "She's waiting to tell you."

"All right! I'd much rather hear it from that charming woman than from you," says he, and goes into the house in a mighty hurry.

What do you think of that, Inspector Theakstone? Would you like to stand in Mr. Sharpin's shoes? I shouldn't, I can promise you.

FROM CHIEF INSPECTOR THEAKSTONE TO MR. MATTHEW SHARPIN.

July 12th.

SIR,

Sergeant Bulmer has already told you to consider yourself suspended until further notice. I have now authority to add that your services as a member of the Detective Police are positively declined. You will please to take this letter as notifying officially your dismissal from the force.

I may inform you, privately, that your rejection is not intended to cast any reflections on your character. It merely implies that you are not quite sharp enough for our purposes. If we *are* to have a new recruit among us, we should infinitely prefer Mrs. Yatman.

Your obedient servant,

FRANCIS THEAKSTONE.

NOTE ON THE PRECEDING CORRESPONDENCE, ADDED BY MR. THEAKSTONE.

The inspector is not in a position to append any explanation of importance to the last of the letters. It has been discovered that Mr. Matthew Sharpin left the house in Rutherford Street five minutes after his interview outside of it with Sergeant Bulmer, his manner expressing the liveliest emotions of terror and astonishment, and his left cheek displaying a bright patch of red, which looked as if it might have been the result of what is popularly termed a smart box on the ear. He was also heard by the shopman at Rutherford Street to use a very shocking expression in reference to Mrs. Yatman, and was seen to clench his fist vindictively as he ran round the corner of the street. Nothing more has been heard of him; and it is conjectured that he has left London with the intention of offering his valuable services to the provincial police.

On the interesting domestic subject of Mr. and Mrs. Yatman still less is known. It has, however, been positively ascertained that the medical attendant of the family was sent for in a great hurry on the day when Mr. Yatman returned from the milliner's shop. The neighbouring chemist received, soon afterward, a prescription of a soothing nature to make up for Mrs. Yatman. The day after, Mr. Yatman purchased some smelling-salts at the shop, and afterward appeared at the circulating library to ask for a novel descriptive of high life that would amuse an invalid lady. It has been inferred from these circumstances that he has not thought it desirable to carry out his threat of separating from his wife, at least in the present (presumed) condition of that lady's sensitive nervous system.

R. Austin Freeman

DR. R. AUSTIN FREEMAN (1862-1943) WAS A BRITISH AUTHOR OF detective fiction, whose most important contribution to the genre was the invention of the 'inverted' detective story — one in which the details of the crime and the identity of the perpetrator are revealed at the beginning of the story, and the rest of the story follows the detective's attempt to solve the mystery.

He created the detective Dr. John Thorndyke, a medical doctor turned forensic investigator aided by his close friend and biographer Christopher Jervis. Thorndyke distinguished himself from other fictional detectives of the time by his method of collecting all the data he could gather and making deductions from them before proceeding to investigate the suspects and their motives.

7

THE BLUE SEQUIN

R. Austin Freeman

THORNDYKE STOOD LOOKING UP AND DOWN THE PLATFORM WITH anxiety that increased as the time drew near for the departure of the train.

"This is very unfortunate," he said, reluctantly stepping into an empty smoking compartment as the guard executed a flourish with his green flag. "I am afraid we have missed our friend." He closed the door, and, as the train began to move, thrust his head out of the window.

"Now I wonder if that will be he," he continued. "If so, he has caught the train by the skin of his teeth, and is now in one of the rear compartments."

The subject of Thorndyke's speculations was Mr. Edward Stopford, of the firm of Stopford and Myers, of Portugal Street, solicitors, and his connection with us at present arose out of a telegram that had reached our chambers on the preceding evening. It was reply-paid, and ran thus:

> *"Can you come here to-morrow to direct defence? Important case. All costs undertaken by us."*
>
> *—STOPFORD AND MYERS*

Thorndyke's reply had been in the affirmative, and early on this present morning a further telegram—evidently posted overnight—had been delivered:

> *"Shall leave for Woldhurst by 8.25 from Charing Cross. Will call for you if possible."*
>
> *—EDWARD STOPFORD*

He had not called, however, and, since he was unknown personally to us both, we could not judge whether or not he had been among the passengers on the platform.

"It is most unfortunate," Thorndyke repeated, "for it deprives us of that preliminary consideration of the case which is so invaluable." He filled his pipe thoughtfully, and, having made a fruitless inspection of the platform at London Bridge, took up the paper that he had bought at the bookstall, and began to turn over the leaves, running his eye quickly down the columns, unmindful of the journalistic baits in paragraph or article.

"It is a great disadvantage," he observed, while still glancing through the paper, "to come plump into an inquiry without preparation—to be confronted with the details before one has a chance of considering the case in general terms. For instance—"

He paused, leaving the sentence unfinished, and as I looked up inquiringly I saw that he had turned over another page, and was now reading attentively.

"This looks like our case, Jervis," he said presently, handing me the paper and indicating a paragraph at the top of the page. It was quite brief, and was headed "Terrible Murder in Kent," the account being as follows:

"A shocking crime was discovered yesterday morning at the little town of Woldhurst, which lies on the branch line from Halbury Junction. The discovery was made by a porter who was inspecting the carriages of the train which had just come in. On opening the door of a first-class compartment, he was horrified to find the body of a fashionably-dressed woman stretched upon the floor. Medical aid was immediately summoned, and on the arrival of the divisional surgeon, Dr. Morton, it was ascertained that the woman had not been dead more than a few minutes.

"The state of the corpse leaves no doubt that a murder of a most brutal kind has been perpetrated, the cause of death being a penetrating wound of the head, inflicted with some pointed implement, which must have been used with terrible violence, since it has perforated the skull and entered the brain. That robbery was not the motive of the crime is made clear by the fact that an expensively fitted dressing-bag was found on the rack, and that the dead woman's jewellery, including several valuable diamond rings, was untouched. It is rumoured that an arrest has been made by the local police."

"A gruesome affair," I remarked, as I handed back the paper, "but the report does not give us much information."

"It does not," Thorndyke agreed, "and yet it gives us something to consider. Here is a perforating wound of the skull, inflicted with some pointed implement—that is, assuming that it is not a bullet wound. Now, what kind of implement would be capable of inflicting such an injury? How would such an implement be used in the confined space of a railway-carriage, and what sort of person would be in possession of such an implement? These are preliminary questions that are worth considering, and I commend them to you, together with the further problems of the possible motive—excluding robbery—and any circumstances other than murder which might account for the injury."

"The choice of suitable implements is not very great," I observed.

"It is very limited, and most of them, such as a plasterer's pick or a geological hammer, are associated with certain definite occupations. You have a notebook?"

I had, and, accepting the hint, I produced it and pursued my further reflections in silence, while my companion, with his notebook also on his knee, gazed steadily out of the window. And thus he remained, wrapped in thought, jotting down an entry now and again in his book, until the train slowed down at

Halbury Junction, where we had to change on to a branch line.

As we stepped out, I noticed a well-dressed man hurrying up the platform from the rear and eagerly scanning the faces of the few passengers who had alighted. Soon he espied us, and, approaching quickly, asked, as he looked from one of us to the other:

"Dr. Thorndyke?"

"Yes," replied my colleague, adding: "And you, I presume, are Mr. Edward Stopford?"

The solicitor bowed. "This is a dreadful affair," he said, in an agitated manner. "I see you have the paper. A most shocking affair. I am immensely relieved to find you here. Nearly missed the train, and feared I should miss you."

"There appears to have been an arrest," Thorndyke began.

"Yes—my brother. Terrible business. Let us walk up the platform; our train won't start for a quarter of an hour yet."

We deposited our joint Gladstone and Thorndyke's travelling-case in an empty first-class compartment, and then, with the solicitor between us, strolled up to the unfrequented end of the platform.

"My brother's position," said Mr. Stopford, "fills me with dismay—but let me give you the facts in order, and you shall judge for yourself. This poor creature who has been murdered so brutally was a Miss Edith Grant. She was formerly an artist's model, and as such was a good deal employed by my brother, who is a painter—Harold Stopford, you know, A.R.A. now—"

"I know his work very well, and charming work it is."

"I think so, too. Well, in those days he was quite a youngster—about twenty—and he became very intimate with Miss Grant, in quite an innocent way, though not very discreet; but she was a nice respectable girl, as most English models are, and no one thought any harm. However, a good many letters passed between them, and some little presents, amongst which was a beaded chain carrying a locket, and in this he was fool enough to put his portrait and the inscription, 'Edith, from Harold.'

"Later on Miss Grant, who had a rather good voice, went

on the stage, in the comic opera line, and, in consequence, her habits and associates changed somewhat; and, as Harold had meanwhile become engaged, he was naturally anxious to get his letters back, and especially to exchange the locket for some less compromising gift. The letters she eventually sent him, but refused absolutely to part with the locket.

"Now, for the last month Harold has been staying at Halbury, making sketching excursions into the surrounding country, and yesterday morning he took the train to Shinglehurst, the third station from here, and the one before Woldhurst.

"On the platform here he met Miss Grant, who had come down from London, and was going on to Worthing. They entered the branch train together, having a first-class compartment to themselves. It seems she was wearing his locket at the time, and he made another appeal to her to make an exchange, which she refused, as before. The discussion appears to have become rather heated and angry on both sides, for the guard and a porter at Munsden both noticed that they seemed to be quarrelling; but the upshot of the affair was that the lady snapped the chain, and tossed it together with the locket to my brother, and they parted quite amiably at Shinglehurst, where Harold got out. He was then carrying his full sketching kit, including a large holland umbrella, the lower joint of which is an ash staff fitted with a powerful steel spike for driving into the ground.

"It was about half-past ten when he got out at Shinglehurst; by eleven he had reached his pitch and got to work, and he painted steadily for three hours. Then he packed up his traps, and was just starting on his way back to the station, when he was met by the police and arrested.

"And now, observe the accumulation of circumstantial evidence against him. He was the last person seen in company with the murdered woman—for no one seems to have seen her after they left Munsden; he appeared to be quarrelling with her when she was last seen alive, he had a reason for possibly wishing for her death, he was provided with an implement—a spiked staff—capable of inflicting the injury which caused her death,

THE DISCOVERY.

and, when he was searched, there was found in his possession the locket and broken chain, apparently removed from her person with violence.

"Against all this is, of course, his known character—he is the gentlest and most amiable of men—and his subsequent conduct—imbecile to the last degree if he had been guilty; but, as a lawyer, I can't help seeing that appearances are almost hopelessly against him."

"We won't say 'hopelessly,'" replied Thorndyke, as we took our places in the carriage, "though I expect the police are pretty cocksure. When does the inquest open?"

"To-day at four. I have obtained an order from the coroner for you to examine the body and be present at the *post-mortem*."

"Do you happen to know the exact position of the wound?"

"Yes; it is a little above and behind the left ear—a horrible round hole, with a ragged cut or tear running from it to the side of the forehead."

"And how was the body lying?"

"Right along the floor, with the feet close to the off-side door."

"Was the wound on the head the only one?"

"No; there was a long cut or bruise on the right cheek—a contused wound the police surgeon called it, which he believes to have been inflicted with a heavy and rather blunt weapon. I have not heard of any other wounds or bruises."

"Did anyone enter the train yesterday at Shinglehurst?" Thorndyke asked.

"No one entered the train after it left Halbury."

Thorndyke considered these statements in silence, and presently fell into a brown study, from which he roused only as the train moved out of Shinglehurst station.

"It would be about here that the murder was committed," said Mr. Stopford; "at least, between here and Woldhurst."

Thorndyke nodded rather abstractedly, being engaged at the moment in observing with great attention the objects that were visible from the windows.

"I notice," he remarked presently, "a number of chips scattered about between the rails, and some of the chair-wedges look new. Have there been any platelayers at work lately?"

"Yes," answered Stopford, "they are on the line now, I believe—at least, I saw a gang working near Woldhurst yesterday, and they are said to have set a rick on fire; I saw it smoking when I came down."

"Indeed; and this middle line of rails is, I suppose, a sort of siding?"

"Yes; they shunt the goods trains and empty trucks on to it. There are the remains of the rick—still smouldering, you see."

Thorndyke gazed absently at the blackened heap until an empty cattle-truck on the middle track hid it from view. This was succeeded by a line of goods-waggons, and these by a passenger coach, one compartment of which—a first-class—was closed up and sealed. The train now began to slow down rather suddenly, and a couple of minutes later we brought up in Woldhurst station.

It was evident that rumours of Thorndyke's advent had preceded us, for the entire staff—two porters, an inspector, and the station-master—were waiting expectantly on the platform, and the latter came forward, regardless of his dignity, to help us with our luggage.

"Do you think I could see the carriage?" Thorndyke asked the solicitor.

"Not the inside, sir," said the station-master, on being appealed to. "The police have sealed it up. You would have to ask the inspector."

"Well, I can have a look at the outside, I suppose?" said Thorndyke, and to this the station-master readily agreed, and offered to accompany us.

"What other first-class passengers were there?" Thorndyke asked.

"None, sir. There was only one first-class coach, and the deceased was the only person in it. It has given us all a dreadful turn, this affair has," he continued, as we set off up the line. "I was on the platform when the train came in. We were watching a rick that was burning up the line, and a rare blaze it made, too; and I was just saying that we should have to move the cattle-truck that was on the mid-track, because, you see, sir, the smoke and sparks were blowing across, and I thought it would frighten the poor beasts. And Mr. Felton he don't like his beasts handled roughly. He says it spoils the meat."

"No doubt he is right," said Thorndyke. "But now, tell me, do you think it is possible for any person to board or leave the train on the off-side unobserved? Could a man, for instance, enter a compartment on the off-side at one station and drop off as the train was slowing down at the next, without being seen?"

"I doubt it," replied the station-master. "Still, I wouldn't say it is impossible."

"Thank you. Oh, and there's another question. You have a gang of men at work on the line, I see. Now, do those men belong to the district?"

"No, sir; they are strangers, every one, and pretty rough diamonds some of 'em are. But I shouldn't say there was any real harm in 'em. If you was suspecting any of 'em of being mixed up in this—"

"I am not," interrupted Thorndyke rather shortly. "I suspect nobody; but I wish to get all the facts of the case at the outset."

"Naturally, sir," replied the abashed official; and we pursued our way in silence.

"Do you remember, by the way," said Thorndyke, as we approached the empty coach, "whether the off-side door of the compartment was closed and locked when the body was discovered?"

"It was closed, sir, but not locked. Why, sir, did you think—?"

"Nothing, nothing. The sealed compartment is the one, of course?"

Without waiting for a reply, he commenced his survey of the coach, while I gently restrained our two companions from shadowing him, as they were disposed to do. The off-side footboard occupied his attention specially, and when he had scrutinized minutely the part opposite the fatal compartment, he walked slowly from end to end with his eyes but a few inches from its surface, as though he was searching for something.

Near what had been the rear end he stopped, and drew from his pocket a piece of paper; then, with a moistened finger-tip he picked up from the footboard some evidently minute object, which he carefully transferred to the paper, folding the latter and placing it in his pocket-book.

He next mounted the footboard, and, having peered in through the window of the sealed compartment, produced from his pocket a small insufflator or powder-blower, with which he blew a stream of impalpable smoke-like powder on to the edges of the middle window, bestowing the closest attention on the irregular dusty patches in which it settled, and even measuring one on the jamb of the window with a pocket-rule. At length he stepped down, and, having carefully looked over the near-side footboard, announced that he had finished for the present.

As we were returning down the line, we passed a working man, who seemed to be viewing the chairs and sleepers with more than casual interest.

"That, I suppose, is one of the plate-layers?" Thorndyke suggested to the station-master.

"Yes, the foreman of the gang," was the reply.

"I'll just step back and have a word with him, if you will walk on slowly." And my colleague turned back briskly and overtook the man, with whom he remained in conversation for some minutes.

"I think I see the police inspector on the platform," remarked Thorndyke, as we approached the station.

"Yes, there he is," said our guide. "Come down to see what you are after, sir, I expect." Which was doubtless the case, although the officer professed to be there by the merest chance.

"You would like to see the weapon, sir, I suppose?" he remarked, when he had introduced himself.

"The umbrella-spike," Thorndyke corrected. "Yes, if I may. We are going to the mortuary now."

"Then you'll pass the station on the way; so, if you care to look in, I will walk up with you."

This proposition being agreed to, we all proceeded to the police-station, including the station-master, who was on the very tiptoe of curiosity.

"There you are, sir," said the inspector, unlocking his office, and ushering us in. "Don't say we haven't given every facility to the defence. There are all the effects of the accused, including the very weapon the deed was done with."

"Come, come," protested Thorndyke; "we mustn't be premature." He took the stout ash staff from the officer, and, having examined the formidable spike through a lens, drew from his pocket a steel calliper-gauge, with which he carefully measured the diameter of the spike, and the staff to which it was fixed. "And now," he said, when he had made a note of the measurements in his book, "we will look at the colour-box and the sketch. Ha! a very orderly man, your brother. Mr. Stopford. Tubes all in their places, palette-knives wiped clean, palette cleaned off and rubbed bright, brushes wiped—they ought to be washed before they stiffen—all this is very significant." He unstrapped the sketch from the blank canvas to which it was pinned, and, standing it on a chair in a good light, stepped back to look at it.

"And you tell me that that is only three hours' work!" he exclaimed, looking at the lawyer. "It is really a marvellous achievement."

"My brother is a very rapid worker," replied Stopford dejectedly.

"Yes, but this is not only amazingly rapid; it is in his very happiest vein—full of spirit and feeling. But we mustn't stay to look at it longer." He replaced the canvas on its pins, and having glanced at the locket and some other articles that lay in a drawer, thanked the inspector for his courtesy and withdrew.

"That sketch and the colour-box appear very suggestive to me," he remarked, as we walked up the street.

"To me also," said Stopford gloomily, "for they are under

lock and key, like their owner, poor old fellow."

He sighed heavily, and we walked on in silence.

The mortuary-keeper had evidently heard of our arrival, for he was waiting at the door with the key in his hand, and, on being shown the coroner's order, unlocked the door, and we entered together; but, after a momentary glance at the ghostly, shrouded figure lying upon the slate table, Stopford turned pale and retreated, saying that he would wait for us outside with the mortuary-keeper.

As soon as the door was closed and locked on the inside, Thorndyke glanced curiously round the bare, whitewashed building. A stream of sunlight poured in through the skylight, and fell upon the silent form that lay so still under its covering-sheet, and one stray beam glanced into a corner by the door, where, on a row of pegs and a deal table, the dead woman's clothing was displayed.

"There is something unspeakably sad in these poor relics, Jervis," said Thorndyke, as we stood before them. "To me they are more tragic, more full of pathetic suggestion, than the corpse itself. See the smart, jaunty hat, and the costly skirts hanging there, so desolate and forlorn; the dainty *lingerie* on the table, neatly folded—by the mortuary-man's wife, I hope—the little French shoes and open-work silk stockings. How pathetically eloquent they are of harmless, womanly vanity, and the gay, careless life, snapped short in the twinkling of an eye. But we must not give way to sentiment. There is another life threatened, and it is in our keeping."

He lifted the hat from its peg, and turned it over in his hand. It was, I think, what is called a "picture-hat"—a huge, flat, shapeless mass of gauze and ribbon and feather, spangled over freely with dark-blue sequins. In one part of the brim was a ragged hole, and from this the glittering sequins dropped off in little showers when the hat was moved.

"This will have been worn tilted over on the left side," said Thorndyke, "judging by the general shape and the position of the hole."

"Yes," I agreed. "Like that of the Duchess of Devonshire in Gainsborough's portrait."

"Exactly."

He shook a few of the sequins into the palm of his hand, and, replacing the hat on its peg, dropped the little discs into an envelope, on which he wrote, "From the hat," and slipped it into his pocket. Then, stepping over to the table, he drew back the sheet reverently and even tenderly from the dead woman's face, and looked down at it with grave pity. It was a comely face, white as marble, serene and peaceful in expression, with half-closed eyes, and framed with a mass of brassy, yellow hair; but its beauty was marred by a long linear wound, half cut, half bruise, running down the right cheek from the eye to the chin.

"A handsome girl," Thorndyke commented—"a dark-haired blonde. What a sin to have disfigured herself so with that horrible peroxide." He smoothed the hair back from her forehead, and added: "She seems to have applied the stuff last about ten days ago. There is about a quarter of an inch of dark hair at the roots. What do you make of that wound on the cheek?"

"It looks as if she had struck some sharp angle in falling, though, as the seats are padded in first-class carriages, I don't see what she could have struck."

"No. And now let us look at the other wound. Will you note down the description?" He handed me his notebook, and I wrote down as he dictated: "A clean-punched circular hole in skull, an inch behind and above margin of left ear—diameter, an inch and seven-sixteenths; starred fracture of parietal bone; membranes perforated, and brain entered deeply; ragged scalp-wound, extending forward to margin of left orbit; fragments of gauze and sequins in edges of wound. That will do for the present. Dr. Morton will give us further details if we want them."

He pocketed his callipers and rule, drew from the bruised scalp one or two loose hairs, which he placed in the envelope with the sequins, and, having looked over the body for other wounds or bruises (of which there were none), replaced the sheet, and prepared to depart.

As we walked away from the mortuary, Thorndyke was silent and deeply thoughtful, and I gathered that he was piecing together the facts that he had acquired. At length Mr. Stopford, who had several times looked at him curiously, said:

"The *post-mortem* will take place at three, and it is now only half-past eleven. What would you like to do next?"

Thorndyke, who, in spite of his mental preoccupation, had been looking about him in his usual keen, attentive way, halted suddenly.

"Your reference to the *post-mortem*," said he, "reminds me that I forgot to put the ox-gall into my case."

"Ox-gall!" I exclaimed, endeavouring vainly to connect this substance with the technique of the pathologist. "What were you going to do with—"

But here I broke off, remembering my friend's dislike of any discussion of his methods before strangers.

"I suppose," he continued, "there would hardly be an artist's colourman in a place of this size?"

"I should think not," said Stopford. "But couldn't you got the stuff from a butcher? There's a shop just across the road."

"So there is," agreed Thorndyke, who had already observed the shop. "The gall ought, of course, to be prepared, but we can filter it ourselves—that is, if the butcher has any. We will try him, at any rate."

He crossed the road towards the shop, over which the name "Felton" appeared in gilt lettering, and, addressing himself to the proprietor, who stood at the door, introduced himself and explained his wants.

"Ox-gall?" said the butcher. "No, sir, I haven't any just now; but I am having a beast killed this afternoon, and I can let you have some then. In fact," he added, after a pause, "as the matter is of importance, I can have one killed at once if you wish it."

"That is very kind of you," said Thorndyke, "and it would greatly oblige me. Is the beast perfectly healthy?"

"They're in splendid condition, sir. I picked them out of the herd myself. But you shall see them—ay, and choose the one that you'd like killed."

"You are really very good," said Thorndyke warmly. "I will just run into the chemist's next door, and get a suitable bottle, and then I will avail myself of your exceedingly kind offer."

He hurried into the chemist's shop, from which he presently emerged, carrying a white paper parcel; and we then followed the butcher down a narrow lane by the side of his shop. It led to an enclosure containing a small pen, in which were confined three handsome steers, whose glossy, black coats contrasted in a very striking manner with their long, greyish-white, nearly straight horns.

"These are certainly very fine beasts, Mr. Felton," said Thorndyke, as we drew up beside the pen, "and in excellent condition, too."

He leaned over the pen and examined the beasts critically, especially as to their eyes and horns; then, approaching the nearest one, he raised his stick and bestowed a smart tap on the under-side of the right horn, following it by a similar tap on the left one, a proceeding that the beast viewed with stolid surprise.

"The state of the horns," explained Thorndyke, as he moved on to the next steer, "enables one to judge, to some extent, of the beast's health."

"Lord bless you, sir," laughed Mr. Felton, "they haven't got no feeling in their horns, else what good 'ud their horns be to 'em?"

Apparently he was right, for the second steer was as indifferent to a sounding rap on either horn as the first. Nevertheless, when Thorndyke approached the third steer, I unconsciously drew nearer to watch; and I noticed that, as the stick struck the horn, the beast drew back in evident alarm, and that when the blow was repeated, it became manifestly uneasy.

"He don't seem to like that," said the butcher. "Seems as if—Hullo, that's queer!"

Thorndyke had just brought his stick up against the left horn, and immediately the beast had winced and started back, shaking his head and moaning. There was not, however, room for him to back out of reach, and Thorndyke, by leaning into the pen, was able to inspect the sensitive horn, which he did with the closest attention, while the butcher looked on with obvious perturbation.

"You don't think there's anything wrong with this beast, sir, I hope," said he.

"I can't say without a further examination," replied Thorndyke. "It may be the horn only that is affected. If you will have it sawn off close to the head, and sent up to me at the hotel, I will look at it and tell you. And, by way of preventing any mistakes, I will mark it and cover it up, to protect it from injury in the slaughter-house."

He opened his parcel and produced from it a wide-mouthed bottle labelled "Ox-gall," a sheet of gutta-percha tissue, a roller bandage, and a stick of sealing-wax. Handing the bottle to Mr. Felton, he encased the distal half of the horn in a covering by means of the tissue and the bandage, which he fixed securely with the sealing-wax.

"I'll saw the horn off and bring it up to the hotel myself, with the ox-gall," said Mr. Felton. "You shall have them in half an hour."

He was as good as his word, for in half an hour Thorndyke was seated at a small table by the window of our private sitting-room in the Black Bull Hotel. The table was covered with newspaper, and on it lay the long grey horn and Thorndyke's travelling-case, now open and displaying a small microscope and its accessories. The butcher was seated solidly in an armchair waiting, with a half-suspicious eye on Thorndyke for the report; and I was endeavouring by cheerful talk to keep Mr. Stopford from sinking into utter despondency, though I, too, kept a furtive watch on my colleague's rather mysterious proceedings.

I saw him unwind the bandage and apply the horn to his ear, bending it slightly to and fro. I watched him, as he scanned the surface closely through a lens, and observed him as he scraped some substance from the pointed end on to a glass slide, and, having applied a drop of some reagent, began to tease out the scraping with a pair of mounted needles. Presently he placed the slide under the microscope, and, having observed it attentively for a minute or two, turned round sharply.

"Come and look at this, Jervis," said he.

I wanted no second bidding, being on tenterhooks of curiosity, but came over and applied my eye to the instrument.

"Well, what is it?" he asked.

"A multipolar nerve corpuscle—very shrivelled, but unmistakable."

"And this?"

He moved the slide to a fresh spot.

"Two pyramidal nerve corpuscles and some portions of fibres."

"And what do you say the tissue is?"

"Cortical brain substance, I should say, without a doubt."

"I entirely agree with you. And that being so," he added, turning to Mr. Stopford, "we may say that the case for the defence is practically complete."

"What, in Heaven's name, do you mean?" exclaimed Stopford, starting up.

"I mean that we can now prove when and where and how Miss Grant met her death. Come and sit down here, and I will explain. No, you needn't go away, Mr. Felton. We shall have to subpoena you. Perhaps," he continued, "we had better go over the facts and see what they suggest. And first we note the position of the body, lying with the feet close to the off-side door, showing that, when she fell, the deceased was sitting, or more probably standing, close to that door. Next there is this." He drew from his pocket a folded paper, which he opened, displaying a tiny blue disc. "It is one of the sequins with which her hat was trimmed, and I have in this envelope several more which I took from the hat itself.

"This single sequin I picked up on the rear end of the off side footboard, and its presence there makes it nearly certain that at some time Miss Grant had put her head out of the window on that side.

"The next item of evidence I obtained by dusting the margins of the off-side window with a light powder, which made visible a greasy impression three and a quarter inches long on the sharp corner of the right-hand jamb (right-hand from the inside, I mean).

"And now as to the evidence furnished by the body. The wound in the skull is behind and above the left ear, is roughly circular, and measures one inch and seven-sixteenths at most, and a ragged scalp-wound runs from it towards the left eye. On the right cheek is a linear contused wound three and a quarter inches long. There are no other injuries.

"Our next facts are furnished by this." He took up the horn and tapped it with his finger, while the solicitor and Mr. Felton stared at him in speechless wonder. "You notice it is a left horn, and you remember that it was highly sensitive. If you put your ear to it while I strain it, you will hear the grating of a fracture in the bony core. Now look at the pointed end, and you will see several deep scratches running lengthwise, and where those scratches end the diameter of the horn is, as you see by this calliper-gauge, one inch and seven-sixteenths. Covering the scratches is a dry blood-stain, and at the extreme tip is a small mass of a dried substance which Dr. Jervis and I have examined with the microscope and are satisfied is brain tissue."

"Good God!" exclaimed Stopford eagerly. "Do you mean to say—"

"Let us finish with the facts, Mr. Stopford," Thorndyke interrupted. "Now, if you look closely at that blood-stain, you will see a short piece of hair stuck to the horn, and through this lens you can make out the root-bulb. It is a golden hair, you notice, but near the root it is black, and our calliper-gauge shows us that the black portion is fourteen sixty-fourths of an inch long. Now, in this envelope are some hairs that I removed from the dead woman's head. They also are golden hairs, black at the roots, and when I measure the black portion I find it to be fourteen sixty-fourths of an inch long. Then, finally, there is this."

He turned the horn over, and pointed to a small patch of dried blood. Embedded in it was a blue sequin.

Mr. Stopford and the butcher both gazed at the horn in silent amazement; then the former drew a deep breath and looked up at Thorndyke.

"No doubt," said he, "you can explain this mystery, but for my part I am utterly bewildered, though you are filling me with hope."

"And yet the matter is quite simple," returned Thorndyke, "even with these few facts before us, which are only a selection from the body of evidence in our possession. But I will state my theory, and you shall judge." He rapidly sketched a rough plan on a sheet of paper, and continued: "These were the conditions when the train was approaching Woldhurst: Here was the passenger-coach, here was the burning rick, and here was a cattle-truck. This steer was in that truck. Now my hypothesis is that at that time Miss Grant was standing with her head out of the off-side window, watching the burning rick. Her wide hat, worn on the left side, hid from her view the cattle-truck which she was approaching, and then this is what happened." He sketched another plan to a larger scale. "One of the steers—this one—had thrust its long horn out through the bars. The point of that horn struck the deceased's head, driving her face violently against the corner of the window, and then, in disengaging, ploughed its way through the scalp, and suffered a fracture of its core from the violence of the wrench. This hypothesis is inherently probable, it fits all the facts, and those facts admit of no other explanation."

The solicitor sat for a moment as though dazed; then he rose impulsively and seized Thorndyke's hands. "I don't know what to say to you," he exclaimed huskily, "except that you have saved my brother's life, and for that may God reward you!"

The butcher rose from his chair with a slow grin.

"It seems to me," said he, "as if that ox-gall was what you might call a blind, eh, sir?"

And Thorndyke smiled an inscrutable smile.

When we returned to town on the following day we were a party of four, which included Mr. Harold Stopford. The verdict of "Death by misadventure," promptly returned by the coroner's jury, had been shortly followed by his release from custody, and he now sat with his brother and me, listening with rapt attention to Thorndyke's analysis of the case.

"So, you see," the latter concluded, "I had six possible theories of the cause of death worked out before I reached Halbury, and it only remained to select the one that fitted the facts. And when I had seen the cattle-truck, had picked up that sequin, had heard the description of the steers, and had seen the hat and the wounds, there was nothing left to do but the filling in of details."

"And you never doubted my innocence?" asked Harold Stopford.

Thorndyke smiled at his quondam client.

"Not after I had seen your colour-box and your sketch," said he, "to say nothing of the spike."

Anton Chekhov

ANTON CHEKHOV (1860-1904) WAS A RUSSIAN AUTHOR, playwright, and doctor who is considered one of the finest writers of short fiction in history, having written hundreds of short stories, seven plays, and one novel. His works fall into the genre of realism and deftly explore the quirks and foibles of the human condition.

8

THE SAFETY MATCH

Anton Chekhov

I

ON THE MORNING OF OCTOBER 6, 1885, IN THE OFFICE OF THE Inspector of Police of the second division of S— District, there appeared a respectably dressed young man, who announced that his master, Marcus Ivanovitch Klausoff, a retired officer of the Horse Guards, separated from his wife, had been murdered. While making this announcement the young man was white and terribly agitated. His hands trembled and his eyes were full of terror.

"Whom have I the honour of addressing?" asked the inspector.

"Psyekoff, Lieutenant Klausoff's agent; agriculturist and mechanician!"

The inspector and his deputy, on visiting the scene of the occurrence in company with Psyekoff, found the following: Near the wing in which Klausoff had lived was gathered a dense crowd. The news of the murder had sped swift as lightning through the neighbourhood, and the peasantry, thanks to the fact that the day was a holiday, had hurried together from all the neighbouring villages. There was much commotion and talk.

Here and there, pale, tear-stained faces were seen. The door of Klausoff's bedroom was found locked. The key was inside.

"It is quite clear that the scoundrels got in by the window!" said Psyekoff as they examined the door.

They went to the garden, into which the bedroom window opened. The window looked dark and ominous. It was covered by a faded green curtain. One corner of the curtain was slightly turned up, which made it possible to look into the bedroom.

"Did any of you look into the window?" asked the inspector.

"Certainly not, your worship!" answered Ephraim, the gardener, a little gray-haired old man, who looked like a retired sergeant. "Who's going to look in, if all their bones are shaking?"

"Ah, Marcus Ivanovitch, Marcus Ivanovitch!" sighed the inspector, looking at the window, "I told you you would come to a bad end! I told the dear man, but he wouldn't listen! Dissipation doesn't bring any good!"

"Thanks to Ephraim," said Psyekoff; "but for him, we would never have guessed. He was the first to guess that something was wrong. He comes to me this morning, and says: 'Why is the master so long getting up? He hasn't left his bedroom for a whole week!' The moment he said that, it was just as if someone had hit me with an axe. The thought flashed through my mind, 'We haven't had a sight of him since last Saturday, and to-day is Sunday'! Seven whole days—not a doubt of it!"

"Ay, poor fellow!" again sighed the inspector. "He was a clever fellow, finely educated, and kind-hearted at that! And in society, nobody could touch him! But he was a waster, God rest his soul! I was prepared for anything since he refused to live with Olga Petrovna. Poor thing, a good wife, but a sharp tongue! Stephen!" the inspector called to one of his deputies, "go over to my house this minute, and send Andrew to the captain to lodge an information with him! Tell him that Marcus Ivanovitch has been murdered. And run over to the orderly; why should he sit there, kicking his heels? Let him come here! And go as fast as you can to the examining magistrate, Nicholas Yermolaïyevitch. Tell him to come over here! Wait; I'll write him a note!"

The inspector posted sentinels around the wing, wrote a letter to the examining magistrate, and then went over to the director's for a glass of tea. Ten minutes later he was sitting on a stool, carefully nibbling a lump of sugar, and swallowing the scalding tea.

"There you are!" he was saying to Psyekoff; "there you are! A noble by birth! a rich man—a favourite of the gods, you may say, as Pushkin has it, and what did he come to? He drank and dissipated and—there you are—he's murdered."

After a couple of hours the examining magistrate drove up. Nicholas Yermolaïyevitch Chubikoff—for that was the magistrate's name—was a tall, fleshy old man of sixty, who had been wrestling with the duties of his office for a quarter of a century. Everybody in the district knew him as an honest man, wise, energetic, and in love with his work. He was accompanied to the scene of the murder by his inveterate companion, fellow worker, and secretary, Dukovski, a tall young fellow of twenty-six.

"Is it possible, gentlemen?" cried Chubikoff, entering Psyekoff's room, and quickly shaking hands with everyone. "Is it possible? Marcus Ivanovitch? Murdered? No! It is impossible! Im-poss-i-ble!"

"Go in there!" sighed the inspector.

"Lord, have mercy on us! Only last Friday I saw him at the fair in Farabankoff. I had a drink of vodka with him, save the mark!"

"Go in there!" again sighed the inspector.

They sighed, uttered exclamations of horror, drank a glass of tea each, and went to the wing.

"Get back!" the orderly cried to the peasants.

Going to the wing, the examining magistrate began his work by examining the bedroom door. The door proved to be of pine, painted yellow, and was uninjured. Nothing was found which could serve as a clue. They had to break in the door.

"Everyone not here on business is requested to keep away!" said the magistrate, when, after much hammering and shaking, the door yielded to axe and chisel. "I request this, in the interest of the investigation. Orderly, don't let anyone in!"

Chubikoff, his assistant, and the inspector opened the door, and hesitatingly, one after the other, entered the room. Their eyes met the following sight: Beside the single window stood the big wooden bed with a huge feather mattress. On the crumpled feather bed lay a tumbled, crumpled quilt. The pillow, in a cotton pillow-case, also much crumpled, was dragging on the floor. On the table beside the bed lay a silver watch and a silver twenty-kopeck piece. Beside them lay some sulphur matches. Beside the bed, the little table, and the single chair, there was no furniture in the room. Looking under the bed, the inspector saw a couple of dozen empty bottles, an old straw hat, and a quart of vodka. Under the table lay one top boot, covered with dust. Casting a glance around the room, the magistrate frowned and grew red in the face.

"Scoundrels!" he muttered, clenching his fists.

"And where is Marcus Ivanovitch?" asked Dukovski in a low voice.

"Mind your own business!" Chubikoff answered roughly. "Be good enough to examine the floor! This is not the first case of the kind I have had to deal with! Eugraph Kuzmitch," he said, turning to the inspector, and lowering his voice, "in 1870 I had another case like this. But you must remember it—the murder of the merchant Portraitoff. It was just the same there. The scoundrels murdered him, and dragged the corpse out through the window—"

Chubikoff went up to the window, pulled the curtain to one side, and carefully pushed the window. The window opened.

"It opens, you see! It wasn't fastened. Hm! There are tracks under the window. Look! There is the track of a knee! Somebody got in there. We must examine the window thoroughly."

"There is nothing special to be found on the floor," said Dukovski. "No stains or scratches. The only thing I found was a struck safety match. Here it is! So far as I remember, Marcus Ivanovitch did not smoke. And he always used sulphur matches, never safety matches. Perhaps this safety match may serve as a clue!"

"Oh, do shut up!" cried the magistrate deprecatingly. "You go on about your match! I can't abide these dreamers! Instead of chasing matches, you had better examine the bed!"

After a thorough examination of the bed, Dukovski reported:

"There are no spots, either of blood or of anything else. There are likewise no new torn places. On the pillow there are signs of teeth. The quilt is stained with something which looks like beer and smells like beer. The general aspect of the bed gives grounds for thinking that a struggle took place on it."

"I know there was a struggle, without your telling me! You are not being asked about a struggle. Instead of looking for struggles, you had better—"

"Here is one top boot, but there is no sign of the other."

"Well, and what of that?"

"It proves that they strangled him, while he was taking his boots off. He hadn't time to take the second boot off when—"

"There you go!—and how do you know they strangled him?"

"There are marks of teeth on the pillow. The pillow itself is badly crumpled, and thrown a couple of yards from the bed."

"Listen to his foolishness! Better come into the garden. You would be better employed examining the garden than digging around here. I can do that without you!"

When they reached the garden they began by examining the grass. The grass under the window was crushed and trampled. A bushy burdock growing under the window close to the wall was also trampled. Dukovski succeeded in finding on it some broken twigs and a piece of cotton wool. On the upper branches were found some fine hairs of dark blue wool.

"What colour was his last suit?" Dukovski asked Psyekoff.

"Yellow crash."

"Excellent! You see they wore blue!"

A few twigs of the burdock were cut off, and carefully wrapped in paper by the investigators. At this point Police

Captain Artsuybasheff Svistakovski and Dr. Tyutyeff arrived. The captain bade them "Good day!" and immediately began to satisfy his curiosity. The doctor, a tall, very lean man, with dull eyes, a long nose, and a pointed chin, without greeting anyone or asking about anything, sat down on a log, sighed, and began:

"The Servians are at war again! What in heaven's name can they want now? Austria, it's all your doing!"

The examination of the window from the outside did not supply any conclusive data. The examination of the grass and the bushes nearest to the window yielded a series of useful clues. For example, Dukovski succeeded in discovering a long, dark streak, made up of spots, on the grass, which led some distance into the centre of the garden. The streak ended under one of the lilac bushes in a dark brown stain. Under this same lilac bush was found a top boot, which turned out to be the fellow of the boot already found in the bedroom.

"That is a blood stain made some time ago," said Dukovski, examining the spot.

At the word "blood" the doctor rose, and going over lazily, looked at the spot.

"Yes, it is blood!" he muttered.

"That shows he wasn't strangled, if there was blood," said Chubikoff, looking sarcastically at Dukovski.

"They strangled him in the bedroom; and here, fearing he might come round again, they struck him a blow with some sharp-pointed instrument. The stain under the bush proves that he lay there a considerable time, while they were looking about for some way of carrying him out of the garden."

"Well, and how about the boot?"

"The boot confirms completely my idea that they murdered him while he was taking his boots off before going to bed. He had already taken off one boot, and the other, this one here, he had only had time to take half off. The half-off boot came off of itself, while the body was dragged over, and fell—"

"There's a lively imagination for you!" laughed Chubikoff. "He goes on and on like that! When will you learn enough to drop your deductions? Instead of arguing and deducing, it would be much better if you took some of the blood-stained grass for analysis!"

When they had finished their examination, and drawn a plan of the locality, the investigators went to the director's office to write their report and have breakfast. While they were breakfasting they went on talking:

"The watch, the money, and so on—all untouched—" Chubikoff began, leading off the talk, "show as clearly as that two and two are four that the murder was not committed for the purpose of robbery."

"The murder was committed by an educated man!" insisted Dukovski.

"What evidence have you of that?"

"The safety match proves that to me, for the peasants hereabouts are not yet acquainted with safety matches. Only the landowners use them, and by no means all of them. And it is evident that there was not one murderer, but at least three. Two held him, while one killed him. Klausoff was strong, and the murderers must have known it!"

"What good would his strength be, supposing he was asleep?"

"The murderers came on him while he was taking off his boots. If he was taking off his boots, that proves that he wasn't asleep!"

"Stop inventing your deductions! Better eat!"

"In my opinion, your worship," said the gardener Ephraim, setting the samovar on the table, "it was nobody but Nicholas who did this dirty trick!"

"Quite possible," said Psyekoff.

"And who is Nicholas?"

"The master's valet, your worship," answered Ephraim. "Who else could it be? He's a rascal, your worship! He's a drunkard and a blackguard, the like of which Heaven should not permit! He always took the master his vodka and put the master to bed. Who else could it be? And I also venture to point out to your worship, he once boasted at the public house that he would kill the master! It happened on account of Aquilina, the woman, you know. He was making up to a soldier's widow. She pleased the master; the master made friends with her himself, and Nicholas—naturally, he was mad! He is rolling about drunk in the kitchen now. He is crying, and telling lies, saying he is sorry for the master—"

The examining magistrate ordered Nicholas to be brought. Nicholas, a lanky young fellow, with a long, freckled nose, narrow-chested, and wearing an old jacket of his master's, entered Psyekoff's room, and bowed low before the magistrate. His face was sleepy and tear-stained. He was tipsy and could hardly keep his feet.

"Where is your master?" Chubikoff asked him.

"Murdered! your worship!"

As he said this, Nicholas blinked and began to weep.

"We know he was murdered. But where is he now? Where is his body?"

"They say he was dragged out of the window and buried in the garden!"

"Hum! The results of the investigation are known in the kitchen already!—That's bad! Where were you, my good fellow, the night the master was murdered? Saturday night, that is."

Nicholas raised his head, stretched his neck, and began to think.

"I don't know, your worship," he said. "I was drunk and don't remember."

"An alibi!" whispered Dukovski, smiling, and rubbing his hands.

"So-o! And why is there blood under the master's window?"

Nicholas jerked his head up and considered.

"Hurry up!" said the Captain of Police.

"Right away! That blood doesn't amount to anything, your worship! I was cutting a chicken's throat. I was doing it quite simply, in the usual way, when all of a sudden it broke away and started to run. That is where the blood came from."

Ephraim declared that Nicholas did kill a chicken every evening, and always in some new place, but that nobody ever heard of a half-killed chicken running about the garden, though of course it wasn't impossible.

"An alibi," sneered Dukovski; "and what an asinine alibi!"

"Did you know Aquilina?"

"Yes, your worship, I know her."

"And the master cut you out with her?"

"Not at all. *He* cut me out—Mr. Psyekoff there, Ivan Mikhailovitch; and the master cut Ivan Mikhailovitch out. That is how it was."

Psyekoff grew confused and began to scratch his left eye. Dukovski looked at him attentively, noted his confusion, and started. He noticed that the director had dark blue trousers, which he had not observed before. The trousers reminded him of the dark blue threads found on the burdock. Chubikoff in his turn glanced suspiciously at Psyekoff.

"Go!" he said to Nicholas. "And now permit me to put a question to you, Mr. Psyekoff. Of course you were here last Saturday evening?"

"Yes! I had supper with Marcus Ivanovitch about ten o'clock."

"And afterward?"

"Afterward—afterward—Really, I do not remember," stammered Psyekoff. "I had a good deal to drink at supper. I don't remember when or where I went to sleep. Why are you all looking at me like that, as if I was the murderer?"

"Where were you when you woke up?"

"I was in the servants' kitchen, lying behind the stove! They can all confirm it. How I got behind the stove I don't know—"

"Do not get agitated. Did you know Aquilina?"

"There's nothing extraordinary about that—"

"She first liked you and then preferred Klausoff?"

"Yes. Ephraim, give us some more mushrooms! Do you want some more tea, Eugraph Kuzmitch?"

A heavy, oppressive silence began and lasted fully five

minutes. Dukovski silently kept his piercing eyes fixed on Psyekoff's pale face. The silence was finally broken by the examining magistrate:

"We must go to the house and talk with Maria Ivanovna, the sister of the deceased. Perhaps she may be able to supply some clues."

Chubikoff and his assistant expressed their thanks for the breakfast, and went toward the house. They found Klausoff's sister, Maria Ivanovna, an old maid of forty-five, at prayer before the big case of family icons. When she saw the portfolios in her guests' hands, and their official caps, she grew pale.

"Let me begin by apologizing for disturbing, so to speak, your devotions," began the gallant Chubikoff, bowing and scraping. "We have come to you with a request. Of course, you have heard already. There is a suspicion that your dear brother, in some way or other, has been murdered. The will of God, you know. No one can escape death, neither czar nor ploughman. Could you not help us with some clue, some explanation—?"

"Oh, don't ask me!" said Maria Ivanovna, growing still paler, and covering her face with her hands. "I can tell you nothing. Nothing! I beg you! I know nothing—What can I do? Oh, no! no!—not a word about my brother! If I die, I won't say anything!"

Maria Ivanovna began to weep, and left the room. The investigators looked at each other, shrugged their shoulders, and beat a retreat.

"Confound the woman!" scolded Dukovski, going out of the house. "It is clear she knows something, and is concealing it! And the chambermaid has a queer expression too! Wait, you wretches! We'll ferret it all out!"

In the evening Chubikoff and his deputy, lit on their road by the pale moon, wended their way homeward. They sat in their carriage and thought over the results of the day. Both were tired and kept silent. Chubikoff was always unwilling to talk while travelling, and the talkative Dukovski remained silent, to fall in with the elder man's humour. But at the end of their journey the deputy could hold in no longer, and said:

"It is quite certain," he said, "that Nicholas had something to do with the matter. *Non dubitandum est!* You can see by his face what sort of a case he is! His alibi betrays him, body and bones. But it is also certain that he did not set the thing going. He was only the stupid hired tool. You agree? And the humble Psyekoff was not without some slight share in the matter. His dark blue breeches, his agitation, his lying behind the stove in terror after the murder, his alibi and—Aquilina—"

"'Grind away, Emilian; it's your week!' So, according to you, whoever knew Aquilina is the murderer! Hothead! You ought to be sucking a bottle, and not handling affairs! You were one of Aquilina's admirers yourself—does it follow that you are implicated too?"

"Aquilina was cook in your house for a month. I am saying nothing about that! The night before that Saturday I was playing cards with you, and saw you, otherwise I should be after you too! It isn't the woman that matters, old chap! It is the mean, nasty, low spirit of jealousy that matters. The retiring young man was not pleased when they got the better of him, you see! His vanity, don't you see? He wanted revenge. Then, those thick lips of his suggest passion. So there you have it: wounded self-love and passion. That is quite enough motive for a murder. We have two of them in our hands; but who is the third? Nicholas and Psyekoff held him, but who smothered him? Psyekoff is shy, timid, an all-round coward. And Nicholas would not know how to smother with a pillow. His sort use an axe or a club. Some third person did the smothering; but who was it?"

Dukovski crammed his hat down over his eyes and pondered. He remained silent until the carriage rolled up to the magistrate's door.

"Eureka!" he said, entering the little house and throwing off his overcoat. "Eureka, Nicholas Yermolaïyevitch! The only thing I can't understand is, how it did not occur to me sooner! Do you know who the third person was?"

"Oh, for goodness sake, shut up! There is supper! Sit down to your evening meal!"

The magistrate and Dukovski sat down to supper. Dukovski poured himself out a glass of vodka, rose, drew himself up, and said, with sparkling eyes:

"Well, learn that the third person, who acted in concert with that scoundrel Psyekoff, and did the smothering, was a woman! Yes-s! I mean—the murdered man's sister, Maria Ivanovna!"

Chubikoff choked over his vodka, and fixed his eyes on Dukovski.

"You aren't—what's-its-name? Your head isn't what-do-you-call-it? You haven't a pain in it?"

"I am perfectly well! Very well, let us say that I am crazy; but how do you explain her confusion when we appeared? How do you explain her unwillingness to give us any information? Let us admit that these are trifles. Very well! All right! But remember their relations. She detested her brother. She never forgave him for living apart from his wife. She of the Old Faith, while in her eyes he is a godless profligate. There is where the germ of her hate was hatched. They say he succeeded in making her believe that he was an angel of Satan. He even went in for spiritualism in her presence!"

"Well, what of that?"

"You don't understand? She, as a member of the Old Faith, murdered him through fanaticism. It was not only that she was putting to death a weed, a profligate—she was freeing the world of an anti-christ!—and there, in her opinion, was her service, her religious achievement! Oh, you don't know those old maids of the Old Faith. Read Dostoyevsky! And what does Lyeskoff say about them, or Petcherski? It was she, and nobody else, even if you cut me open. She smothered him! O treacherous woman! wasn't that the reason why she was kneeling before the icons, when we came in, just to take our attention away? 'Let me kneel down and pray,' she said to herself, 'and they will think I am tranquil and did not expect them!' That is the plan of all novices in crime, Nicholas Yermolaïyevitch, old pal! My dear old man, won't you intrust this business to me? Let me personally bring it through! Friend, I began it and I will finish it!"

Chubikoff shook his head and frowned.

"We know how to manage difficult matters ourselves," he said; "and your business is not to push yourself in where you don't belong. Write from dictation when you are dictated to; that is your job!"

Dukovski flared up, banged the door, and disappeared.

"Clever rascal!" muttered Chubikoff, glancing after him. "Awfully clever! But too much of a hothead. I must buy him a cigar case at the fair as a present."

The next day, early in the morning, a young man with a big head and a pursed-up mouth, who came from Klausoff's place, was introduced to the magistrate's office. He said he was the shepherd Daniel, and brought a very interesting piece of information.

"I was a bit drunk," he said. "I was with my pal till midnight. On my way home, as I was drunk, I went into the river for a bath. I was taking a bath, when I looked up. Two men were walking along the dam, carrying something black. 'Shoo!' I cried at them. They got scared, and went off like the wind toward Makareff's cabbage garden. Strike me dead, if they weren't carrying away the master!"

That same day, toward evening, Psyekoff and Nicholas were arrested and brought under guard to the district town. In the town they were committed to the cells of the prison.

II

A fortnight passed.

It was morning. The magistrate Nicholas Yermolaïyevitch was sitting in his office before a green table, turning over the papers of the "Klausoff case"; Dukovski was striding restlessly up and down like a wolf in a cage.

"You are convinced of the guilt of Nicholas and Psyekoff," he said, nervously plucking at his young beard. "Why will you not believe in the guilt of Maria Ivanovna? Are there not proofs enough for you?"

"I don't say I am not convinced. I am convinced, but somehow I don't believe it! There are no real proofs, but just a kind of philosophizing—fanaticism, this and that—"

"You can't do without an axe and bloodstained sheets. Those jurists! Very well, I'll prove it to you! You will stop sneering at the psychological side of the affair! To Siberia with your Maria Ivanovna! I will prove it! If philosophy is not enough for you, I have something substantial for you. It will show you how correct my philosophy is. Just give me permission—"

"What are you going on about?"

"About the safety match! Have you forgotten it? I haven't! I am going to find out who struck it in the murdered man's room. It was not Nicholas that struck it; it was not Psyekoff, for neither of them had any matches when they were examined; it was the third person, Maria Ivanovna. I will prove it to you. Just give me permission to go through the district to find out."

"That's enough! Sit down. Let us go on with the examination."

Dukovski sat down at a little table, and plunged his long nose in a bundle of papers.

"Bring in Nicholas Tetekhoff!" cried the examining magistrate.

They brought Nicholas in. Nicholas was pale and thin as a rail. He was trembling.

"Tetekhoff!" began Chubikoff. "In 1879 you were tried in the Court of the First Division, convicted of theft, and sentenced to imprisonment. In 1882 you were tried a second time for theft, and were again imprisoned. We know all—"

Astonishment was depicted on Nicholas's face. The examining magistrate's omniscience startled him. But soon his expression of astonishment changed to extreme indignation. He began to cry and requested permission to go and wash his face and quiet down. They led him away.

"Bring in Psyekoff!" ordered the examining magistrate.

They brought in Psyekoff. The young man had changed greatly during the last few days. He had grown thin and pale, and looked haggard. His eyes had an apathetic expression.

"Sit down, Psyekoff," said Chubikoff. "I hope that to-day you are going to be reasonable, and will not tell lies, as you did before. All these days you have denied that you had anything to do with the murder of Klausoff, in spite of all the proofs that testify against you. That is foolish. Confession will lighten your guilt. This is the last time I am going to talk to you. If you do not confess to-day, to-morrow it will be too late. Come, tell me all—"

"I know nothing about it. I know nothing about your proofs," answered Psyekoff, almost inaudibly.

"It's no use! Well, let me relate to you how the matter took place. On Saturday evening you were sitting in Klausoff's sleeping room, and drinking vodka and beer with him." (Dukovski fixed his eyes on Psyekoff's face, and kept them there all through the examination.) "Nicholas was waiting on you. At one o'clock, Marcus Ivanovitch announced his intention of going to bed. He always went to bed at one o'clock. When he was taking off his boots, and was giving you directions about details of management, you and Nicholas, at a given signal, seized your drunken master and threw him on the bed. One of you sat on his legs, the other on his head. Then a third person came in from the passage—a woman in a black dress, whom you know well, and who had previously arranged with you as to her share in your criminal deed. She seized a pillow and began to smother him. While the struggle was going on the candle went out. The woman took a box of safety matches from her pocket, and lit the candle. Was it not so? I see by your face that I am speaking the truth. But to go on. After you had smothered him, and saw that he had ceased breathing, you and Nicholas pulled him out through the window and laid him down near the burdock. Fearing that he might come round again, you struck him with something sharp. Then you carried him away, and laid him down under a lilac bush for a short time. After resting awhile and considering, you carried him across the fence. Then you entered the road. After that comes the dam. Near the dam, a peasant frightened you. Well, what is the matter with you?"

"I am suffocating!" replied Psyekoff. "Very well—have it so.

Only let me go out, please!"

They led Psyekoff away.

"At last! He has confessed!" cried Chubikoff, stretching himself luxuriously. "He has betrayed himself! And didn't I get round him cleverly! Regularly caught him napping—"

"And he doesn't deny the woman in the black dress!" exulted Dukovski. "But all the same, that safety match is tormenting me frightfully. I can't stand it any longer. Good-bye! I am off!"

Dukovski put on his cap and drove off. Chubikoff began to examine Aquilina. Aquilina declared that she knew nothing whatever about it.

At six that evening Dukovski returned. He was more agitated than he had ever been before. His hands trembled so that he could not even unbutton his greatcoat. His cheeks glowed. It was clear that he did not come empty-handed.

"*Veni, vidi, vici!*" he cried, rushing into Chubikoff's room, and falling into an armchair. "I swear to you on my honour, I begin to believe that I am a genius! Listen, devil take us all! It is funny, and it is sad. We have caught three already—isn't that so? Well, I have found the fourth, and a woman at that. You will never believe who it is! But listen. I went to Klausoff's village, and began to make a spiral round it. I visited all the little shops, public houses, dram shops on the road, everywhere asking for safety matches. Everywhere they said they hadn't any. I made a wide round. Twenty times I lost faith, and twenty times I got it back again. I knocked about the whole day, and only an hour ago I got on the track. Three versts from here. They gave me a packet of ten boxes. One box was missing. Immediately: 'Who bought the other box?' 'Such-a-one! She was pleased with them!' Old man! Nicholas Yermolaïyevitch! See what a fellow who was expelled from the seminary and who has read Gaboriau can do! From to-day on I begin to respect myself! Oof! Well, come!"

"Come where?"

"To her, to number four! We must hurry, otherwise—otherwise I'll burst with impatience! Do you know who she is? You'll never guess! Olga Petrovna, Marcus Ivanovitch's wife—

his own wife—that's who it is! She is the person who bought the matchbox!"

"You—you—you are out of your mind!"

"It's quite simple! To begin with, she smokes. Secondly, she was head and ears in love with Klausoff, even after he refused to live in the same house with her, because she was always scolding his head off. Why, they say she used to beat him because she loved him so much. And then he positively refused to stay in the same house. Love turned sour. 'Hell hath no fury like a woman scorned.' But come along! Quick, or it will be dark. Come!"

"I am not yet sufficiently crazy to go and disturb a respectable honourable woman in the middle of the night for a crazy boy!"

"Respectable, honourable! Do honourable women murder their husbands? After that you are a rag, and not an examining magistrate! I never ventured to call you names before, but now you compel me to. Rag! Dressing-gown!—Dear Nicholas Yermolaïyevitch, do come, I beg of you—!"

The magistrate made a deprecating motion with his hand.

"I beg of you! I ask, not for myself, but in the interests of justice. I beg you! I implore you! Do what I ask you to, just this once!"

Dukovski went down on his knees.

"Nicholas Yermolaïyevitch! Be kind! Call me a blackguard, a ne'er-do-weel, if I am mistaken about this woman. You see what an affair it is. What a case it is. A romance! A woman murdering her own husband for love! The fame of it will go all over Russia. They will make you investigator in all important cases. Understand, O foolish old man!"

The magistrate frowned, and undecidedly stretched his hand toward his cap.

"Oh, the devil take you!" he said. "Let us go!"

It was dark when the magistrate's carriage rolled up to the porch of the old country house in which Olga Petrovna had taken refuge with her brother.

"What pigs we are," said Chubikoff, taking hold of the bell, "to disturb a poor woman like this!"

"It's all right! It's all right! Don't get frightened! We can say that we have broken a spring."

Chubikoff and Dukovski were met at the threshold by a tall buxom woman of three and twenty, with pitch-black brows and juicy red lips. It was Olga Petrovna herself, apparently not the least distressed by the recent tragedy.

"Oh, what a pleasant surprise!" she said, smiling broadly. "You are just in time for supper. Kuzma Petrovitch is not at home. He is visiting the priest, and has stayed late. But we'll get on without him! Be seated. You have come from the examination?"

"Yes. We broke a spring, you know," began Chubikoff, entering the sitting room and sinking into an armchair.

"Take her unawares—at once!" whispered Dukovski; "take her unawares!"

"A spring—hum—yes—so we came in."

"Take her unawares, I tell you! She will guess what the matter is if you drag things out like that."

"Well, do it yourself as you want. But let me get out of it," muttered Chubikoff, rising and going to the window.

"Yes, a spring," began Dukovski, going close to Olga Petrovna and wrinkling his long nose. "We did not drive over here—to take supper with you or—to see Kuzma Petrovitch. We came here to ask you, respected madam, where Marcus Ivanovitch is, whom you murdered!"

"What? Marcus Ivanovitch murdered?" stammered Olga Petrovna, and her broad face suddenly and instantaneously flushed bright scarlet. "I don't—understand!"

"I ask you in the name of the law! Where is Klausoff? We know all!"

"Who told you?" Olga Petrovna asked in a low voice, unable to endure Dukovski's glance.

"Be so good as to show us where he is!"

"But how did you find out? Who told you?"

"We know all! I demand it in the name of the law!"

The examining magistrate, emboldened by her confusion, came forward and said:

"Show us, and we will go away. Otherwise, we—"

"What do you want with him?"

"Madam, what is the use of these questions? We ask you to show us! You tremble, you are agitated. Yes, he has been murdered, and, if you must have it, murdered by you! Your accomplices have betrayed you!"

Olga Petrovna grew pale.

"Come!" she said in a low voice, wringing her hands.

"I have him—hid—in the bath house! Only for heaven's sake, do not tell Kuzma Petrovitch. I beg and implore you! He will never forgive me!"

Olga Petrovna took down a big key from the wall, and led her guests through the kitchen and passage to the courtyard. The courtyard was in darkness. Fine rain was falling. Olga Petrovna walked in advance of them. Chubikoff and Dukovski strode behind her through the long grass, as the odour of wild hemp and dishwater splashing under their feet reached them. The courtyard was wide. Soon the dishwater ceased, and they felt freshly broken earth under their feet. In the darkness appeared the shadowy outlines of trees, and among the trees a little house with a crooked chimney.

"That is the bath house," said Olga Petrovna. "But I implore you, do not tell my brother! If you do, I'll never hear the end of it!"

Going up to the bath house, Chubikoff and Dukovski saw a huge padlock on the door.

"Get your candle and matches ready," whispered the examining magistrate to his deputy.

Olga Petrovna unfastened the padlock, and let her guests into the bath house. Dukovski struck a match and lit up the anteroom. In the middle of the anteroom stood a table. On the table, beside a sturdy little samovar, stood a soup tureen with cold cabbage soup and a plate with the remnants of some sauce.

"Forward!"

They went into the next room, where the bath was. There was a table there also. On the table was a dish with some ham, a bottle of vodka, plates, knives, forks.

"But where is it—where is the murdered man?" asked the examining magistrate.

"On the top tier," whispered Olga Petrovna, still pale and trembling.

Dukovski took the candle in his hand and climbed up to the top tier of the sweating frame. There he saw a long human body lying motionless on a large feather bed. A slight snore came from the body.

"You are making fun of us, devil take it!" cried Dukovski. "That is not the murdered man! Some live fool is lying here. Here, whoever you are, the devil take you!"

The body drew in a quick breath and stirred. Dukovski stuck his elbow into it. It raised a hand, stretched itself, and lifted its head.

"Who is sneaking in here?" asked a hoarse, heavy bass. "What do you want?"

Dukovski raised the candle to the face of the unknown, and cried out. In the red nose, dishevelled, unkempt hair, the pitch-black moustache, one of which was jauntily twisted and pointed insolently toward the ceiling, he recognized the gallant cavalryman Klausoff.

"You—Marcus—Ivanovitch? Is it possible?"

The examining magistrate glanced sharply up at him, and stood spellbound.

"Yes, it is I. That's you, Dukovski? What the devil do you want here? And who's that other mug down there? Great snakes! It is the examining magistrate! What fate has brought him here?"

Klausoff rushed down and threw his arms round Chubikoff in a cordial embrace. Olga Petrovna slipped through the door.

"How did you come here? Let's have a drink, devil take it! Tra-ta-ti-to-tum—let us drink! But who brought you here? How did you find out that I was here? But it doesn't matter! Let's have a drink!"

Klausoff lit the lamp and poured out three glasses of vodka.

"That is—I don't understand you," said the examining

magistrate, running his hands over him. "Is this you or not you!"

"Oh, shut up! You want to preach me a sermon? Don't trouble yourself! Young Dukovski, empty your glass! Friends, let us bring this—What are you looking at? Drink!"

"All the same, I do not understand!" said the examining magistrate, mechanically drinking off the vodka. "What are you here for?"

"Why shouldn't I be here, if I am all right here?"

Klausoff drained his glass and took a bite of ham.

"I am in captivity here, as you see. In solitude, in a cavern, like a ghost or a bogey. Drink! She carried me off and locked me up, and—well, I am living here, in the deserted bath house, like a hermit. I am fed. Next week I think I'll try to get out. I'm tired of it here!"

"Incomprehensible!" said Dukovski.

"What is incomprehensible about it?"

"Incomprehensible! For Heaven's sake, how did your boot get into the garden?"

"What boot?"

"We found one boot in the sleeping room and the other in the garden."

"And what do you want to know that for? It's none of your business! Why don't you drink, devil take you? If you wakened me, then drink with me! It is an interesting tale, brother, that of the boot! I didn't want to go with Olga. I don't like to be bossed. She came under the window and began to abuse me. She always was a termagant. You know what women are like, all of them. I was a bit drunk, so I took a boot and heaved it at her. Ha-ha-ha! Teach her not to scold another time! But it didn't! Not a bit of it! She climbed in at the window, lit the lamp, and began to hammer poor tipsy me. She thrashed me, dragged me over here, and locked me in. She feeds me now—on love, vodka, and ham! But where are you off to, Chubikoff? Where are you going?"

The examining magistrate swore, and left the bath house. Dukovski followed him, crestfallen. They silently took their seats in the carriage and drove off. The road never seemed to them so long and disagreeable as it did that time. Both remained silent. Chubikoff trembled with rage all the way. Dukovski hid his nose in the collar of his overcoat, as if he was afraid that the darkness and the drizzling rain might read the shame in his face.

When they reached home, the examining magistrate found Dr. Tyutyeff awaiting him. The doctor was sitting at the table, and, sighing deeply, was turning over the pages of the *Neva*.

"Such goings on there are in the world!" he said, meeting the examining magistrate with a sad smile. "Austria is at it again! And Gladstone also to some extent—"

Chubikoff threw his cap under the table, and shook himself.

"Devils' skeletons! Don't plague me! A thousand times I have told you not to bother me with your politics! This is no question of politics! And you," said Chubikoff, turning to Dukovski and shaking his fist, "I won't forget this in a thousand years!"

"But the safety match? How could I know?"

"Choke yourself with your safety match! Get out of my way! Don't make me mad, or the devil only knows what I'll do to you! Don't let me see a trace of you!"

Dukovski sighed, took his hat, and went out.

"I'll go and get drunk," he decided, going through the door, and gloomily wending his way to the public house.

Arthur Morrison

ARTHUR MORRISON (1863-1945) WAS AN ENGLISH AUTHOR AND journalist famous for his realist novels depicting life in London's East End, and his detective fiction featuring the character Martin Hewitt.

In contrast to the conventional detective Hewitt, Morrison later invented the character Horace Dorrington, who flipped the trope on its head – Dorrington was a more gritty, realistic depiction of a corrupt private eye who would do anything to make money, whether it involved larceny, deception, murder or worse.

9

THE NARRATIVE OF MR. JAMES RIGBY

Arthur Morrison

I SHALL HERE SET DOWN IN LANGUAGE AS SIMPLE AND straightforward as I can command, the events which followed my recent return to England; and I shall leave it to others to judge whether or not my conduct has been characterised by foolish fear and ill-considered credulity. At the same time I have my own opinion as to what would have been the behaviour of any other man of average intelligence and courage in the same circumstances; more especially a man of my exceptional upbringing and retired habits.

I was born in Australia, and I have lived there all my life till quite recently, save for a single trip to Europe as a boy, in company with my father and mother. It was then that I lost my father. I was less than nine years old at the time, but my memory of the events of that European trip is singularly vivid.

My father had emigrated to Australia at the time of his marriage, and had become a rich man by singularly fortunate speculations in land in and about Sydney. As a family we were most uncommonly self-centred and isolated. From my parents I never heard a word as to their relatives in England; indeed to this day I do not as much as know what was the Christian name of my grandfather. I have often supposed that some serious family quarrel or great misfortune must have preceded or accompanied my father's marriage. Be that as it may, I was never able to learn anything of my relatives, either on my mother's or my father's side. Both parents, however, were educated people, and indeed I fancy that their habit of seclusion must first have arisen from this circumstance, since the colonists about them in the early days, excellent people as they were, were not as a class distinguished for extreme intellectual culture. My father had his library stocked from England, and added to by fresh arrivals from time to time; and among his books he would pass most of his days, taking, however, now and again an excursion with a gun in search of some new specimen to add to his museum of natural history, which occupied three long rooms in our house by the Lane Cove river.

I was, as I have said, eight years of age when I started with my parents on a European tour, and it was in the year 1873. We stayed but a short while in England at first arrival, intending to make a longer stay on our return from the Continent. We made our tour, taking Italy last, and it was here that my father encountered a dangerous adventure.

We were at Naples, and my father had taken an odd fancy for a picturesque-looking ruffian who had attracted his attention by a complexion unusually fair for an Italian, and in whom he professed to recognise a likeness to Tasso the poet. This man became his guide in excursions about the neighbourhood of Naples, though he was not one of the regular corps of guides, and indeed seemed to have no regular occupation of a definite sort. "Tasso," as my father always called him, seemed a civil fellow enough, and was fairly intelligent; but my mother disliked him extremely from the first, without being able to offer any very distinct reason for her aversion. In the event her instinct was proved true.

"Tasso"—his correct name, by the way, was Tommaso Marino—persuaded my father that something interesting was to be seen at the Astroni crater, four miles west of the city, or thereabout; persuaded him, moreover, to make the journey on foot; and the two accordingly set out. All went well enough till the crater was reached, and then, in a lonely and broken part of the hill, the guide suddenly turned and attacked my father with a knife, his intention, without a doubt, being murder and the acquisition of the Englishman's valuables. Fortunately my father had a hip-pocket with a revolver in it, for he had been warned of the danger a stranger might at that time run wandering in the country about Naples. He received a wound in the flesh of his left arm in an attempt to ward off a stab, and fired, at wrestling distance, with the result that his assailant fell dead on the spot. He left the place with all speed, tying up his arm as he went, sought the British consul at Naples, and informed him of the whole circumstances. From the authorities there was no great difficulty. An examination or two, a few signatures, some particular exertions on the part of the consul, and my father was free, so far as the officers of the law were concerned. But while these formalities were in progress no less than three attempts were made on his life—two by the knife and one by shooting—and in each his escape was little short of miraculous. For the dead ruffian, Marino, had been a member of the dreaded Camorra, and the Camorristi were eager to avenge his death. To anybody acquainted with the internal history of Italy—more particularly the history of the old kingdom of Naples—the name of the Camorra will be familiar enough. It was one of the worst and most powerful of the many powerful and evil secret societies of Italy, and had none of the excuses for existence which have been from time to time put forward on behalf of the others. It was a gigantic club for the commission of crime and the extortion of money. So powerful was it that it actually imposed a regular tax on all food material entering Naples—a tax collected and paid with far more regularity than were any of the taxes due to the lawful Government of the country. The carrying of smuggled goods was a monopoly of the Camorra, a perfect organisation existing for the purpose throughout the kingdom. The whole

"HIS ASSAILANT FELL DEAD."

population was terrorised by this detestable society, which had no less than twelve centres in the city of Naples alone. It contracted for the commission of crime just as systematically and calmly as a railway company contracts for the carriage of merchandise. A murder was so much, according to circumstances, with extras for disposing of the body; arson was dealt in profitably; maimings and kidnappings were carried out with promptitude and despatch; and any diabolical outrage imaginable was a mere matter of price. One of the staple vocations of the concern was of course brigandage. After the coming of Victor Emanuel and the fusion of Italy into one kingdom the Camorra lost some of its power, but for a long time gave considerable trouble. I have heard that in the year after the matters I am describing two hundred Camorristi were banished from Italy.

As soon as the legal forms were complied with, my father received the broadest possible official hint that the sooner and the more secretly he left the country the better it would be for himself and his family. The British consul, too, impressed it upon him that the law would be entirely unable to protect him against the machinations of the Camorra; and indeed it needed but little persuasion to induce us to leave, for my poor mother was in a state of constant terror lest we were murdered together in our hotel; so that we lost no time in returning to England and bringing our European trip to a close.

In London we stayed at a well-known private hotel near Bond Street. We had been but three days here when my father came in one evening with a firm conviction that he had been followed for something like two hours, and followed very skilfully too. More than once he had doubled suddenly with a view to confront the pursuers, who he felt were at his heels, but he had met nobody of a suspicious appearance. The next afternoon I heard my mother telling my governess (who was travelling with us) of an unpleasant-looking man, who had been hanging about opposite the hotel door, and who, she felt sure, had afterwards been following her and my father as they were walking. My mother grew nervous, and communicated her fears to my father. He, however, pooh-poohed the thing, and took little thought of its meaning. Nevertheless the dogging continued, and my father, who was never able to fix upon the persons who caused the annoyance—indeed he rather felt their presence by instinct, as one does in such cases, than otherwise—grew extremely angry, and had some idea of consulting the police. Then one morning my mother discovered a little paper label stuck on the outside of the door of the bedroom occupied by herself and my father. It was a small thing, circular, and about the size of a sixpenny-piece, or even smaller, but my mother was quite certain that it had not been there when she last entered the door the night before, and she was much terrified. For the label carried a tiny device, drawn awkwardly in ink—a pair of knives of curious shape, crossed: the sign of the Camorra.

Nobody knew anything of this label, or how it came where it had been found. My mother urged my father to place himself under the protection of the police at once, but he delayed. Indeed, I fancy he had a suspicion that the label might be the production of some practical joker staying at the hotel who had heard of his Neapolitan adventure (it was reported in many newspapers) and designed to give him a fright. But that very evening my poor father was found dead, stabbed in a dozen places, in a short, quiet street not forty yards from the hotel. He had merely gone out to buy a few cigars of a particular brand which he fancied, at a shop two streets away, and in less than half an hour of his departure the police were at the hotel door with the news of his death, having got his address from letters in his pockets.

It is no part of my present design to enlarge on my mother's grief, or to describe in detail the incidents that followed my father's death, for I am going back to this early period of my life merely to make more clear the bearings of what has recently happened to myself. It will be sufficient therefore to say that at the inquest the jury returned a verdict of wilful murder against some person or persons unknown; that it was several times reported that the police had obtained a most important clue, and that being so, very naturally there was never any arrest. We returned to Sydney, and there I grew up.

I should perhaps have mentioned ere this that my profession—or I should rather say my hobby—is that of an artist. Fortunately or unfortunately, as you may please to consider it, I have no need to follow any profession as a means of livelihood, but since I was sixteen years of age my whole time has been engrossed in drawing and painting. Were it not for my mother's invincible objection to parting with me, even for the shortest space of time, I should long ago have come to Europe to work and to study in the regular schools. As it was I made shift to do my best in Australia, and wandered about pretty freely, struggling with the difficulties of moulding into artistic form the curious Australian landscape. There is an odd, desolate, uncanny note in characteristic Australian scenery, which most people are apt to regard as of little value for the purposes of the landscape painter, but with which I have always been convinced that an able painter could do great things. So I did my feeble best.

Two years ago my mother died. My age was then twenty-eight, and I was left without a friend in the world, and, so far as I know, without a relative. I soon found it impossible any longer to inhabit the large house by the Lane Cove river. It was beyond my simple needs, and the whole thing was an embarrassment, to say nothing of the associations of the house with my dead mother, which exercised a painful and depressing effect on me. So I sold the house, and cut myself adrift. For a year or more I pursued the life of a lonely vagabond in New South Wales, painting as well as I could its scattered forests of magnificent trees, with their curious upturned foliage. Then, miserably dissatisfied with my performance, and altogether filled with a restless spirit, I determined to quit the colony and live in England, or at any rate somewhere in Europe. I would paint at the Paris schools, I promised myself, and acquire that technical mastery of my material that I now felt the lack of.

The thing was no sooner resolved on than begun. I instructed my solicitors in Sydney to wind up my affairs and to communicate with their London correspondents in order that, on my arrival in England, I might deal with business matters through them. I had more than half resolved to transfer all my property to England, and to make the old country my permanent headquarters; and in three weeks from the date of my resolve I had started. I carried with me the necessary letters of introduction to the London solicitors, and the deeds appertaining to certain land in South Australia, which my father had bought just before his departure on the fatal European trip. There was workable copper in this land, it had since been ascertained, and I believed I might profitably dispose of the property to a company in London.

I found myself to some extent out of my element on board a great passenger steamer. It seemed no longer possible for me in the constant association of shipboard to maintain that reserve which had become with me a second nature. But so much had it become my nature that I shrank ridiculously from breaking it, for, grown man as I was, it must be confessed that I was absurdly shy, and indeed I fear little better than an overgrown schoolboy in my manner. But somehow I was scarce a day at sea before falling into a most pleasant acquaintanceship with another passenger, a man of thirty-eight or forty, whose name was Dorrington. He was a tall, well-built fellow, rather handsome, perhaps, except for a certain extreme roundness of face and fulness of feature; he had a dark military moustache, and carried himself erect, with a swing as of a cavalryman, and his eyes had, I think, the most penetrating quality I ever saw. His manners were extremely engaging, and he was the only good talker I had ever met. He knew everybody, and had been everywhere. His fund of illustration and anecdote was inexhaustible, and during all my acquaintance with him I never heard him tell the same story twice. Nothing could happen—not a bird could fly by the ship, not a dish could be put on the table, but Dorrington was ready with a pungent remark and the appropriate anecdote. And he never bored nor wearied one. With all his ready talk he never appeared unduly obtrusive nor in the least egotistic. Mr. Horace Dorrington was altogether the most charming person I had ever met. Moreover we discovered a community of taste in cigars.

"By the way," said Dorrington to me one magnificent evening as we leaned on the rail and smoked, "Rigby isn't a very common name in Australia, is it? I seem to remember a case, twenty years ago or more, of an Australian gentleman of that name being very badly treated in London—indeed, now I think of it, I'm not sure that he wasn't murdered. Ever hear anything of it?"

"Yes," I said, "I heard a great deal, unfortunately. He was my father, and he *was* murdered."

"Your father? There—I'm awfully sorry. Perhaps I shouldn't have mentioned it; but of course I didn't know."

"Oh," I replied, "that's all right. It's so far back now that I don't mind speaking about it. It was a very extraordinary thing altogether." And then, feeling that I owed Dorrington a story of some sort, after listening to the many he had been telling me, I described to him the whole circumstances of my father's death.

"Ah," said Dorrington when I had finished, "I have heard of the Camorra before this—I know a thing or two about it, indeed. As a matter of fact it still exists; not quite the widespread and open thing it once was, of course, and much smaller; but pretty active in a quiet way, and pretty mischievous. They were a mighty bad lot, those Camorristi. Personally I'm rather surprised that you heard no more of them. They were the sort of people who would rather any day murder three people than one, and their usual idea of revenge went a good way beyond the mere murder of the offending party; they had a way of including his wife and family, and as many relatives as possible. But at any rate *you* seem to have got off all right, though I'm inclined to call it rather a piece of luck than otherwise."

Then, as was his invariable habit, he launched into anecdote. He told me of the crimes of the Maffia, that Italian secret society, larger even and more powerful than the Camorra, and almost as criminal; tales of implacable revenge visited on father, son, and grandson in succession, till the race was extirpated. Then he talked of the methods; of the large funds at the disposal of the Camorra and the Maffia, and of the cunning patience with which their schemes were carried into execution; of the victims who had discovered too late that their most trusted servants were sworn to their destruction, and of those who had fled to remote parts of the earth and hoped to be lost and forgotten, but who had been shadowed and slain with barbarous ferocity in their most trusted hiding-places. Wherever Italians were, there was apt to be a branch of one of the societies, and one could never tell where they might or might not turn up. The two Italian forecastle hands on board at that moment might be members, and might or might not have some business in hand not included in their signed articles.

I asked if he had ever come into personal contact with either of these societies or their doings.

"With the Camorra, no, though I know things about them that would probably surprise some of them not a little. But I have had professional dealings with the Maffia—and that without coming off second best, too. But it was not so serious a case as your father's; one of a robbery of documents and blackmail."

"Professional dealings?" I queried.

Dorrington laughed. "Yes," he answered. "I find I've come very near to letting the cat out of the bag. I don't generally tell people who I am when I travel about, and indeed I don't always use my own name, as I am doing now. Surely you've heard the name at some time or another?"

I had to confess that I did not remember it. But I excused myself by citing my secluded life, and the fact that I had never left Australia since I was a child.

"Ah," he said, "of course we should be less heard of in Australia. But in England we're really pretty well known, my partner and I. But, come now, look me all over and consider, and I'll give you a dozen guesses and bet you a sovereign you can't tell me my trade. And it's not such an uncommon or unheard-of trade, neither."

Guessing would have been hopeless, and I said so. He did not seem the sort of man who would trouble himself about a trade at all. I gave it up.

"Well," he said, "I've no particular desire to have it known all over the ship, but I don't mind telling you—you'd find it out probably before long if you settle in the old country—that we are what is called private inquiry agents—detectives—secret service men—whatever you like to call it."

"Indeed!"

"Yes, indeed. And I think I may claim that we stand as high as any—if not a trifle higher. Of course I can't tell you, but you'd be rather astonished if you heard the names of some of our clients. We have had dealings with certain royalties, European and Asiatic, that would startle you a bit if I could tell them. Dorrington & Hicks is the name of the firm, and we are both pretty busy men, though we keep going a regiment of assistants and correspondents. I have been in Australia three months over a rather awkward and complicated matter, but I fancy I've pulled it through pretty well, and I mean to reward myself with a little holiday when I get back. There—now you know the worst of me. And D. & H. present their respectful compliments, and trust that by unfailing punctuality and a strict attention to business they may hope to receive your esteemed commands whenever you may be so unfortunate as to require their services. Family secrets extracted, cleaned, scaled, or stopped with gold. Special attention given to wholesale orders." He laughed and pulled out his cigar-case. "You haven't another cigar in your pocket," he said, "or you wouldn't smoke that stump so low. Try one of these."

I took the cigar and lit it at my remainder. "Ah, then," I said, "I take it that it is the practice of your profession that has given you such a command of curious and out-of-the-way information and anecdote. Plainly you must have been in the midst of many curious affairs."

"Yes, I believe you," Dorrington replied. "But, as it happens, the most curious of my experiences I am unable to relate, since they are matters of professional confidence. Such as I *can* tell I usually tell with altered names, dates, and places. One learns discretion in such a trade as mine."

"As to your adventure with the Maffia, now. Is there any secrecy about that?"

Dorrington shrugged his shoulders. "No," he said, "none in particular. But the case was not particularly interesting. It was in Florence. The documents were the property of a wealthy American, and some of the Maffia rascals managed to steal them. It doesn't matter what the documents were—that's a private matter—but their owner would have parted with a great deal to get them back, and the Maffia held them for ransom. But they had such a fearful notion of the American's wealth, and of what he ought to pay, that, badly as he wanted the papers back, he couldn't stand their demands, and employed us to negotiate and to do our best for him. I think I might have managed to get the things stolen back again—indeed I spent some time thinking a plan over—but I decided in the end that it wouldn't pay. If the Maffia were tricked in that way they might consider it appropriate to stick somebody with a knife, and that was not an easy thing to provide against. So I took a little time and went another way to work. The details don't matter—they're quite uninteresting, and to tell you them would be to talk mere professional 'shop'; there's a deal of dull and patient work to be done in my business. Anyhow, I contrived to find out exactly in whose hands the documents lay. He wasn't altogether a blameless creature, and there were two or three little things that, properly handled, might have brought him into awkward complications with the law. So I delayed the negotiations while I got my nets effectually round this gentleman, who was the president of that particular branch of the Maffia, and when all was ready I had a friendly interview with him, and just showed him my hand of cards. They served as no other argument would have done, and in the end we concluded quite an amicable arrangement on easy terms for both parties, and my client got his property back, including all expenses, at about a fifth of the price he expected to have to pay. That's all. I learnt a deal about the Maffia while the business lasted, and at that and other times I learnt a good deal about the Camorra too."

Dorrington and I grew more intimate every day of the voyage, till he knew every detail of my uneventful little history, and I knew many of his own most curious experiences. In truth he was a man with an irresistible fascination for a dull home-bird like myself. With all his gaiety he never forgot business, and at most of our stopping places he sent off messages by cable to his partner. As the voyage drew near its end he grew anxious and impatient lest he should not arrive in time to enable him to get to Scotland for grouse-shooting on the twelfth of August. His one amusement, it seemed, was shooting, and the holiday he had promised himself was to be spent on a grouse-moor which he rented in Perthshire. It would be a great nuisance to miss the twelfth, he said, but it would apparently be a near shave. He thought, however, that in any case it might be done by leaving the ship at Plymouth, and rushing up to London by the first train.

"Yes," he said, "I think I shall be able to do it that way, even if the boat is a couple of days late. By the way," he added suddenly, "why not come along to Scotland with me? You haven't any particular business in hand, and I can promise you a week or two of good fun."

The invitation pleased me. "It's very good of you," I said, "and as a matter of fact I haven't any very urgent business in London. I must see those solicitors I told you of, but that's not a matter of hurry; indeed an hour or two on my way through London would be enough. But as I don't know any of your party and—"

"Pooh, pooh, my dear fellow," answered Dorrington, with a snap of his fingers, "that's all right. I shan't have a party. There won't be time to get it together. One or two might come down a little later, but if they do they'll be capital fellows, delighted to make your acquaintance, I'm sure. Indeed you'll do me a great favour if you'll come, else I shall be all alone, without a soul to say a word to. Anyway, I *won't* miss the twelfth, if it's to be done by any possibility. You'll really have to come, you know—you've no excuse. I can lend you guns and anything you want, though

I believe you've such things with you. Who is your London solicitor, by the way?"

"Mowbray, of Lincoln's Inn Fields."

"Oh, Mowbray? We know him well; his partner died last year. When I say *we* know him well, I mean as a firm. I have never met him personally, though my partner (who does the office work) has regular dealings with him. He's an excellent man, but his managing clerk's frightful; I wonder Mowbray keeps him. Don't you let him do anything for you on his own hook; he makes the most disastrous messes, and I rather fancy he drinks. Deal with Mowbray himself; there's nobody better in London. And by the way, now I think of it, it's lucky you've nothing urgent for him, for he's sure to be off out of town for the twelfth; he's a rare old gunner, and never misses a season. So that now you haven't a shade of an excuse for leaving me in the lurch, and we'll consider the thing settled."

Settled accordingly it was, and the voyage ended uneventfully. But the steamer was late, and we left it at Plymouth and rushed up to town on the tenth. We had three or four hours to prepare before leaving Euston by the night train. Dorrington's moor was a long drive from Crieff station, and he calculated that at best we could not arrive there before the early evening of the following day, which would, however, give us comfortable time for a good long night's rest before the morning's sport opened. Fortunately I had plenty of loose cash with me, so that there was nothing to delay us in that regard. We made ready in Dorrington's rooms (he was a bachelor) in Conduit Street, and got off comfortably by the ten o'clock train from Euston.

Then followed a most delightful eight days. The weather was fine, the birds were plentiful, and my first taste of grouse-shooting was a complete success. I resolved for the future to come out of my shell and mix in the world that contained such charming fellows as Dorrington, and such delightful sports as that I was then enjoying. But on the eighth day Dorrington received a telegram calling him instantly to London.

"It's a shocking nuisance," he said; "here's my holiday either knocked on the head altogether or cut in two, and I fear it's the first rather than the second. It's just the way in such an uncertain profession as mine. There's no possible help for it, however; I must go, as you'd understand at once if you knew the case. But what chiefly annoys me is leaving you all alone."

I reassured him on this point, and pointed out that I had for a long time been used to a good deal of my own company. Though indeed, with Dorrington away, life at the shooting-lodge threatened to be less pleasant than it had been.

"But you'll be bored to death here," Dorrington said, his thoughts jumping with my own. "But on the other hand it won't be much good going up to town yet. Everybody's out of town, and Mowbray among them. There's a little business of ours that's waiting for him at this moment—my partner mentioned it in his letter yesterday. Why not put in the time with a little tour round? Or you might work up to London by irregular stages, and look about you. As an artist you'd like to see a few of the old towns—probably, Edinburgh, Chester, Warwick, and so on. It isn't a great programme, perhaps, but I hardly know what else to suggest. As for myself I must be off as I am by the first train I can get."

I begged him not to trouble about me, but to attend to his business. As a matter of fact, I was disposed to get to London and take chambers, at any rate for a little while. But Chester was a place I much wanted to see—a real old town, with walls round it—and I was not indisposed to take a day at Warwick. So in the end I resolved to pack up and make for Chester the following day, and from there to take train for Warwick. And in half an hour Dorrington was gone.

Chester was all delight to me. My recollections of the trip to Europe in my childhood were vivid enough as to the misfortunes that followed my father, but of the ancient buildings we visited I remembered little. Now in Chester I found the mediæval town I had so often read of. I wandered for hours together in the quaint old "Rows," and walked on the city wall. The evening after my arrival was fine and moonlight, and I was tempted from my

"I MADE A QUICK RUSH."

hotel. I took a stroll about the town and finished by a walk along the wall from the Watergate toward the cathedral. The moon, flecked over now and again by scraps of cloud, and at times obscured for half a minute together, lighted up all the Roodee in the intervals, and touched with silver the river beyond. But as I walked I presently grew aware of a quiet shuffling footstep some little way behind me. I took little heed of it at first, though I could see nobody near me from whom the sound might come. But soon I perceived that when I stopped, as I did from time to time to gaze over the parapet, the mysterious footsteps stopped also, and when I resumed my walk the quiet shuffling tread began again. At first I thought it might be an echo; but a moment's reflection dispelled that idea. Mine was an even, distinct walk, and this which followed was a soft, quick, shuffling step—a mere scuffle. Moreover, when, by way of test, I took a few silent steps on tip-toe, the shuffle still persisted. I was being followed.

Now I do not know whether or not it may sound like a childish fancy, but I confess I thought of my father. When last I had been in England, as a child, my father's violent death had been preceded by just such followings. And now after all these years, on my return, on the very first night I walked abroad alone, there were strange footsteps in my track. The walk was narrow, and nobody could possibly pass me unseen. I turned suddenly, therefore, and hastened back. At once I saw a dark figure rise from the shadow of the parapet and run. I ran too, but I could not gain on the figure, which receded farther and more indistinctly before me. One reason was that I felt doubtful of my footing on the unfamiliar track. I ceased my chase, and continued my stroll. It might easily have been some vagrant thief, I thought, who had a notion to rush, at a convenient opportunity, and snatch my watch. But here I was far past the spot where I had turned there was the shuffling footstep behind me again. For a little while I feigned not to notice it; then, swinging round as swiftly as I could, I made a quick rush. Useless again, for there in the distance scuttled that same indistinct figure, more rapidly than I could run. What did it mean? I liked the affair so little that I left the walls and walked toward my hotel.

The streets were quiet. I had traversed two, and was about emerging into one of the two main streets, where the Rows are, when, from the farther part of the dark street behind me, there came once more the sound of the now unmistakable footstep. I stopped; the footsteps stopped also. I turned and walked back a few steps, and as I did it the sounds went scuffling away at the far end of the street.

It could not be fancy. It could not be chance. For a single incident perhaps such an explanation might serve, but not for this persistent recurrence. I hurried away to my hotel, resolved, since I could not come at my pursuer, to turn back no more. But before I reached the hotel there were the shuffling footsteps again, and not far behind.

It would not be true to say that I was alarmed at this stage of the adventure, but I was troubled to know what it all might mean, and altogether puzzled to account for it. I thought a great deal, but I went to bed and rose in the morning no wiser than ever.

Whether or not it was a mere fancy induced by the last night's experience I cannot say, but I went about that day with a haunting feeling that I was watched, and to me the impression was very real indeed. I listened often, but in the bustle of the day, even in quiet old Chester, the individual characters of different footsteps were not easily recognisable. Once, however, as I descended a flight of steps from the Rows, I fancied I heard the quick shuffle in the curious old gallery I had just quitted. I turned up the steps again and looked. There was a shabby sort of man looking in one of the windows, and leaning so far as to hide his head behind the heavy oaken pilaster that supported the building above. It might have been his footstep, or it might have been my fancy. At any rate I would have a look at him. I mounted the top stair, but as I turned in his direction the man ran off, with his face averted and his head ducked, and vanished down another stair. I made all speed after him, but when I reached the street he was nowhere to be seen.

What *could* it all mean? The man was rather above the middle height, and he wore one of those soft felt hats familiar on the head of the London organ-grinder. Also his hair was black and bushy, and protruded over the back of his coat-collar. Surely *this* was no delusion; surely I was not imagining an Italian aspect for this man simply because of the recollection of my father's fate?

Perhaps I was foolish, but I took no more pleasure in Chester. The embarrassment was a novel one for me, and I could not forget it. I went back to my hotel, paid my bill, sent my bag to the railway station, and took train for Warwick by way of Crewe.

It was dark when I arrived, but the night was near as fine as last night had been at Chester. I took a very little late dinner at my hotel, and fell into a doubt what to do with myself. One rather fat and very sleepy commercial traveller was the only other customer visible, and the billiard room was empty. There seemed to be nothing to do but to light a cigar and take a walk.

I could just see enough of the old town to give me good hopes of to-morrow's sight-seeing. There was nothing visible of quite such an interesting character as one might meet in Chester, but there were a good few fine old sixteenth century houses, and there were the two gates with the chapels above them. But of course the castle was the great show-place, and that I should visit on the morrow, if there were no difficulties as to permission. There were some very fine pictures there, if I remembered aright what I had read. I was walking down the incline from one of the gates, trying to remember who the painters of these pictures were, besides Van Dyck and Holbein, when—that shuffling step was behind me again!

I admit that it cost me an effort, this time, to turn on my pursuer. There was something uncanny in that persistent, elusive footstep, and indeed there was something alarming in my circumstances, dogged thus from place to place, and unable to shake off my enemy, or to understand his movements or his motive. Turn I did, however, and straightway the shuffling step went off at a hastened pace in the shadow of the gate. This time I made no more than half-a-dozen steps back. I turned again, and pushed my way to the hotel. And as I went the shuffling step came after.

The thing was serious. There must be some object in this unceasing watching, and the object could bode no good to me. Plainly some unseen eye had been on me the whole of that day, had noted my goings and comings and my journey from Chester. Again, and irresistibly, the watchings that preceded my father's death came to mind, and I could not forget them. I could have no doubt now that I had been closely watched from the moment I had set foot at Plymouth. But who could have been waiting to watch me at Plymouth, when indeed I had only decided to land at the last moment? Then I thought of the two Italian forecastle hands on the steamer—the very men whom Dorrington had used to illustrate in what unexpected quarters members of the terrible Italian secret societies might be found. And the Camorra was not satisfied with single revenge; it destroyed the son after the father, and it waited for many years, with infinite patience and cunning.

Dogged by the steps, I reached the hotel and went to bed. I slept but fitfully at first, though better rest came as the night wore on. In the early morning I woke with a sudden shock, and with an indefinite sense of being disturbed by somebody about me. The window was directly opposite the foot of the bed, and there, as I looked, was the face of a man, dark, evil, and grinning, with a bush of black hair about his uncovered head, and small rings in his ears.

It was but a flash, and the face vanished. I was struck by the terror that one so often feels on a sudden and violent awakening from sleep, and it was some seconds ere I could leave my bed and get to the window. My room was on the first floor, and the window looked down on a stable-yard. I had a momentary glimpse of a human figure leaving the gate of the yard, and it was the figure that had fled before me in the Rows, at Chester. A ladder belonging to the yard stood under the window, and that was all.

I rose and dressed; I could stand this sort of thing no longer. If it were only something tangible, if there were only somebody I could take hold of, and fight with if necessary, it would not have been so bad. But I was surrounded by some mysterious machination, persistent, unexplainable, that it was altogether impossible to tackle or to face. To complain to the police would have been absurd—they would take me for a lunatic. They are indeed just such complaints that lunatics so often make to the police—complaints of being followed by indefinite enemies, and of being besieged by faces that look in at windows. Even if they did not set me down a lunatic, what could the police of a provincial town do for me in a case like this? No, I must go and consult Dorrington.

I had my breakfast, and then decided that I would at any rate try the castle before leaving. Try it I did accordingly, and was allowed to go over it. But through the whole morning I was oppressed by the horrible sense of being watched by malignant eyes. Clearly there was no comfort for me while this lasted; so after lunch I caught a train which brought me to Euston soon after half-past six.

I took a cab straight to Dorrington's rooms, but he was out, and was not expected home till late. So I drove to a large hotel near Charing Cross—I avoid mentioning its name for reasons which will presently be understood—sent in my bag, and dined.

I had not the smallest doubt but that I was still under the observation of the man or the men who had so far pursued me; I had, indeed, no hope of eluding them, except by the contrivance of Dorrington's expert brain. So as I had no desire to hear that shuffling footstep again—indeed it had seemed, at Warwick, to have a physically painful effect on my nerves—I stayed within and got to bed early.

I had no fear of waking face to face with a grinning Italian here. My window was four floors up, out of reach of anything but a fire-escape. And, in fact, I woke comfortably and naturally, and saw nothing from my window but the bright sky, the buildings opposite, and the traffic below. But as I turned to close my door behind me as I emerged into the corridor, there, on the muntin of the frame, just below the bedroom number, was a little round paper label, perhaps a trifle smaller than a sixpence, and on the label, drawn awkwardly in ink, was a device of two crossed knives of curious, crooked shape. The sign of the Camorra!

I will not attempt to describe the effect of this sign upon me. It may best be imagined, in view of what I have said of the incidents preceding the murder of my father. It was the sign of an inexorable fate, creeping nearer step by step, implacable, inevitable, and mysterious. In little more than twelve hours after seeing that sign my father had been a mangled corpse. One of the hotel servants passed as I stood by the door, and I made shift to ask him if he knew anything of the label. He looked at the paper, and then, more curiously, at me, but he could offer no explanation. I spent little time over breakfast, and then went by cab to Conduit Street. I paid my bill and took my bag with me.

Dorrington had gone to his office, but he had left a message that if I called I was to follow him; and the office was in Bedford Street, Covent Garden. I turned the cab in that direction forthwith.

"Why," said Dorrington as we shook hands, "I believe you look a bit out of sorts! Doesn't England agree with you?"

"Well," I answered, "it has proved rather trying so far." And then I described, in exact detail, my adventures as I have set them down here.

Dorrington looked grave. "It's really extraordinary," he said, "most extraordinary; and it isn't often that I call a thing extraordinary neither, with my experience. But it's plain something must be done—something to gain time at any rate. We're in the dark at present, of course, and I expect I shall have to fish about a little before I get at anything to go on. In the meantime I think you must disappear as artfully as we can manage it." He sat silent for a little while, thoughtfully tapping his forehead with his finger-tips. "I wonder," he said presently, "whether or not those Italian fellows on the steamer *are* in it or not. I suppose you haven't made yourself known anywhere, have you?"

"Nowhere. As you know, you've been with me all the time till you left the moor, and since then I have been with nobody and called on nobody."

"Now there's no doubt it's the Camorra," Dorrington said—"that's pretty plain. I think I told you on the steamer that it was rather wonderful that you had heard nothing of them after your father's death. What has caused them all this delay there's no telling—they know best themselves; it's been lucky for you, anyway, so far. What I'd like to find out now is how they have identified you, and got on your track so promptly. There's no guessing where these fellows get their information—it's just wonderful; but if we can find out, then perhaps we can stop the supply, or turn on something that will lead them into a pit. If you had called anywhere on business and declared yourself—as you might have done, for instance, at Mowbray's—I might be inclined to suspect that they got the tip in some crooked way from there. But you haven't. Of course, if those Italian chaps on the steamer *are* in it, you're probably identified pretty certainly; but if they're not, they may only have made a guess. We two landed together, and kept together, till a day or two ago; as far as any outsider would know, I might be Rigby and you might be Dorrington. Come, we'll work on those lines. I think I smell a plan. Are you staying anywhere?"

"No. I paid my bill at the hotel and came along here with my bag."

"Very well. Now there's a house at Highgate kept by a very trustworthy man, whom I know very well, where a man might be pretty comfortable for a few days, or even for a week, if he doesn't mind staying indoors, and keeping himself out of sight. I expect your friends of the Camorra are watching in the street outside at this moment; but I think it will be fairly easy to get you away to Highgate without letting them into the secret, if you don't mind secluding yourself for a bit. In the circumstances, I take it you won't object at all?"

"Object? I should think not."

"Very well, that's settled. You can call yourself Dorrington or not, as you please, though perhaps it will be safest not to shout 'Rigby' too loud. But as for myself, for a day or two at least I'm going to be Mr. James Rigby. Have you your card-case handy?"

"Yes, here it is. But then, as to taking my name, won't you run serious risk?"

Dorrington winked merrily. "I've run a risk or two before now," he said, "in course of my business. And if *I* don't mind the risk, you needn't grumble, for I warn you I shall charge for risk when I send you my bill. And I think I can take care of myself fairly well, even with the Camorra about. I shall take you to this place at Highgate, and then you won't see me for a few days. It won't do for me, in the character of Mr. James Rigby, to go dragging a trail up and down between this place and your retreat. You've got some other identifying papers, haven't you?"

"Yes, I have." I produced the letter from my Sydney lawyers to Mowbray, and the deeds of the South Australian property from my bag.

"Ah," said Dorrington, "I'll just give you a formal receipt for these, since they're valuable; it's a matter of business, and we'll do it in a business-like way. I may want something solid like this to support any bluff I may have to make. A mere case of cards won't always act, you know. It's a pity old Mowbray's out of town, for there's a way in which he might give a little help, I fancy. But never mind—leave it all to me. There's your receipt. Keep it snug away somewhere, where inquisitive people can't read it."

He handed me the receipt, and then took me to his partner's room and introduced me. Mr. Hicks was a small, wrinkled man, older than Dorrington, I should think, by fifteen or twenty years, and with all the aspect and manner of a quiet old professional man.

Dorrington left the room, and presently returned with his hat in his hand. "Yes," he said, "there's a charming dark gentleman with a head like a mop, and rings in his ears, skulking about at the next corner. If it was he who looked in at your window, I don't wonder you were startled. His dress suggests the organ-grinding interest, but he looks as though cutting a throat would be more in his line than grinding a tune; and no doubt he has friends as engaging as himself close at call. If you'll come with me now I think we shall give him the slip. I have a growler ready for you—a hansom's a bit too glassy and public. Pull down the blinds and sit back when you get inside."

He led me to a yard at the back of the building wherein the office stood, from which a short flight of steps led to a basement. We followed a passage in this basement till we reached another flight, and ascending these, we emerged into the corridor of another building. Out at the door at the end of this, and we passed a large block of model dwellings, and were in Bedfordbury. Here a four-wheeler was waiting, and I shut myself in it without delay.

I was to proceed as far as King's Cross in this cab, Dorrington had arranged, and there he would overtake me in a swift hansom. It fell out as he had settled, and, dismissing the hansom, he came the rest of the journey with me in the four-wheeler.

We stopped at length before one of a row of houses, apparently recently built—houses of the over-ornamented, gabled and tiled sort that abound in the suburbs.

"Crofting is the man's name," Dorrington said, as we alighted. "He's rather an odd sort of customer, but quite decent in the main, and his wife makes coffee such as money won't buy in most places."

A woman answered Dorrington's ring—a woman of most extreme thinness. Dorrington greeted her as Mrs. Crofting, and we entered.

"We've just lost our servant again, Mr. Dorrington," the woman said in a shrill voice, "and Mr. Crofting ain't at home. But I'm expecting him before long."

"I don't think I need wait to see him, Mrs. Crofting," Dorrington answered. "I'm sure I can't leave my friend in better hands than yours. I hope you've a vacant room?"

"Well, for a friend of yours, Mr. Dorrington, no doubt we can find room."

"That's right. My friend Mr."—Dorrington gave me a

meaning look—"Mr. Phelps, would like to stay here for a few days. He wants to be quite quiet for a little—do you understand?"

"Oh, yes, Mr. Dorrington, I understand."

"Very well, then, make him as comfortable as you can, and give him some of your very best coffee. I believe you've got quite a little library of books, and Mr. Phelps will be glad of them. Have you got any cigars?" Dorrington added, turning to me.

"Yes; there are some in my bag."

"Then I think you'll be pretty comfortable now. Goodbye. I expect you'll see me in a few days—or at any rate you'll get a message. Meantime be as happy as you can."

Dorrington left, and the woman showed me to a room upstairs, where I placed my bag. In front, on the same floor, was a sitting-room, with, I suppose, some two or three hundred books, mostly novels, on shelves. The furniture of the place was of the sort one expects to find in an ordinary lodging-house—horsehair sofas, loo tables, lustres, and so forth. Mrs. Crofting explained to me that the customary dinner hour was two, but that I might dine when I liked. I elected, however, to follow the custom of the house, and sat down to a cigar and a book.

At two o'clock the dinner came, and I was agreeably surprised to find it a very good one, much above what the appointments of the house had led me to expect. Plainly Mrs. Crofting was a capital cook. There was no soup, but there was a very excellent sole, and some well-done cutlets with peas, and an omelet; also a bottle of Bass. Come, I felt that I should not do so badly in this place after all. I trusted that Dorrington would be as comfortable in his half of the transaction, bearing my responsibilities and troubles. I had heard a heavy, blundering tread on the floor below, and judged from this that Mr. Crofting had returned.

After dinner I lit a cigar, and Mrs. Crofting brought her coffee. Truly it was excellent coffee, and brewed as I like it—strong and black, and plenty of it. It had a flavour of its own too, novel, but not unpleasing. I took one cupful, and brought another to my side as I lay on the sofa with my book. I had not read six lines before I was asleep.

I woke with a sensation of numbing cold in my right side, a terrible stiffness in my limbs, and a sound of loud splashing in my ears. All was pitch dark, and—what was this? Water! Water all about me. I was lying in six inches of cold water, and more was pouring down upon me from above. My head was afflicted with a splitting ache. But where was I? Why was it dark? And whence all the water? I staggered to my feet, and instantly struck my head against a hard roof above me. I raised my hand; there was the roof or whatever place it was, hard, smooth and cold, and little more than five feet from the floor, so that I bent as I stood. I spread my hand to the side; that was hard, smooth and cold too. And then the conviction struck me like a blow—I was in a covered iron tank, and the water was pouring in to drown me!

I dashed my hands frantically against the lid, and strove to raise it. It would not move. I shouted at the top of my voice, and turned about to feel the extent of my prison. One way I could touch the opposite sides at once easily with my hands, the other way it was wider—perhaps a little more than six feet altogether. What was this? Was this to be my fearful end, cooped in this tank while the water rose by inches to choke me? Already the water was a foot deep. I flung myself at the sides, I beat the pitiless iron with fists, face and head, I screamed and implored. Then it struck me that I might at least stop the inlet of water. I put out my hand and felt the falling stream, then found the inlet and stopped it with my fingers. But water still poured in with a resounding splash; there was another opening at the opposite end, which I could not reach without releasing the one I now held! I was but prolonging my agony. Oh, the devilish cunning that had devised those two inlets, so far apart! Again I beat the sides, broke my nails with tearing at the corners, screamed and entreated in my agony. I was mad, but with no dulling of the senses, for the horrors of my awful, helpless state, overwhelmed my brain, keen and perceptive to every ripple of the unceasing water.

In the height of my frenzy I held my breath, for I heard a

sound from outside. I shouted again—implored some quicker death. Then there was a scraping on the lid above me, and it was raised at one edge, and let in the light of a candle. I sprang from my knees and forced the lid back, and the candle flame danced before me. The candle was held by a dusty man, a workman apparently, who stared at me with scared eyes, and said nothing but, "Goo' lor'!"

Overhead were the rafters of a gabled roof, and tilted against them was the thick beam which, jammed across from one sloping rafter to another, had held the tank-lid fast. "Help me!" I gasped. "Help me out!"

The man took me by the armpits and hauled me, dripping and half dead, over the edge of the tank, into which the water still poured, making a noise in the hollow iron that half drowned our voices. The man had been at work on the cistern of a neighbouring house, and hearing an uncommon noise, he had climbed through the spaces left in the party walls to give passage along under the roofs to the builders' men. Among the joists at our feet was the trap-door through which, drugged and insensible, I had been carried, to be flung into that horrible cistern.

With the help of my friend the workman I made shift to climb through by the way he had come. We got back to the house where he had been at work, and there the people gave me brandy and lent me dry clothes. I made haste to send for the police, but when they arrived Mrs. Crofting and her respectable spouse had gone. Some unusual noise in the roof must have warned them. And when the police, following my directions further, got to the offices of Dorrington and Hicks, those acute professional men had gone too, but in such haste that the contents of the office, papers and everything else, had been left just as they stood.

The plot was clear now. The followings, the footsteps, the face at the window, the label on the door—all were a mere humbug arranged by Dorrington for his own purpose, which was to drive me into his power and get my papers from me. Armed with these, and with his consummate address and knowledge of affairs, he could go to Mr. Mowbray in the character of Mr. James Rigby, sell my land in South Australia, and have the whole of my property transferred to himself from Sydney. The rest of my baggage was at his rooms; if any further proof were required it might be found there. He had taken good care that I should not meet Mr. Mowbray—who, by the way, I afterwards found had not left his office, and had never fired a gun in his life. At first I wondered that Dorrington had not made some murderous attempt on me at the shooting place in Scotland. But a little thought convinced me that that would have been bad policy for him. The disposal of the body would be difficult, and he would have to account somehow for my sudden disappearance. Whereas, by the use of his Italian assistant and his murder apparatus at Highgate I was made to efface my own trail, and could be got rid of in the end with little trouble; for my body, stripped of everything that might identify me, would be simply that of a drowned man unknown, whom nobody could identify. The whole plot was contrived upon the information I myself had afforded Dorrington during the voyage home. And it all sprang from his remembering the report of my father's death. When the papers in the office came to be examined, there each step in the operations was plainly revealed. There was a code telegram from Suez directing Hicks to hire a grouse moor. There were telegrams and letters from Scotland giving directions as to the later movements; indeed the thing was displayed completely. The business of Dorrington and Hicks had really been that of private inquiry agents, and they had done much *bonâ fide* business; but many of their operations had been of a more than questionable sort. And among their papers were found complete sets, neatly arranged in dockets, each containing in skeleton a complete history of a case. Many of these cases were of a most interesting character, and I have been enabled to piece together, out of the material thus supplied, the narratives which will follow this. As to my own case, it only remains to say that as yet neither Dorrington, Hicks, nor the Croftings have been caught. They played in the end for a high stake (they might have made six figures of me if they had killed me, and the first figure would not have been a one) and they lost by a mere accident. But I have often wondered how many of the bodies which the coroners' juries of London have returned to be "Found Drowned" were drowned, not where they were picked up, but in that horrible tank at Highgate. What the drug was that gave Mrs. Crofting's coffee its value in Dorrington's eyes I do not know, but plainly it had not been sufficient in my case to keep me unconscious against the shock of cold water till I could be drowned altogether. Months have passed since my adventure, but even now I sweat at the sight of an iron tank.

Edgar Allan Poe

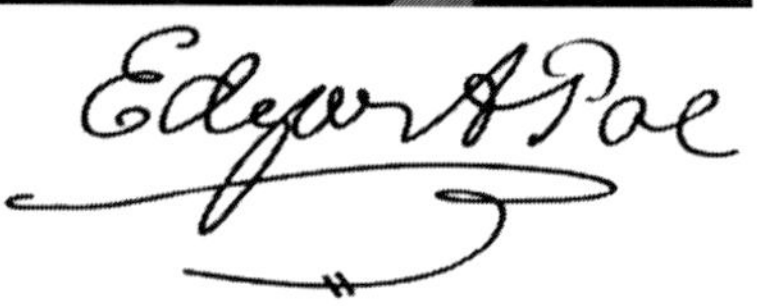

EDGAR ALLAN POE (1809-1849) WAS AN AMERICAN AUTHOR, poet, and literary critic and the progenitor of modern detective fiction and a major contributor to the then-emerging genre of science fiction.

Poe wrote a series of three short stories involving the character C. Auguste Dupin, an amateur detective who relies on deductive reasoning and his preternaturally good ability to read people to solve crimes.

10

THE MURDERS IN THE RUE MORGUE

Edgar Allan Poe

What song the Syrens sang, or what name Achilles assumed when he hid himself among women, although puzzling questions, are not beyond all conjecture.

—Sir Thomas Browne.

THE MENTAL FEATURES DISCOURSED OF AS THE ANALYTICAL, ARE, in themselves, but little susceptible of analysis. We appreciate them only in their effects. We know of them, among other things, that they are always to their possessor, when inordinately possessed, a source of the liveliest enjoyment. As the strong man exults in his physical ability, delighting in such exercises as call his muscles into action, so glories the analyst in that moral activity which *disentangles.* He derives pleasure from even the most trivial occupations bringing his talent into play. He is fond of enigmas, of conundrums, of hieroglyphics; exhibiting in his solutions of each a degree of *acumen* which appears to the ordinary apprehension præternatural. His results, brought about by the very soul and essence of method, have, in truth, the whole air of intuition.

The faculty of re-solution is possibly much invigorated by mathematical study, and especially by that highest branch of it which, unjustly, and merely on account of its retrograde operations, has been called, as if *par excellence*, analysis. Yet to calculate is not in itself to analyse. A chess-player, for example, does the one without effort at the other. It follows that the game of chess, in its effects upon mental character, is greatly misunderstood. I am not now writing a treatise, but simply prefacing a somewhat peculiar narrative by observations very much at random; I will, therefore, take occasion to assert that the higher powers of the reflective intellect are more decidedly and more usefully tasked by the unostentatious game of draughts than by all the elaborate frivolity of chess. In this latter, where the pieces have different and *bizarre* motions, with various and variable values, what is only complex is mistaken (a not unusual error) for what is profound. The *attention* is here called powerfully into play. If it flag for an instant, an oversight is committed resulting in injury or defeat. The possible moves being not only manifold but involute, the chances of such oversights are multiplied; and in nine cases out of ten it is the more concentrative rather than the more acute player who conquers. In draughts, on the contrary, where the moves are *unique* and have but little variation, the probabilities of inadvertence are diminished, and the mere attention being left comparatively unemployed, what advantages are obtained by either party are obtained by superior *acumen*. To be less abstract—Let us suppose a game of draughts where the pieces are reduced to four kings, and where, of course, no oversight is to be expected. It is obvious that here the victory can be decided (the players being at all equal) only by some *recherché* movement, the result of some strong exertion of the intellect. Deprived of ordinary resources, the analyst throws himself into the spirit of his opponent, identifies himself therewith, and not unfrequently sees thus, at a glance, the sole methods (sometime indeed absurdly simple ones) by which he may seduce into error or hurry into miscalculation.

Whist has long been noted for its influence upon what is

termed the calculating power; and men of the highest order of intellect have been known to take an apparently unaccountable delight in it, while eschewing chess as frivolous. Beyond doubt there is nothing of a similar nature so greatly tasking the faculty of analysis. The best chess-player in Christendom *may* be little more than the best player of chess; but proficiency in whist implies capacity for success in all those more important undertakings where mind struggles with mind. When I say proficiency, I mean that perfection in the game which includes a comprehension of *all* the sources whence legitimate advantage may be derived. These are not only manifold but multiform, and lie frequently among recesses of thought altogether inaccessible to the ordinary understanding. To observe attentively is to remember distinctly; and, so far, the concentrative chess-player will do very well at whist; while the rules of Hoyle (themselves based upon the mere mechanism of the game) are sufficiently and generally comprehensible. Thus to have a retentive memory, and to proceed by "the book," are points commonly regarded as the sum total of good playing. But it is in matters beyond the limits of mere rule that the skill of the analyst is evinced. He makes, in silence, a host of observations and inferences. So, perhaps, do his companions; and the difference in the extent of the information obtained, lies not so much in the validity of the inference as in the quality of the observation. The necessary knowledge is that of *what* to observe. Our player confines himself not at all; nor, because the game is the object, does he reject deductions from things external to the game. He examines the countenance of his partner, comparing it carefully with that of each of his opponents. He considers the mode of assorting the cards in each hand; often counting trump by trump, and honor by honor, through the glances bestowed by their holders upon each. He notes every variation of face as the play progresses, gathering a fund of thought from the differences in the expression of certainty, of surprise, of triumph, or of chagrin. From the manner of gathering up a trick he judges whether the person taking it can make another in the suit. He recognises what is played through feint, by the air with which it is thrown upon the table. A casual or inadvertent word; the accidental dropping or turning of a card, with the accompanying anxiety or carelessness in regard to its concealment; the counting of the tricks, with the order of their arrangement; embarrassment, hesitation, eagerness or trepidation—all afford, to his apparently intuitive perception, indications of the true state of affairs. The first two or three rounds having been played, he is in full possession of the contents of each hand, and thenceforward puts down his cards with as absolute a precision of purpose as if the rest of the party had turned outward the faces of their own.

The analytical power should not be confounded with ample ingenuity; for while the analyst is necessarily ingenious, the ingenious man is often remarkably incapable of analysis. The constructive or combining power, by which ingenuity is usually manifested, and to which the phrenologists (I believe erroneously) have assigned a separate organ, supposing it a primitive faculty, has been so frequently seen in those whose intellect bordered otherwise upon idiocy, as to have attracted general observation among writers on morals. Between ingenuity and the analytic ability there exists a difference far greater, indeed, than that between the fancy and the imagination, but of a character very strictly analogous. It will be found, in fact, that the ingenious are always fanciful, and the *truly* imaginative never otherwise than analytic.

The narrative which follows will appear to the reader somewhat in the light of a commentary upon the propositions just advanced.

Residing in Paris during the spring and part of the summer of 18—, I there became acquainted with a Monsieur C. Auguste Dupin. This young gentleman was of an excellent—indeed of an illustrious family, but, by a variety of untoward events, had been reduced to such poverty that the energy of his character succumbed beneath it, and he ceased to bestir himself in the world, or to care for the retrieval of his fortunes. By courtesy of his creditors, there still remained in his possession a small remnant of his patrimony; and, upon the income arising from this, he managed, by means of a rigorous economy, to procure the necessaries of life, without troubling himself about its superfluities. Books, indeed, were his sole luxuries, and in Paris these are easily obtained.

Our first meeting was at an obscure library in the Rue Montmartre, where the accident of our both being in search of the same very rare and very remarkable volume, brought us into closer communion. We saw each other again and again. I was deeply interested in the little family history which he detailed to me with all that candor which a Frenchman indulges whenever mere self is his theme. I was astonished, too, at the vast extent of his reading; and, above all, I felt my soul enkindled within me by the wild fervor, and the vivid freshness of his imagination. Seeking in Paris the objects I then sought, I felt that the society of such a man would be to me a treasure beyond price; and this feeling I frankly confided to him. It was at length arranged that we should live together during my stay in the city; and as my worldly circumstances were somewhat less embarrassed than his own, I was permitted to be at the expense of renting, and furnishing in a style which suited the rather fantastic gloom of our common temper, a time-eaten and grotesque mansion, long deserted through superstitions into which we did not inquire, and tottering to its fall in a retired and desolate portion of the Faubourg St. Germain.

Had the routine of our life at this place been known to the world, we should have been regarded as madmen—although, perhaps, as madmen of a harmless nature. Our seclusion was perfect. We admitted no visitors. Indeed the locality of our retirement had been carefully kept a secret from my own former associates; and it had been many years since Dupin had ceased to know or be known in Paris. We existed within ourselves alone.

It was a freak of fancy in my friend (for what else shall I call it?) to be enamored of the Night for her own sake; and into this *bizarrerie*, as into all his others, I quietly fell; giving myself up to his wild whims with a perfect *abandon*. The sable divinity would not herself dwell with us always; but we could counterfeit her presence. At the first dawn of the morning we closed all the messy shutters of our old building; lighting a couple of tapers which, strongly perfumed, threw out only the ghastliest and feeblest of rays. By the aid of these we then busied our souls in dreams—reading, writing, or conversing, until warned by the clock of the advent of the true Darkness. Then we sallied forth into the streets arm in arm, continuing the topics of the day, or roaming far and wide until a late hour, seeking, amid the wild lights and shadows of the populous city, that infinity of mental excitement which quiet observation can afford.

At such times I could not help remarking and admiring (although from his rich ideality I had been prepared to expect it) a peculiar analytic ability in Dupin. He seemed, too, to take an eager delight in its exercise—if not exactly in its display—and did not hesitate to confess the pleasure thus derived. He boasted to me, with a low chuckling laugh, that most men, in respect to himself, wore windows in their bosoms, and was wont to follow up such assertions by direct and very startling proofs of his intimate knowledge of my own. His manner at these moments was frigid and abstract; his eyes were vacant in expression; while his voice, usually a rich tenor, rose into a treble which would have sounded petulantly but for the deliberateness and entire distinctness of the enunciation. Observing him in these moods, I often dwelt meditatively upon the old philosophy of the Bi-Part Soul, and amused myself with the fancy of a double Dupin—the creative and the resolvent.

Let it not be supposed, from what I have just said, that I am detailing any mystery, or penning any romance. What I have described in the Frenchman, was merely the result of an excited, or perhaps of a diseased intelligence. But of the character of his remarks at the periods in question an example will best convey the idea.

We were strolling one night down a long dirty street in the vicinity of the Palais Royal. Being both, apparently, occupied with thought, neither of us had spoken a syllable for fifteen minutes at least. All at once Dupin broke forth with these words:

"He is a very little fellow, that's true, and would do better for the *Théâtre des Variétés.*"

"There can be no doubt of that," I replied unwittingly, and not at first observing (so much had I been absorbed in reflection) the extraordinary manner in which the speaker had chimed in with my meditations. In an instant afterward I recollected myself, and my astonishment was profound.

"Dupin," said I, gravely, "this is beyond my comprehension. I do not hesitate to say that I am amazed, and can scarcely credit my senses. How was it possible you should know I was thinking of —-?" Here I paused, to ascertain beyond a doubt whether he really knew of whom I thought.

—"of Chantilly," said he, "why do you pause? You were remarking to yourself that his diminutive figure unfitted him for tragedy."

This was precisely what had formed the subject of my reflections. Chantilly was a *quondam* cobbler of the Rue St. Denis, who, becoming stage-mad, had attempted the *rôle* of Xerxes, in Crébillon's tragedy so called, and been notoriously Pasquinaded for his pains.

"Tell me, for Heaven's sake," I exclaimed, "the method—if method there is—by which you have been enabled to fathom my soul in this matter." In fact I was even more startled than I would have been willing to express.

"It was the fruiterer," replied my friend, "who brought you to the conclusion that the mender of soles was not of sufficient height for Xerxes *et id genus omne.*"

"The fruiterer!—you astonish me—I know no fruiterer whomsoever."

"The man who ran up against you as we entered the street—it may have been fifteen minutes ago."

I now remembered that, in fact, a fruiterer, carrying upon his head a large basket of apples, had nearly thrown me down, by accident, as we passed from the Rue C — into the thoroughfare where we stood; but what this had to do with Chantilly I could not possibly understand.

There was not a particle of *charlatanerie* about Dupin. "I will explain," he said, "and that you may comprehend all clearly, we will first retrace the course of your meditations, from the moment in which I spoke to you until that of the *rencontre* with the fruiterer in question. The larger links of the chain run thus—Chantilly, Orion, Dr. Nichols, Epicurus, Stereotomy, the street stones, the fruiterer."

There are few persons who have not, at some period of their lives, amused themselves in retracing the steps by which particular conclusions of their own minds have been attained. The occupation is often full of interest and he who attempts it for the first time is astonished by the apparently illimitable distance and incoherence between the starting-point and the goal. What, then, must have been my amazement when I heard the Frenchman speak what he had just spoken, and when I could not help acknowledging that he had spoken the truth. He continued:

"We had been talking of horses, if I remember aright, just before leaving the Rue C —. This was the last subject we discussed. As we crossed into this street, a fruiterer, with a large basket upon his head, brushing quickly past us, thrust you upon a pile of paving stones collected at a spot where the causeway is undergoing repair. You stepped upon one of the loose fragments, slipped, slightly strained your ankle, appeared vexed or sulky, muttered a few words, turned to look at the pile, and then proceeded in silence. I was not particularly attentive to what you did; but observation has become with me, of late, a species of necessity.

"You kept your eyes upon the ground—glancing, with a petulant expression, at the holes and ruts in the pavement, (so that I saw you were still thinking of the stones,) until we reached the little alley called Lamartine, which has been paved, by way of experiment, with the overlapping and riveted blocks. Here your countenance brightened up, and, perceiving your lips move, I could not doubt that you murmured the word 'stereotomy,' a term very affectedly applied to this species of pavement. I knew that you could not say to yourself 'stereotomy' without being brought to think of atomies, and thus of the theories of Epicurus; and since, when we discussed this subject not very long ago, I mentioned to you how singularly, yet with how little notice, the vague guesses of that noble Greek had met with confirmation in the late nebular cosmogony, I felt that you could not avoid casting your eyes upward to the great *nebula* in Orion, and I certainly expected that you would do so. You did look up; and I was now assured that I had correctly followed your steps. But in that bitter *tirade* upon Chantilly, which appeared in yesterday's '*Musée*,' the satirist, making some disgraceful allusions to the cobbler's change of name upon assuming the buskin, quoted a Latin line about which we have often conversed. I mean the line

Perdidit antiquum litera sonum.

"I had told you that this was in reference to Orion, formerly written Urion; and, from certain pungencies connected with this explanation, I was aware that you could not have forgotten it. It was clear, therefore, that you would not fail to combine the two ideas of Orion and Chantilly. That you did combine them I saw by the character of the smile which passed over your lips. You thought of the poor cobbler's immolation. So far, you had been stooping in your gait; but now I saw you draw yourself up to your full height. I was then sure that you reflected upon the diminutive figure of Chantilly. At this point I interrupted your meditations to remark that as, in fact, he was a very little fellow—that Chantilly—he would do better at the *Théâtre des Variétés*."

Not long after this, we were looking over an evening edition of the "Gazette des Tribunaux," when the following paragraphs arrested our attention.

"EXTRAORDINARY MURDERS — This morning, about three o'clock, the inhabitants of the Quartier St. Roch were aroused from sleep by a succession of terrific shrieks, issuing, apparently, from the fourth story of a house in

the Rue Morgue, known to be in the sole occupancy of one Madame L'Espanaye, and her daughter Mademoiselle Camille L'Espanaye. After some delay, occasioned by a fruitless attempt to procure admission in the usual manner, the gateway was broken in with a crowbar, and eight or ten of the neighbors entered accompanied by two gendarmes. By this time the cries had ceased; but, as the party rushed up the first flight of stairs, two or more rough voices in angry contention were distinguished and seemed to proceed from the upper part of the house. As the second landing was reached, these sounds, also, had ceased and everything remained perfectly quiet. The party spread themselves and hurried from room to room. Upon arriving at a large back chamber in the fourth story, (the door of which, being found locked, with the key inside, was forced open,) a spectacle presented itself which struck every one present not less with horror than with astonishment.

"The apartment was in the wildest disorder—the furniture broken and thrown about in all directions. There was only one bedstead; and from this the bed had been removed, and thrown into the middle of the floor. On a chair lay a razor, besmeared with blood. On the hearth were two or three long and thick tresses of grey human hair, also dabbled in blood, and seeming to have been pulled out by the roots. Upon the floor were found four Napoleons, an ear-ring of topaz, three large silver spoons, three smaller of métal d'Alger, and two bags, containing nearly four thousand francs in gold. The drawers of a bureau, which stood in one corner were open, and had been, apparently, rifled, although many articles still remained in them. A small iron safe was discovered under the bed (not under the bedstead). It was open, with the key still in the door. It had no contents beyond a few old letters, and other papers of little consequence.

"Of Madame L'Espanaye no traces were here seen; but an

unusual quantity of soot being observed in the fire-place, a search was made in the chimney, and (horrible to relate!) the corpse of the daughter, head downward, was dragged therefrom; it having been thus forced up the narrow aperture for a considerable distance. The body was quite warm. Upon examining it, many excoriations were perceived, no doubt occasioned by the violence with which it had been thrust up and disengaged. Upon the face were many severe scratches, and, upon the throat, dark bruises, and deep indentations of finger nails, as if the deceased had been throttled to death.

"After a thorough investigation of every portion of the house, without farther discovery, the party made its way into a small paved yard in the rear of the building, where lay the corpse of the old lady, with her throat so entirely cut that, upon an attempt to raise her, the head fell off. The body, as well as the head, was fearfully mutilated—the former so much so as scarcely to retain any semblance of humanity.

"To this horrible mystery there is not as yet, we believe, the slightest clue."

The next day's paper had these additional particulars.

"The Tragedy in the Rue Morgue. *Many individuals have been examined in relation to this most extraordinary and frightful affair.* [The word 'affaire' has not yet, in France, that levity of import which it conveys with us,] *"but nothing whatever has transpired to throw light upon it. We give below all the material testimony elicited.*

"Pauline Dubourg, *laundress, deposes that she has known both the deceased for three years, having washed for them during that period. The old lady and her daughter seemed on good terms—very affectionate towards each other. They were excellent pay. Could not speak in regard to their mode or means of living. Believed that Madame L. told fortunes for a living. Was reputed to have money put by. Never met any persons in the house when she called for the clothes or took them home. Was sure that they had no servant in employ. There appeared to be no furniture in any part of the building except in the fourth story.*

"Pierre Moreau, *tobacconist, deposes that he has been in the habit of selling small quantities of tobacco and snuff to Madame L'Espanaye for nearly four years. Was born in the neighborhood, and has always resided there. The deceased and her daughter had occupied the house in which the corpses were found, for more than six years. It was formerly occupied by a jeweller, who under-let the upper rooms to various persons. The house was the property of Madame L. She became dissatisfied with the abuse of the premises by her tenant, and moved into them herself, refusing to let any portion. The old lady was childish. Witness had seen the daughter some five or six times during the six years. The two lived an exceedingly retired life—were reputed to have money. Had heard it said among the neighbors that Madame L. told fortunes—did not believe it. Had never seen any person enter the door except the old lady and her daughter, a porter once or twice, and a physician some eight or ten times.*

"Many other persons, neighbors, gave evidence to the same effect. No one was spoken of as frequenting the house. It was not known whether there were any living connexions of Madame L. and her daughter. The shutters of the front windows were seldom opened. Those in the rear were always closed, with the exception of the large back room, fourth story. The house was a good house—not very old.

"Isidore Muset, *gendarme, deposes that he was called to the house about three o'clock in the morning, and found some twenty or thirty persons at the gateway, endeavoring to gain admittance. Forced it open, at length, with a bayonet—not with a crowbar. Had but little difficulty in getting it open, on account of its being a double or folding gate, and bolted neither at bottom not top. The shrieks were continued until the gate was forced—and then suddenly ceased. They seemed to be screams of some person (or persons) in great agony—were loud and drawn out, not short and quick. Witness led the way up stairs. Upon reaching the first landing, heard two voices in loud and angry contention—the one a gruff voice, the other much shriller—a very strange voice. Could distinguish some words of the former, which was that of a Frenchman. Was positive that it was not a woman's voice. Could distinguish the words 'sacré' and 'diable.' The shrill voice was that of a foreigner. Could not be sure whether it was the voice of a man or of a woman. Could not make out what was said, but believed the language to be Spanish. The state of the room and of the bodies was described by this witness as we described them yesterday.*

"Henri Duval, *a neighbor, and by trade a silver-smith, deposes that he was one of the party who first entered the house. Corroborates the testimony of Muset in general. As soon as they forced an entrance, they reclosed the door, to keep out the crowd, which collected very fast, notwithstanding the lateness of the hour. The shrill voice, this witness thinks, was that of an Italian. Was certain it was not French. Could not be sure that it was a man's voice. It might have been a woman's. Was not acquainted with the Italian language. Could not distinguish the words, but was convinced by the intonation that the speaker was an Italian. Knew Madame L. and her daughter. Had conversed with both frequently. Was sure that the shrill voice was not that of either of the deceased.*

"—Odenheimer, restaurateur. *This witness volunteered his testimony. Not speaking French, was examined through an interpreter. Is a native of Amsterdam. Was passing the house at the time of the shrieks. They lasted for several minutes—probably ten. They were long and loud—very awful and distressing. Was one of those who entered the building. Corroborated the previous evidence in every respect but one. Was sure that the shrill voice was that of a man—of a Frenchman. Could not distinguish the words uttered. They were loud and quick—unequal—spoken apparently in fear as well as in anger. The voice was harsh—not so much shrill as harsh. Could not call it a shrill voice. The gruff voice said repeatedly 'sacré,' 'diable,' and once 'mon Dieu.'*

"Jules Mignaud, *banker, of the firm of Mignaud et Fils, Rue Deloraine. Is the elder Mignaud. Madame L'Espanaye had some property. Had opened an account with his banking house in the spring of the year—(eight years previously). Made frequent deposits in small sums. Had checked for nothing until the third day before her death, when she took out in person the sum of 4000 francs. This sum was paid in gold, and a clerk went home with the money.*

"Adolphe Le Bon, *clerk to Mignaud et Fils, deposes that on the day in question, about noon, he accompanied Madame L'Espanaye to her residence with the 4000 francs, put up in two bags. Upon the door being opened, Mademoiselle L. appeared and took from his hands one of the bags, while the old lady relieved him of the other. He then bowed and departed. Did not see any person in the street at the time. It is a bye-street—very lonely.*

"William Bird, *tailor deposes that he was one of the party who entered the house. Is an Englishman. Has lived in Paris two years. Was one of the first to ascend the stairs. Heard the voices in contention. The gruff voice was that of a Frenchman. Could make out several words, but cannot now remember all. Heard distinctly 'sacré' and 'mon Dieu.' There was a sound at the moment as if of several persons struggling—a scraping and scuffling sound. The shrill voice was very loud—louder than the gruff one. Is sure that it was not the voice of an Englishman. Appeared to be that of a German. Might have been a woman's voice. Does not understand German.*

"Four of the above-named witnesses, being recalled, deposed that the door of the chamber in which was found the body of Mademoiselle L. was locked on the inside when the party reached it. Every thing was perfectly silent—no groans or noises of any kind. Upon forcing the door no person was seen. The windows, both of the back and front room, were down and firmly fastened from within. A door between the two rooms was closed, but not locked. The door leading from the front room into the passage was locked, with the key on the inside. A small room in the front of the house, on the fourth story, at the head of the passage was open, the door being ajar. This room was crowded with old beds, boxes, and so forth. These were carefully removed and searched. There was not an inch of any portion of the house which was not carefully searched. Sweeps were sent up and down the chimneys. The house was a four story one, with garrets (mansardes.) A trap-door on the roof was nailed down very securely—did not appear to have been opened for years. The time elapsing between the hearing of the voices in contention and the breaking open of the room door, was variously stated by the witnesses. Some made it as short as three minutes—some as long as five. The door was opened with difficulty.

"Alfonzo Garcio, *undertaker, deposes that he resides in the Rue Morgue. Is a native of Spain. Was one of the party who entered the house. Did not proceed up stairs. Is nervous, and was apprehensive of the consequences of agitation. Heard the voices in contention. The gruff voice was that of a Frenchman. Could not distinguish what was said. The shrill voice was that of an Englishman—is sure of this. Does not understand the English language, but judges by the intonation.*

"Alberto Montani, *confectioner, deposes that he was among the first to ascend the stairs. Heard the voices in question. The gruff voice was that of a Frenchman. Distinguished several words. The speaker appeared to be expostulating. Could not make out the words of the shrill voice. Spoke quick and unevenly. Thinks it the voice of a Russian. Corroborates the general testimony. Is an Italian. Never conversed with a native of Russia.*

"Several witnesses, recalled, here testified that the chimneys of all the rooms on the fourth story were too narrow to admit the passage of a human being. By 'sweeps' were meant cylindrical sweeping brushes, such as are employed by those who clean chimneys. These brushes were passed up and down every flue in the house. There is no back passage by which any one could have descended while the party proceeded up stairs. The body of Mademoiselle L'Espanaye was so firmly wedged in the chimney that it could not be got down until four or five of the party united their strength.

"Paul Dumas, *physician, deposes that he was called to view the bodies about day-break. They were both then lying on the sacking of the bedstead in the chamber where Mademoiselle L. was found. The corpse of the young lady was much bruised and excoriated. The fact that it had been thrust up the chimney would sufficiently account for these appearances. The throat was greatly chafed. There were several deep scratches just below the chin, together with a series of livid spots which were evidently the impression of fingers. The face was fearfully discolored, and the eye-balls protruded. The tongue had been partially bitten through. A large bruise was discovered upon the pit of the stomach, produced, apparently, by the pressure of a knee. In the opinion of M. Dumas, Mademoiselle L'Espanaye had been throttled to death by some person or persons unknown. The corpse of the mother was horribly mutilated. All the bones of the right leg and arm were more or less shattered. The left tibia much splintered, as well as all the ribs of the left side. Whole body dreadfully bruised and discolored. It was not possible to say how the injuries had been inflicted. A heavy club of wood, or a broad bar of iron—a chair—any large, heavy, and obtuse weapon would have produced such results, if wielded by the hands of a very powerful man. No woman could have inflicted the blows with any weapon. The head of the deceased, when seen by witness, was entirely separated from the body, and was also greatly shattered. The throat had evidently been cut with some very sharp instrument—probably with a razor.*

"Alexandre Etienne, *surgeon, was called with M. Dumas to view the bodies. Corroborated the testimony, and the opinions of M. Dumas.*

"Nothing farther of importance was elicited, although several other persons were examined. A murder so mysterious, and so perplexing in all its particulars, was never before committed in Paris—if indeed a murder has been committed at all. The police are entirely at fault—an unusual occurrence in affairs of this nature. There is not, however, the shadow of a clue apparent."

The evening edition of the paper stated that the greatest excitement still continued in the Quartier St. Roch—that the premises in question had been carefully re-searched, and fresh examinations of witnesses instituted, but all to no purpose. A postscript, however, mentioned that Adolphe Le Bon had been arrested and imprisoned—although nothing appeared to criminate him, beyond the facts already detailed.

Dupin seemed singularly interested in the progress of this affair—at least so I judged from his manner, for he made no comments. It was only after the announcement that Le Bon had been imprisoned, that he asked me my opinion respecting the murders.

I could merely agree with all Paris in considering them an insoluble mystery. I saw no means by which it would be possible to trace the murderer.

"We must not judge of the means," said Dupin, "by this shell of an examination. The Parisian police, so much extolled for *acumen*, are cunning, but no more. There is no method in their proceedings, beyond the method of the moment. They make a vast parade of measures; but, not unfrequently, these are so ill adapted to the objects proposed, as to put us in mind of Monsieur Jourdain's calling for his *robe-de-chambre—pour mieux entendre la musique.* The results attained by them are not unfrequently surprising, but, for the most part, are brought about by simple diligence and activity. When these qualities are unavailing, their schemes fail. Vidocq, for example, was a good guesser and a persevering man. But, without educated thought, he erred continually by the very intensity of his investigations. He impaired his vision by holding the object too close. He might see, perhaps, one or two points with unusual clearness, but in so doing he, necessarily, lost sight of the matter as a whole. Thus there is such a thing as being too profound. Truth is not always in a well. In fact, as regards the more important knowledge, I do believe that she is invariably superficial. The depth lies in the valleys where we seek her, and not upon the mountain-tops where she is found. The modes and sources of this kind of error are well typified in the contemplation of the heavenly bodies. To look at a star by glances—to view it in a side-long way, by turning toward it the exterior portions of the *retina* (more susceptible of feeble impressions of light than the interior), is to behold the star distinctly—is to have the best appreciation of its lustre—a lustre which grows dim just in proportion as we turn our vision *fully* upon it. A greater number of rays actually fall upon the eye in the latter case, but, in the former, there is the more refined capacity for comprehension. By undue profundity we perplex and enfeeble thought; and it is possible to make even Venus herself vanish from the firmament by a scrutiny too sustained, too concentrated, or too direct.

"As for these murders, let us enter into some examinations for ourselves, before we make up an opinion respecting them. An inquiry will afford us amusement," [I thought this an odd term, so applied, but said nothing] "and, besides, Le Bon once rendered me a service for which I am not ungrateful. We will go and see the premises with our own eyes. I know G—, the Prefect of Police, and shall have no difficulty in obtaining the necessary permission."

The permission was obtained, and we proceeded at once to the Rue Morgue. This is one of those miserable thoroughfares which intervene between the Rue Richelieu and the Rue St. Roch. It was late in the afternoon when we reached it; as this quarter is at a great distance from that in which we resided. The house was readily found; for there were still many persons gazing up at the closed shutters, with an objectless curiosity, from the opposite side of the way. It was an ordinary Parisian house, with a gateway, on one side of which was a glazed watch-box, with a sliding panel in the window, indicating a *loge de concierge.* Before going in we walked up the street, turned down an alley, and then, again turning, passed in the rear of the building—Dupin, meanwhile examining the whole neighborhood, as well as the house, with a minuteness of attention for which I could see no possible object.

Retracing our steps, we came again to the front of the dwelling, rang, and, having shown our credentials, were admitted by the agents in charge. We went up stairs—into the chamber where the body of Mademoiselle L'Espanaye had been found, and where both the deceased still lay. The disorders of the room had, as usual, been suffered to exist. I saw nothing beyond what had been stated in the "Gazette des Tribunaux." Dupin scrutinized every thing—not excepting the bodies of the victims. We then went into the other rooms, and into the yard; a *gendarme* accompanying us throughout. The examination occupied us until dark, when we took our departure. On our way home my companion stepped in for a moment at the office of one of the daily papers.

I have said that the whims of my friend were manifold, and that *Je les ménageais*:—for this phrase there is no English equivalent. It was his humor, now, to decline all conversation on the subject of the murder, until about noon the next day. He then asked me, suddenly, if I had observed any thing *peculiar* at the scene of the atrocity.

There was something in his manner of emphasizing the word "peculiar," which caused me to shudder, without knowing why.

"No, nothing *peculiar*," I said; "nothing more, at least, than we both saw stated in the paper."

"The 'Gazette,'" he replied, "has not entered, I fear, into the unusual horror of the thing. But dismiss the idle opinions of this print. It appears to me that this mystery is considered insoluble, for the very reason which should cause it to be regarded as easy of solution—I mean for the *outré* character of its features. The police are confounded by the seeming absence of motive—not for the murder itself—but for the atrocity of the murder. They are puzzled, too, by the seeming impossibility of reconciling the voices heard in contention, with the facts that no one was discovered up stairs but the assassinated Mademoiselle L'Espanaye, and that there were no means of egress without the notice of the party ascending. The wild disorder of the room; the corpse thrust, with the head downward, up the chimney; the frightful mutilation of the body of the old lady; these considerations, with those just mentioned, and others which I need not mention, have sufficed to paralyze the powers, by putting completely at fault the boasted *acumen*, of the government agents. They have fallen into the gross but common error of confounding the unusual with the abstruse. But it is by these deviations from the plane of the ordinary, that reason feels its way, if at all, in its search for the true. In investigations such as we are now pursuing, it should not be so much asked 'what has occurred,' as 'what has occurred that has never occurred before.' In fact, the facility with which I shall arrive, or have arrived, at the solution of this mystery, is in the direct ratio of its apparent insolubility in the eyes of the police."

I stared at the speaker in mute astonishment.

"I am now awaiting," continued he, looking toward the

door of our apartment—"I am now awaiting a person who, although perhaps not the perpetrator of these butcheries, must have been in some measure implicated in their perpetration. Of the worst portion of the crimes committed, it is probable that he is innocent. I hope that I am right in this supposition; for upon it I build my expectation of reading the entire riddle. I look for the man here—in this room—every moment. It is true that he may not arrive; but the probability is that he will. Should he come, it will be necessary to detain him. Here are pistols; and we both know how to use them when occasion demands their use."

I took the pistols, scarcely knowing what I did, or believing what I heard, while Dupin went on, very much as if in a soliloquy. I have already spoken of his abstract manner at such times. His discourse was addressed to myself; but his voice, although by no means loud, had that intonation which is commonly employed in speaking to some one at a great distance. His eyes, vacant in expression, regarded only the wall.

"That the voices heard in contention," he said, "by the party upon the stairs, were not the voices of the women themselves, was fully proved by the evidence. This relieves us of all doubt upon the question whether the old lady could have first destroyed the daughter and afterward have committed suicide. I speak of this point chiefly for the sake of method; for the strength of Madame L'Espanaye would have been utterly unequal to the task of thrusting her daughter's corpse up the chimney as it was found; and the nature of the wounds upon her own person entirely preclude the idea of self-destruction. Murder, then, has been committed by some third party; and the voices of this third party were those heard in contention. Let me now advert—not to the whole testimony respecting these voices—but to what was *peculiar* in that testimony. Did you observe any thing peculiar about it?"

I remarked that, while all the witnesses agreed in supposing the gruff voice to be that of a Frenchman, there was much disagreement in regard to the shrill, or, as one individual termed it, the harsh voice.

"That was the evidence itself," said Dupin, "but it was not the peculiarity of the evidence. You have observed nothing distinctive. Yet there *was* something to be observed. The witnesses, as you remark, agreed about the gruff voice; they were here unanimous. But in regard to the shrill voice, the peculiarity is—not that they disagreed—but that, while an Italian, an Englishman, a Spaniard, a Hollander, and a Frenchman attempted to describe it, each one spoke of it as that *of a foreigner*. Each is sure that it was not the voice of one of his own countrymen. Each likens it—not to the voice of an individual of any nation with whose language he is conversant—but the converse. The Frenchman supposes it the voice of a Spaniard, and 'might have distinguished some words *had he been acquainted with the Spanish.*' The Dutchman maintains it to have been that of a Frenchman; but we find it stated that '*not understanding French this witness was examined through an interpreter.*' The Englishman thinks it the voice of a German, and '*does not understand German.*' The Spaniard 'is sure' that it was that of an Englishman, but 'judges by the intonation' altogether, '*as he has no knowledge of the English.*' The Italian believes it the voice of a Russian, but '*has never conversed with a native of Russia.*' A second Frenchman differs, moreover, with the first, and is positive that the voice was that of an Italian; but, *not being cognizant of that tongue*, is, like the Spaniard, 'convinced by the intonation.' Now, how strangely unusual must that voice have really been, about which such testimony as this *could* have been elicited!—in whose *tones*, even, denizens of the five great divisions of Europe could recognise nothing familiar! You will say that it might have been the voice of an Asiatic—of an African. Neither Asiatics nor Africans abound in Paris; but, without denying the inference, I will now merely call your attention to three points. The voice is termed by one witness 'harsh rather than shrill.' It is represented by two others to have been 'quick and *unequal.*' No words—no sounds resembling words—were by any witness mentioned as distinguishable.

"I know not," continued Dupin, "what impression I may have made, so far, upon your own understanding; but I do not hesitate to say that legitimate deductions even from this portion of the testimony—the portion respecting the gruff and shrill voices—are in themselves sufficient to engender a suspicion which should give direction to all farther progress in the investigation of the mystery. I said 'legitimate deductions;' but my meaning is not thus fully expressed. I designed to imply that the deductions are the *sole* proper ones, and that the suspicion arises *inevitably* from them as the single result. What the suspicion is, however, I will not say just yet. I merely wish you to bear in mind that, with myself, it was sufficiently forcible to give a definite form—a certain tendency—to my inquiries in the chamber.

"Let us now transport ourselves, in fancy, to this chamber. What shall we first seek here? The means of egress employed by the murderers. It is not too much to say that neither of us believe in præternatural events. Madame and Mademoiselle L'Espanaye were not destroyed by spirits. The doers of the deed were material, and escaped materially. Then how? Fortunately, there is but one mode of reasoning upon the point, and that mode *must* lead us to a definite decision.—Let us examine, each by each, the possible means of egress. It is clear that the assassins were in the room where Mademoiselle L'Espanaye was found, or at least in the room adjoining, when the party ascended the stairs. It is then only from these two apartments that we have to seek issues. The police have laid bare the floors, the ceilings, and the masonry of the walls, in every direction. No *secret* issues could have escaped their vigilance. But, not trusting to *their* eyes, I examined with my own. There were, then, no secret issues. Both doors leading from the rooms into the passage were securely locked, with the keys inside. Let us turn to the chimneys. These, although of ordinary width for some eight or ten feet above the hearths, will not admit, throughout their extent, the body of a large cat. The impossibility of egress, by means already stated, being thus absolute, we are reduced to the windows. Through those of the front room no one could have escaped without notice from the crowd in the street. The murderers *must* have passed, then, through those of the back room. Now, brought to this conclusion in so unequivocal a manner as we are, it is not our part, as reasoners, to reject it on account of apparent impossibilities. It is only left for us to prove that these apparent 'impossibilities' are, in reality, not such.

"There are two windows in the chamber. One of them is unobstructed by furniture, and is wholly visible. The lower portion of the other is hidden from view by the head of the unwieldy bedstead which is thrust close up against it. The former was found securely fastened from within. It resisted the utmost force of those who endeavored to raise it. A large gimlet-hole had been pierced in its frame to the left, and a very stout nail was found fitted therein, nearly to the head. Upon examining the other window, a similar nail was seen similarly fitted in it; and a vigorous attempt to raise this sash, failed also. The police were now entirely satisfied that egress had not been in these directions. And, *therefore*, it was thought a matter of supererogation to withdraw the nails and open the windows.

"My own examination was somewhat more particular, and was so for the reason I have just given—because here it was, I knew, that all apparent impossibilities *must* be proved to be not such in reality.

"I proceeded to think thus—*a posteriori*. The murderers did escape from one of these windows. This being so, they could not have refastened the sashes from the inside, as they were found fastened;—the consideration which put a stop, through its obviousness, to the scrutiny of the police in this quarter. Yet the sashes *were* fastened. They *must*, then, have the power of fastening themselves. There was no escape from this conclusion. I stepped to the unobstructed casement, withdrew the nail with some difficulty and attempted to raise the sash. It resisted all my efforts, as I had anticipated. A concealed spring must, I now know, exist; and this corroboration of my idea convinced me that my premises at least, were correct, however mysterious still appeared the circumstances attending the nails. A careful search soon brought to light the hidden spring. I pressed it, and, satisfied with the discovery, forbore to upraise the sash.

"I now replaced the nail and regarded it attentively. A person passing out through this window might have reclosed it, and the spring would have caught—but the nail could not have been replaced. The conclusion was plain, and again narrowed in the field of my investigations. The assassins *must* have escaped through the other window. Supposing, then, the springs upon each sash to be the same, as was probable, there *must* be found a difference between the nails, or at least between the modes of their fixture. Getting upon the sacking of the bedstead, I looked over the head-board minutely at the second casement. Passing my hand down behind the board, I readily discovered and pressed the spring, which was, as I had supposed, identical in character with its neighbor. I now looked at the nail. It was as stout as the other, and apparently fitted in the same manner—driven in nearly up to the head.

"You will say that I was puzzled; but, if you think so, you must have misunderstood the nature of the inductions. To use a sporting phrase, I had not been once 'at fault.' The scent had never for an instant been lost. There was no flaw in any link of the chain. I had traced the secret to its ultimate result, and that result was *the nail.* It had, I say, in every respect, the appearance of its fellow in the other window; but this fact was an absolute nullity (conclusive us it might seem to be) when compared with the consideration that here, at this point, terminated the clue. 'There *must* be something wrong,' I said, 'about the nail.' I touched it; and the head, with about a quarter of an inch of the shank, came off in my fingers. The rest of the shank was in the gimlet-hole where it had been broken off. The fracture was an old one (for its edges were incrusted with rust), and had apparently been accomplished by the blow of a hammer, which had partially imbedded, in the top of the bottom sash, the head portion of the nail. I now carefully replaced this head portion in the indentation whence I had taken it, and the resemblance to a perfect nail was complete—the fissure was invisible. Pressing the spring, I gently raised the sash for a few inches; the head went up with it, remaining firm in its bed. I closed the window, and the semblance of the whole nail was again perfect.

"The riddle, so far, was now unriddled. The assassin had escaped through the window which looked upon the bed. Dropping of its own accord upon his exit (or perhaps purposely closed), it had become fastened by the spring; and it was the retention of this spring which had been mistaken by the police for that of the nail, farther inquiry being thus considered unnecessary.

"The next question is that of the mode of descent. Upon this point I had been satisfied in my walk with you around the building. About five feet and a half from the casement in question there runs a lightning-rod. From this rod it would have been impossible for any one to reach the window itself, to say nothing of entering it. I observed, however, that the shutters of the fourth story were of the peculiar kind called by Parisian carpenters *ferrades*—a kind rarely employed at the present day, but frequently seen upon very old mansions at Lyons and Bordeaux. They are in the form of an ordinary door, (a single, not a folding door) except that the lower half is latticed or worked in open trellis—thus affording an excellent hold for the hands. In the present instance these shutters are fully three feet and a half broad. When we saw them from the rear of the house, they were both about half open—that is to say, they stood off at right angles from the wall. It is probable that the police, as well as myself, examined the back of the tenement; but, if so, in looking at these *ferrades* in the line of their breadth (as they must have done), they did not perceive this great breadth itself, or, at all events, failed to take it into due consideration. In fact, having once satisfied themselves that no egress could have been made in this quarter, they would naturally bestow here a very cursory examination. It was clear to me, however, that the shutter belonging to the window at the head of the bed, would, if swung fully back to the wall, reach to within two feet of the lightning-rod. It was also evident that, by exertion of a very unusual degree of activity and courage, an entrance into the window, from the rod, might have been thus effected.—By reaching to the distance of two feet and a half (we now suppose the shutter open to its whole extent) a robber might have taken a firm grasp upon the trellis-work. Letting go, then, his hold upon the rod, placing his feet securely against the wall, and springing boldly from it, he might have swung the shutter so as to close it, and, if we imagine the window open at the time, might even have swung himself into the room.

"I wish you to bear especially in mind that I have spoken of a *very* unusual degree of activity as requisite to success in so hazardous and so difficult a feat. It is my design to show you, first, that the thing might possibly have been accomplished:—but, secondly and *chiefly,* I wish to impress upon your understanding the *very extraordinary*—the almost præternatural character of that agility which could have accomplished it.

"You will say, no doubt, using the language of the law, that 'to make out my case,' I should rather undervalue, than insist upon a full estimation of the activity required in this matter. This may be the practice in law, but it is not the usage of reason. My ultimate object is only the truth. My immediate purpose is to lead you to place in juxtaposition, that *very unusual* activity of which I have just spoken with that *very peculiar* shrill (or harsh) and *unequal* voice, about whose nationality no two persons could be found to agree, and in whose utterance no syllabification could be detected."

At these words a vague and half-formed conception of the meaning of Dupin flitted over my mind. I seemed to be upon the verge of comprehension without power to comprehend—men, at times, find themselves upon the brink of remembrance without being able, in the end, to remember. My friend went on with his discourse.

"You will see," he said, "that I have shifted the question from the mode of egress to that of ingress. It was my design to convey the idea that both were effected in the same manner, at the same point. Let us now revert to the interior of the room. Let us survey the appearances here. The drawers of the bureau, it is said, had been rifled, although many articles of apparel still remained within them. The conclusion here is absurd. It is a mere guess—a very silly one—and no more. How are we to know that the articles found in the drawers were not all these drawers had originally contained? Madame L'Espanaye and her daughter lived an exceedingly retired life—saw no company—seldom went out—had little use for numerous changes of habiliment. Those found were at least of as good quality as any likely to be possessed by these ladies. If a thief had taken any, why did he not take the best—why did he not take all? In a word, why did he abandon four thousand francs in gold to encumber himself with a bundle of linen? The gold *was* abandoned. Nearly the whole sum mentioned by Monsieur Mignaud, the banker, was discovered, in bags, upon the floor. I wish you, therefore, to discard from your thoughts the blundering idea of *motive*, engendered in the brains of the police by that portion of the evidence which speaks of money delivered at the door of the house. Coincidences ten times as remarkable as this (the delivery of the money, and murder committed within three days upon the party receiving it), happen to all of us every hour of our lives, without attracting even momentary notice. Coincidences, in general, are great stumbling-blocks in the way of that class of thinkers who have been educated to know nothing of the theory of probabilities—that theory to which the most glorious objects of human research are indebted for the most glorious of illustration. In the present instance, had the gold been gone, the fact of its delivery three days before would have formed something more than a coincidence. It would have been corroborative of this idea of motive. But, under the real circumstances of the case, if we are to suppose gold the motive of this outrage, we must also imagine the perpetrator so vacillating an idiot as to have abandoned his gold and his motive together.

"Keeping now steadily in mind the points to which I have drawn your attention—that peculiar voice, that unusual agility, and that startling absence of motive in a murder so singularly atrocious as this—let us glance at the butchery itself. Here is a woman strangled to death by manual strength, and thrust up a chimney, head downward. Ordinary assassins employ no such modes of murder as this. Least of all, do they thus dispose of the murdered. In the manner of thrusting the corpse up the chimney, you will admit that there was something *excessively outré*—something altogether irreconcilable with our common notions of human action, even when we suppose the actors the most depraved of men. Think, too, how great must have been that strength which could have thrust the body *up* such an aperture so forcibly that the united vigor of several persons was found barely sufficient to drag it *down!*

"Turn, now, to other indications of the employment of a vigor most marvellous. On the hearth were thick tresses—very thick tresses—of grey human hair. These had been torn out by the roots. You are aware of the great force necessary in tearing thus from the head even twenty or thirty hairs together. You saw the locks in question as well as myself. Their roots (a hideous sight!) were clotted with fragments of the flesh of the scalp—sure token of the prodigious power which had been exerted in uprooting perhaps half a million of hairs at a time. The throat of the old lady was not merely cut, but the head absolutely severed from the body: the instrument was a mere razor. I wish you also to look at the *brutal* ferocity of these deeds. Of the bruises upon the body of Madame L'Espanaye I do not speak. Monsieur Dumas, and his worthy coadjutor Monsieur Etienne, have pronounced that they were inflicted by some obtuse instrument; and so far these gentlemen are very correct. The obtuse instrument was clearly the stone pavement in the yard, upon which the victim had fallen from the window which looked in upon the bed. This idea, however simple it may now seem, escaped the police for the same reason that the breadth of the shutters escaped them—because, by the affair of the nails, their perceptions had been hermetically sealed against the possibility of the windows having ever been opened at all.

"If now, in addition to all these things, you have properly reflected upon the odd disorder of the chamber, we have gone so far as to combine the ideas of an agility astounding, a strength superhuman, a ferocity brutal, a butchery without motive, a *grotesquerie* in horror absolutely alien from humanity, and a voice foreign in tone to the ears of men of many nations, and devoid of all distinct or intelligible syllabification. What result, then, has ensued? What impression have I made upon your fancy?"

I felt a creeping of the flesh as Dupin asked me the question. "A madman," I said, "has done this deed—some raving maniac, escaped from a neighboring *Maison de Santé*."

"In some respects," he replied, "your idea is not irrelevant. But the voices of madmen, even in their wildest paroxysms, are never found to tally with that peculiar voice heard upon the stairs. Madmen are of some nation, and their language, however incoherent in its words, has always the coherence of syllabification. Besides, the hair of a madman is not such as I now hold in my hand. I disentangled this little tuft from the rigidly clutched fingers of Madame L'Espanaye. Tell me what you can make of it."

"Dupin!" I said, completely unnerved; "this hair is most unusual—this is no *human* hair."

"I have not asserted that it is," said he; "but, before we decide this point, I wish you to glance at the little sketch I have here traced upon this paper. It is a *fac-simile* drawing of what has been described in one portion of the testimony as 'dark bruises, and deep indentations of finger nails,' upon the throat of Mademoiselle L'Espanaye, and in another, (by Messrs. Dumas and Etienne,) as a 'series of livid spots, evidently the impression of fingers.'

"You will perceive," continued my friend, spreading out the paper upon the table before us, "that this drawing gives the idea of a firm and fixed hold. There is no *slipping* apparent. Each finger has retained—possibly until the death of the victim—the fearful grasp by which it originally imbedded itself. Attempt, now, to place all your fingers, at the same time, in the respective impressions as you see them."

I made the attempt in vain.

"We are possibly not giving this matter a fair trial," he said.

"The paper is spread out upon a plane surface; but the human throat is cylindrical. Here is a billet of wood, the circumference of which is about that of the throat. Wrap the drawing around it, and try the experiment again."

I did so; but the difficulty was even more obvious than before. "This," I said, "is the mark of no human hand."

"Read now," replied Dupin, "this passage from Cuvier."

It was a minute anatomical and generally descriptive account of the large fulvous Ourang-Outang of the East Indian Islands. The gigantic stature, the prodigious strength and activity, the wild ferocity, and the imitative propensities of these mammalia are sufficiently well known to all. I understood the full horrors of the murder at once.

"The description of the digits," said I, as I made an end of reading, "is in exact accordance with this drawing. I see that no animal but an Ourang-Outang, of the species here mentioned, could have impressed the indentations as you have traced them. This tuft of tawny hair, too, is identical in character with that of the beast of Cuvier. But I cannot possibly comprehend the particulars of this frightful mystery. Besides, there were *two* voices heard in contention, and one of them was unquestionably the voice of a Frenchman."

"True; and you will remember an expression attributed almost unanimously, by the evidence, to this voice, the expression, '*mon Dieu!* This, under the circumstances, has been justly characterized by one of the witnesses (Montani, the confectioner,) as an expression of remonstrance or expostulation. Upon these two words, therefore, I have mainly built my hopes of a full solution of the riddle. A Frenchman was cognizant of the murder. It is possible—indeed it is far more than probable—that he was innocent of all participation in the bloody transactions which took place. The Ourang-Outang may have escaped from him. He may have traced it to the chamber; but, under the agitating circumstances which ensued, he could never have re-captured it. It is still at large. I will not pursue these guesses—for I have no right to call them more—since the shades of reflection upon which they are based are scarcely of sufficient depth to be appreciable by my own intellect, and since I could not pretend to make them intelligible to the understanding of another. We will call them guesses then, and speak of them as such. If the Frenchman in question is indeed, as I suppose, innocent of this atrocity, this advertisement which I left last night, upon our return home, at the office of 'Le Monde,' (a paper devoted to the shipping interest, and much sought by sailors,) will bring him to our residence."

He handed me a paper, and I read thus:

> *CAUGHT — In the Bois de Boulogne, early in the morning of the—inst., (the morning of the murder,) a very large, tawny Ourang-Outang of the Bornese species. The owner, (who is ascertained to be a sailor, belonging to a Maltese vessel,) may have the animal again, upon identifying it satisfactorily, and paying a few charges arising from its capture and keeping. Call at No. —, Rue —, Faubourg St. Germain—au troisième.*

"How was it possible," I asked, "that you should know the man to be a sailor, and belonging to a Maltese vessel?"

"I do *not* know it," said Dupin. "I am not *sure* of it. Here, however, is a small piece of ribbon, which from its form, and from its greasy appearance, has evidently been used in tying the hair in one of those long *queues* of which sailors are so fond. Moreover, this knot is one which few besides sailors can tie, and is peculiar to the Maltese. I picked the ribbon up at the foot of the lightning-rod. It could not have belonged to either of the deceased. Now if, after all, I am wrong in my induction from this ribbon, that the Frenchman was a sailor belonging to a Maltese vessel, still I can have done no harm in saying what I did in the advertisement. If I am in error, he will merely suppose that I have been misled by some circumstance into which he will not take the trouble to inquire. But if I am right, a great point is gained. Cognizant although innocent of the murder, the Frenchman will naturally hesitate about replying to the advertisement—about demanding the Ourang-Outang. He will reason thus:—'I am innocent; I am poor; my Ourang-Outang is of great value—to one in my circumstances a fortune of itself—why should I lose it through idle apprehensions of danger? Here it is, within my grasp. It was found in the Bois de Boulogne—at a vast distance from the scene of that butchery. How can it ever be suspected that a brute beast should have done the deed? The police are at fault—they have failed to procure the slightest clue. Should they even trace the animal, it would be impossible to prove me cognizant of the murder, or to implicate me in guilt on account of that cognizance. Above all, *I am known.* The advertiser designates me as the possessor of the beast. I am not sure to what limit his knowledge may extend. Should I avoid claiming a property of so great value, which it is known that I possess, I will render the animal at least, liable to suspicion. It is not my policy to attract attention either to myself or to the beast. I will answer the advertisement, get the Ourang-Outang, and keep it close until this matter has blown over.'"

At this moment we heard a step upon the stairs.

"Be ready," said Dupin, "with your pistols, but neither use them nor show them until at a signal from myself."

The front door of the house had been left open, and the visitor had entered, without ringing, and advanced several steps upon the staircase. Now, however, he seemed to hesitate. Presently we heard him descending. Dupin was moving quickly to the door, when we again heard him coming up. He did not turn back a second time, but stepped up with decision, and rapped at the door of our chamber.

"Come in," said Dupin, in a cheerful and hearty tone.

A man entered. He was a sailor, evidently, a tall, stout, and muscular-looking person, with a certain dare-devil expression of countenance, not altogether unprepossessing. His face, greatly sunburnt, was more than half hidden by whisker and *mustachio.* He had with him a huge oaken cudgel, but appeared to be otherwise unarmed. He bowed awkwardly, and bade us "good evening," in French accents, which, although somewhat

Neufchatelish, were still sufficiently indicative of a Parisian origin.

"Sit down, my friend," said Dupin. "I suppose you have called about the Ourang-Outang. Upon my word, I almost envy you the possession of him; a remarkably fine, and no doubt a very valuable animal. How old do you suppose him to be?"

The sailor drew a long breath, with the air of a man relieved of some intolerable burden, and then replied, in an assured tone:

"I have no way of telling—but he can't be more than four or five years old. Have you got him here?"

"Oh no, we had no conveniences for keeping him here. He is at a livery stable in the Rue Dubourg, just by. You can get him in the morning. Of course you are prepared to identify the property?"

"To be sure I am, sir."

"I shall be sorry to part with him," said Dupin.

"I don't mean that you should be at all this trouble for nothing, sir," said the man. "Couldn't expect it. Am very willing to pay a reward for the finding of the animal—that is to say, any thing in reason."

"Well," replied my friend, "that is all very fair, to be sure. Let me think!—what should I have? Oh! I will tell you. My reward shall be this. You shall give me all the information in your power about these murders in the Rue Morgue."

Dupin said the last words in a very low tone, and very quietly. Just as quietly, too, he walked toward the door, locked it and put the key in his pocket. He then drew a pistol from his bosom and placed it, without the least flurry, upon the table.

The sailor's face flushed up as if he were struggling with suffocation. He started to his feet and grasped his cudgel, but the next moment he fell back into his seat, trembling violently, and with the countenance of death itself. He spoke not a word. I pitied him from the bottom of my heart.

"My friend," said Dupin, in a kind tone, "you are alarming yourself unnecessarily—you are indeed. We mean you no harm whatever. I pledge you the honor of a gentleman, and of a

Frenchman, that we intend you no injury. I perfectly well know that you are innocent of the atrocities in the Rue Morgue. It will not do, however, to deny that you are in some measure implicated in them. From what I have already said, you must know that I have had means of information about this matter—means of which you could never have dreamed. Now the thing stands thus. You have done nothing which you could have avoided—nothing, certainly, which renders you culpable. You were not even guilty of robbery, when you might have robbed with impunity. You have nothing to conceal. You have no reason for concealment. On the other hand, you are bound by every principle of honor to confess all you know. An innocent man is now imprisoned, charged with that crime of which you can point out the perpetrator."

The sailor had recovered his presence of mind, in a great measure, while Dupin uttered these words; but his original boldness of bearing was all gone.

"So help me God," said he, after a brief pause, "I will tell you all I know about this affair;—but I do not expect you to believe one half I say—I would be a fool indeed if I did. Still, I am innocent, and I will make a clean breast if I die for it."

What he stated was, in substance, this. He had lately made a voyage to the Indian Archipelago. A party, of which he formed one, landed at Borneo, and passed into the interior on an excursion of pleasure. Himself and a companion had captured the Ourang-Outang. This companion dying, the animal fell into his own exclusive possession. After great trouble, occasioned by the intractable ferocity of his captive during the home voyage, he at length succeeded in lodging it safely at his own residence in Paris, where, not to attract toward himself the unpleasant curiosity of his neighbors, he kept it carefully secluded, until such time as it should recover from a wound in the foot, received from a splinter on board ship. His ultimate design was to sell it.

Returning home from some sailors' frolic the night, or rather in the morning of the murder, he found the beast occupying his own bed-room, into which it had broken from a closet adjoining, where it had been, as was thought, securely confined. Razor in hand, and fully lathered, it was sitting before a looking-glass, attempting the operation of shaving, in which it had no doubt previously watched its master through the key-hole of the closet. Terrified at the sight of so dangerous a weapon in the possession of an animal so ferocious, and so well able to use it, the man, for some moments, was at a loss what to do. He had been accustomed, however, to quiet the creature, even in its fiercest moods, by the use of a whip, and to this he now resorted. Upon sight of it, the Ourang-Outang sprang at once through the door of the chamber, down the stairs, and thence, through a window, unfortunately open, into the street.

The Frenchman followed in despair; the ape, razor still in hand, occasionally stopping to look back and gesticulate at its pursuer, until the latter had nearly come up with it. It then again made off. In this manner the chase continued for a long time. The streets were profoundly quiet, as it was nearly three o'clock in the morning. In passing down an alley in the rear of the Rue Morgue, the fugitive's attention was arrested by a light gleaming from the open window of Madame L'Espanaye's chamber, in the fourth story of her house. Rushing to the building, it perceived the lightning rod, clambered up with inconceivable agility, grasped the shutter, which was thrown fully back against the wall, and, by its means, swung itself directly upon the headboard of the bed. The whole feat did not occupy a minute. The shutter was kicked open again by the Ourang-Outang as it entered the room.

The sailor, in the meantime, was both rejoiced and perplexed. He had strong hopes of now recapturing the brute, as it could scarcely escape from the trap into which it had ventured, except by the rod, where it might be intercepted as it came down. On the other hand, there was much cause for anxiety as to what it might do in the house. This latter reflection urged the man still to follow the fugitive. A lightning rod is ascended without difficulty, especially by a sailor; but, when he had arrived as high as the window, which lay far to his left, his career was stopped;

the most that he could accomplish was to reach over so as to obtain a glimpse of the interior of the room. At this glimpse he nearly fell from his hold through excess of horror. Now it was that those hideous shrieks arose upon the night, which had startled from slumber the inmates of the Rue Morgue. Madame L'Espanaye and her daughter, habited in their night clothes, had apparently been occupied in arranging some papers in the iron chest already mentioned, which had been wheeled into the middle of the room. It was open, and its contents lay beside it on the floor. The victims must have been sitting with their backs toward the window; and, from the time elapsing between the ingress of the beast and the screams, it seems probable that it was not immediately perceived. The flapping-to of the shutter would naturally have been attributed to the wind.

As the sailor looked in, the gigantic animal had seized Madame L'Espanaye by the hair, (which was loose, as she had been combing it,) and was flourishing the razor about her face, in imitation of the motions of a barber. The daughter lay prostrate and motionless; she had swooned. The screams and struggles of the old lady (during which the hair was torn from her head) had the effect of changing the probably pacific purposes of the Ourang-Outang into those of wrath. With one determined sweep of its muscular arm it nearly severed her head from her body. The sight of blood inflamed its anger into phrenzy. Gnashing its teeth, and flashing fire from its eyes, it flew upon the body of the girl, and imbedded its fearful talons in her throat, retaining its grasp until she expired. Its wandering and wild glances fell at this moment upon the head of the bed, over which the face of its master, rigid with horror, was just discernible. The fury of the beast, who no doubt bore still in mind the dreaded whip, was instantly converted into fear. Conscious of having deserved punishment, it seemed desirous of concealing its bloody deeds, and skipped about the chamber in an agony of nervous agitation; throwing down and breaking the furniture as it moved, and dragging the bed from the bedstead. In conclusion, it seized first the corpse of the daughter, and thrust it up the chimney, as it was found; then that of the old lady, which it immediately hurled through the window headlong.

As the ape approached the casement with its mutilated burden, the sailor shrank aghast to the rod, and, rather gliding than clambering down it, hurried at once home—dreading the consequences of the butchery, and gladly abandoning, in his terror, all solicitude about the fate of the Ourang-Outang. The words heard by the party upon the staircase were the Frenchman's exclamations of horror and affright, commingled with the fiendish jabberings of the brute.

I have scarcely anything to add. The Ourang-Outang must have escaped from the chamber, by the rod, just before the break of the door. It must have closed the window as it passed through it. It was subsequently caught by the owner himself, who obtained for it a very large sum at the *Jardin des Plantes.* Le Don was instantly released, upon our narration of the circumstances (with some comments from Dupin) at the bureau of the Prefect of Police. This functionary, however well disposed to my friend, could not altogether conceal his chagrin at the turn which affairs had taken, and was fain to indulge in a sarcasm or two, about the propriety of every person minding his own business.

"Let him talk," said Dupin, who had not thought it necessary to reply. "Let him discourse; it will ease his conscience, I am satisfied with having defeated him in his own castle. Nevertheless, that he failed in the solution of this mystery, is by no means that matter for wonder which he supposes it; for, in truth, our friend the Prefect is somewhat too cunning to be profound. In his wisdom is no *stamen.* It is all head and no body, like the pictures of the Goddess Laverna, or, at best, all head and shoulders, like a codfish. But he is a good creature after all. I like him especially for one master stroke of cant, by which he has attained his reputation for ingenuity. I mean the way he has '*de nier ce qui est, et d'expliquer ce qui n'est pas.*'" (Rousseau—Nouvelle Heloise.)

Arthur B. Reeve

Arthur B. Reeve (1880-1936) was an American author, journalist, and mystery writer, best known for his detective stories involving the character Craig Kennedy, sometimes referred to as "the American Sherlock Holmes". He wrote 82 short stories involving Kennedy.

Craig Kennedy is a forensic detective who solves crimes using his vast knowledge of chemistry and psychology plus modern (for the time) equipment, such as polygraph tests and seismographs. Kennedy's sidekick was the newspaper reporter Walter Jameson, with whom he collaborated on many cases.

11

THE BLACK HAND

Arthur B. Reeve

KENNEDY AND I HAD BEEN DINING RATHER LATE ONE EVENING AT Luigi's, a little Italian restaurant on the lower West Side. We had known the place well in our student days, and had made a point of visiting it once a month since, in order to keep in practice in the fine art of gracefully handling long shreds of spaghetti. Therefore we did not think it strange when the proprietor himself stopped a moment at our table to greet us. Glancing furtively around at the other diners, mostly Italians, he suddenly leaned over and whispered to Kennedy:

"I have heard of your wonderful detective work, Professor. Could you give a little advice in the case of a friend of mine?"

"Surely, Luigi. What is the case?" asked Craig, leaning back in his chair.

Luigi glanced around again apprehensively and lowered his voice. "Not so loud, sir. When you pay your check, go out, walk around Washington Square, and come in at the private entrance. I'll be waiting in the hall. My friend is dining privately upstairs."

We lingered a while over our chianti, then quietly paid the check and departed.

True to his word, Luigi was waiting for us in the dark hall. With a motion that indicated silence, he led us up the stairs to the second floor, and quickly opened a door into what seemed to be a fair-sized private dining-room. A man was pacing the floor nervously. On a table was some food, untouched. As the door opened I thought he started as if in fear, and I am sure his dark face blanched, if only for an instant. Imagine our surprise at seeing Gennaro, the great tenor, with whom merely to have a speaking acquaintance was to argue oneself famous.

"Oh, it is you, Luigi," he exclaimed in perfect English, rich and mellow. "And who are these gentlemen?"

Luigi merely replied, "Friends," in English also, and then dropped off into a voluble, low-toned explanation in Italian.

I could see, as we waited, that the same idea had flashed over Kennedy's mind as over my own. It was now three or four days since the papers had reported the strange kidnapping of Gennaro's five-year-old daughter Adelina, his only child, and the sending of a demand for ten thousand dollars ransom, signed, as usual, with the mystic Black Hand—a name to conjure with in blackmail and extortion.

As Signor Gennaro advanced toward us, after his short talk with Luigi, almost before the introductions were over, Kennedy anticipated him by saying: "I understand, Signor, before you ask me. I have read all about it in the papers. You want someone to help you catch the criminals who are holding your little girl."

"No, no!" exclaimed Gennaro excitedly. "Not that. I want to get my daughter first. After that, catch them if you can—yes, I should like to have someone do it. But read this first and tell me what you think of it. How should I act to get my little Adelina back without harming a hair of her head?" The famous singer drew from a capacious pocketbook a dirty, crumpled letter, scrawled on cheap paper.

Kennedy translated it quickly. It read:

Honourable sir: Your daughter is in safe hands. But, by the saints, if you give this letter to the police as you did the other, not only she but your family also, someone near to you, will suffer. We will not fail as we did Wednesday. If you want your *daughter back, go yourself, alone and without telling a soul, to Enrico Albano's Saturday night at the twelfth hour. You must provide yourself with $10,000 in bills hidden in Saturday's* Il Progresso Italiano. *In the back room you will see a man sitting alone at a table. He will have a red flower on his coat. You are to say, "A fine opera is 'I Pagliacci.'" If he answers, "Not without Gennaro," lay the newspaper down on the table. He will pick it up, leaving his own, the* Bolletino. *On the third page you will find written the place where your daughter has been left waiting for you. Go immediately and get her. But, by the God, if you have so much as the shadow of the police near Enrico's your daughter will be sent to you in a box that night. Do not fear to come. We pledge our word to deal fairly if you deal fairly. This is a last warning. Lest you shall forget we will show one other sign of our power to-morrow.*

LA MANO NERA.

The end of this letter was decorated with a skull and crossbones, a rough drawing of a dagger thrust through a bleeding heart, a coffin, and, under all, a huge black hand. There was no doubt about the type of letter. It was such as have of late years become increasingly common in all our large cities.

"You have not showed this to the police, I presume?" asked Kennedy.

"Naturally not."

"Are you going Saturday night?"

"I am afraid to go and afraid to stay away," was the reply, and the voice of the fifty-thousand-dollars-a-season tenor was as human as that of a five-dollar-a-week father, for at bottom all men, high or low, are one.

"'We will not fail as we did Wednesday,'" reread Craig. "What does that mean?"

Gennaro fumbled in his pocketbook again, and at last drew forth a typewritten letter bearing the letterhead of the Leslie Laboratories, Incorporated.

"After I received the first threat," explained Gennaro, "my wife and I went from our apartments at the hotel to her father's, the banker Cesare, you know, who lives on Fifth Avenue. I gave the letter to the Italian Squad of the police. The next morning my father-in-law's butler noticed something peculiar about the milk. He barely touched some of it to his tongue, and he has been violently ill ever since. I at once sent the milk to the laboratory of my friend Doctor Leslie to have it analyzed. This letter shows what the household escaped."

"My dear Gennaro," read Kennedy. "The milk submitted to us for examination on the 10th inst. has been carefully analyzed, and I beg to hand you herewith the result:

"Specific gravity 1.036 at 15 degrees Cent.

Water	84.60	per	cent.
Casein	3.49	"	"
Albumin	.56	"	"
Globulin	1.32	"	"
Lactose	5.08	"	"
Ash	.72	"	"
Fat	3.42	"	"
Ricinus	1.19	"	"

"Ricinus is a new and little-known poison derived from the shell of the castor-oil bean. Professor Ehrlich states that one gram of the pure poison will kill 1,500,000 guinea pigs. Ricinus was lately isolated by Professor Robert, of Rostock, but is seldom found except in an impure state, though still very deadly. It surpasses strychnine, prussic acid, and other commonly known drugs. I congratulate you and yours on escaping and shall of course respect your wishes absolutely regarding keeping secret this attempt on your life. Believe me,

"Very sincerely yours,

"C. W. LESLIE."

As Kennedy handed the letter back, he remarked significantly: "I can see very readily why you don't care to have the police figure in your case. It has got quite beyond ordinary police methods."

"And to-morrow, too, they are going to give another sign of their power," groaned Gennaro, sinking into the chair before his untasted food.

"You say you have left your hotel?" inquired Kennedy.

"Yes. My wife insisted that we would be more safely guarded at the residence of her father, the banker. But we are afraid even there since the poison attempt. So I have come here secretly to Luigi, my old friend Luigi, who is preparing food for us, and in a few minutes one of Cesare's automobiles will be here, and I will take the food up to her—sparing no expense or trouble. She is heartbroken. It will kill her, Professor Kennedy, if anything happens to our little Adelina.

"Ah, sir, I am not poor myself. A month's salary at the opera-house, that is what they ask of me. Gladly would I give it, ten thousand dollars—all, if they asked it, of my contract with Signor Cassinelli, the director. But the police—bah!—they are all for catching the villains. What good will it do me if they catch them and my little Adelina is returned to me dead? It is all very well for the Anglo-Saxon to talk of justice and the law, but I am—what you call it?—an emotional Latin. I want my little daughter—and at any cost. Catch the villains afterward—yes. I will pay double then to catch them so that they cannot blackmail me again. Only first I want my daughter back."

"And your father-in-law?"

"My father-in-law, he has been among you long enough to be one of you. He has fought them. He has put up a sign in his banking-house, 'No money paid on threats.' But I say it is foolish. I do not know America as well as he, but I know this: the police never succeed—the ransom is paid without their knowledge, and they very often take the credit. I say, pay first, then I will swear a righteous vendetta—I will bring the dogs to justice with the money yet on them. Only show me how, show me how."

"First of all," replied Kennedy, "I want you to answer one question, truthfully, without reservation, as to a friend. I am your friend, believe me. Is there any person, a relative or acquaintance of yourself or your wife or your father-in-law, whom you even have reason to suspect of being capable of extorting money from you in this way? I needn't say that is the experience of the district attorney's office in the large majority of cases of this so-called Black Hand."

"No," replied the tenor without hesitation. "I know that, and I have thought about it. No, I can think of no one. I know you Americans often speak of the Black Hand as a myth coined originally by a newspaper writer. Perhaps it has no organization. But, Professor Kennedy, to me it is no myth. What if the real Black Hand is any gang of criminals who choose to use that convenient name to extort money? Is it the less real? My daughter is gone!"

"Exactly," agreed Kennedy. "It is not a theory that confronts you. It is a hard, cold fact. I understand that perfectly. What is the address of this Albano's?"

Luigi mentioned a number on Mulberry Street, and Kennedy made a note of it.

"It is a gambling saloon," explained Luigi. "Albano is a Neapolitan, a Camorrista, one of my countrymen of whom I am thoroughly ashamed, Professor Kennedy."

"Do you think this Albano had anything to do with the letter?"

Luigi shrugged his shoulders.

Just then a big limousine was heard outside. Luigi picked up a huge hamper that was placed in a corner of the room and, followed closely by Signor Gennaro, hurried down to it. As the tenor left us he grasped our hands in each of his.

"I have an idea in my mind," said Craig simply. "I will try to think it out in detail to-night. Where can I find you to-morrow?"

"Come to me at the opera-house in the afternoon, or if you want me sooner at Mr. Cesare's residence. Good night, and a thousand thanks to you, Professor Kennedy, and to you, also, Mr. Jameson. I trust you absolutely because Luigi trusts you."

We sat in the little dining-room until we heard the door of the limousine bang shut and the car shoot off with the rattle of the changing gears.

"One more question, Luigi," said Craig as the door opened again. "I have never been on that block in Mulberry Street where this Albano's is. Do you happen to know any of the shopkeepers on it or near it?"

"I have a cousin who has a drug store on the corner below Albano's, on the same side of the street."

"Good! Do you think he would let me use his store for a few minutes Saturday night—of course without any risk to himself?"

"I think I could arrange it."

"Very well. Then to-morrow, say at nine in the morning, I will stop here, and we will all go over to see him. Good night, Luigi, and many thanks for thinking of me in connection with this case. I've enjoyed Signor Gennaro's singing often enough at the opera to want to render him this service, and I'm only too glad to be able to be of service to all honest Italians; that is, if I succeed in carrying out a plan I have in mind."

A little before nine the following day Kennedy and I dropped into Luigi's again. Kennedy was carrying a suitcase which he had taken over from his laboratory to our rooms the night before. Luigi was waiting for us, and without losing a minute we sallied forth.

By means of the tortuous twists of streets in old Greenwich village we came out at last on Bleecker Street and began walking east amid the hurly-burly of races of lower New York. We had not quite reached Mulberry Street when our attention was attracted by a large crowd on one of the busy corners, held back by a cordon of police who were endeavouring to keep the people moving with that burly good nature which the six-foot Irish policeman displays toward the five-foot burden-bearers of southern and eastern Europe who throng New York.

Apparently, we saw, as we edged up into the front of the crowd, here was a building whose whole front had literally been torn off and wrecked. The thick plate-glass of the windows was smashed to a mass of greenish splinters on the sidewalk, while the windows of the upper floors and for several houses down the block in either street were likewise broken. Some thick iron bars which had formerly protected the windows were now bent and twisted. A huge hole yawned in the floor inside the doorway, and peering in we could see the desk and chairs a tangled mass of kindling.

"What's the matter?" I inquired of an officer near me, displaying my reporter's fire-line badge, more for its moral effect than in the hope of getting any real information in these days of enforced silence toward the press.

"Black Hand bomb," was the laconic reply.

"Whew!" I whistled. "Anyone hurt?"

"They don't usually kill anyone, do they?" asked the officer by way of reply to test my acquaintance with such things.

"No," I admitted. "They destroy more property than lives. But did they get anyone this time? This must have been a thoroughly overloaded bomb, I should judge by the looks of things."

"Came pretty close to it. The bank hadn't any more than opened when, bang! went this gas-pipe-and-dynamite thing. Crowd collected before the smoke had fairly cleared. Man who owns the bank was hurt, but not badly. Now come, beat it down to headquarters if you want to find out any more. You'll find it printed on the pink slips—the 'squeal book'—by this tune. 'Gainst the rules for me to talk," he added with a good-natured grin, then to the crowd: "Gwan, now. You're blockin' traffic. Keep movin'."

I turned to Craig and Luigi. Their eyes were riveted on the big gilt sign, half broken, and all askew overhead. It read:

CIRO DI CESARE & CO. BANKERS
NEW YORK, GENOA, NAPLES, ROME, PALERMO

"This is the reminder so that Gennaro and his father-in-law will not forget," I gasped.

"Yes," added Craig, pulling us away, "and Cesare himself is wounded, too. Perhaps that was for putting up the notice refusing to pay. Perhaps not. It's a queer case—they usually set the bombs off at night when no one is around. There must be more back of this than merely to scare Gennaro. It looks to me as if they were after Cesare, too, first by poison, then by dynamite."

We shouldered our way out through the crowd, and went on until we came to Mulberry Street, pulsing with life. Down we went past the little shops, dodging the children, and making way for women with huge bundles of sweat-shop clothing accurately balanced on their heads or hugged up under their capacious capes. Here was just one little colony of the hundreds of thousands of Italians—a population larger than the Italian population of Rome—of whose life the rest of New York knew and cared nothing.

At last we came to Albano's little wine-shop, a dark, evil, malodorous place on the street level of a five-story, alleged "new-law" tenement. Without hesitation Kennedy entered, and we followed, acting the part of a slumming party. There were a few customers at this early hour, men out of employment and an inoffensive-looking lot, though of course they eyed us sharply. Albano himself proved to be a greasy, low-browed fellow who had a sort of cunning look. I could well imagine such a fellow spreading terror in the hearts of simple folk by merely pressing both temples with his thumbs and drawing his long bony forefinger under his throat—the so-called Black Hand sign that has shut up many a witness in the middle of his testimony even in open court.

We pushed through to the low-ceilinged back room, which was empty, and sat down at a table. Over a bottle of Albano's famous California "red ink" we sat silently. Kennedy was making a mental note of the place. In the middle of the ceiling was a single gas-burner with a big reflector over it. In the back wall of the room was a horizontal oblong window, barred, and with a sash that opened like a transom. The tables were dirty and the chairs rickety. The walls were bare and unfinished, with beams innocent of decoration. Altogether it was as unprepossessing a place as I had ever seen.

Apparently satisfied with his scrutiny, Kennedy got up to go, complimenting the proprietor on his wine. I could see that Kennedy had made up his mind as to his course of action.

"How sordid crime really is," he remarked as we walked on down the street. "Look at that place of Albano's. I defy even the police news reporter on the *Star* to find any glamour in that."

Our next stop was at the corner at the little store kept by the cousin of Luigi, who conducted us back of the partition where prescriptions were compounded, and found us chairs.

A hurried explanation from Luigi brought a cloud to the open face of the druggist, as if he hesitated to lay himself and his little fortune open to the blackmailers. Kennedy saw it and interrupted.

"All that I wish to do," he said, "is to put in a little instrument here and use it to-night for a few minutes. Indeed, there will be no risk to you, Vincenzo. Secrecy is what I desire, and no one will ever know about it."

Vincenzo was at length convinced, and Craig opened his suit-case. There was little in it except several coils of insulated wire, some tools, a couple of packages wrapped up, and a couple of pairs of overalls. In a moment Kennedy had donned overalls and was smearing dirt and grease over his face and hands. Under his direction I did the same.

Taking the bag of tools, the wire, and one of the small packages, we went out on the street and then up through the dark and ill-ventilated hall of the tenement. Half-way up a woman stopped us suspiciously.

"Telephone company," said Craig curtly. "Here's permission from the owner of the house to string wires across the roof."

He pulled an old letter out of his pocket, but as it was too dark to read even if the woman had cared to do so, we went on up as he had expected, unmolested. At last we came to the roof, where there were some children at play a couple of houses down from us.

Kennedy began by dropping two strands of wire down to the ground in the back yard behind Vincenzo's shop. Then he proceeded to lay two wires along the edge of the roof.

We had worked only a little while when the children began to collect. However, Kennedy kept right on until we reached the tenement next to that in which Albano's shop was.

"Walter," he whispered, "just get the children away for a minute now."

"Look here, you kids," I yelled, "some of you will fall off if you get so close to the edge of the roof. Keep back."

It had no effect. Apparently they looked not a bit frightened at the dizzy mass of clothes-lines below us.

"Say, is there a candy store on this block?" I asked in desperation.

"Yes, sir," came the chorus.

"Who'll go down and get me a bottle of ginger ale?" I asked.

A chorus of voices and glittering eyes was the answer. They all would. I took a half-dollar from my pocket and gave it to the oldest.

"All right now, hustle along, and divide the change."

With the scamper of many feet they were gone, and we were alone. Kennedy had now reached Albano's, and as soon as the last head had disappeared below the scuttle of the roof he dropped two long strands down into the back yard, as he had done at Vincenzo's.

I started to go back, but he stopped me. "Oh, that will never do," he said. "The kids will see that the wires end here. I must carry them on several houses farther as a blind and trust to luck that they don't see the wires leading down below."

We were several houses down, still putting up wires when the crowd came shouting back, sticky with cheap trust-made candy and black with East Side chocolate. We opened the ginger ale and forced ourselves to drink it so as to excite no suspicion, then a few minutes later descended the stairs of the tenement, coming out just above Albano's.

I was wondering how Kennedy was going to get into Albano's again without exciting suspicion. He solved it neatly.

"Now, Walter, do you think you could stand another dip

into that red ink of Albano's?"

I said I might in the interests of science and justice—not otherwise.

"Well, your face is sufficiently dirty," he commented, "so that with the overalls you don't look very much as you did the first time you went in. I don't think they will recognize you. Do I look pretty good?"

"You look like a coal-heaver on the job," I said. "I can scarcely restrain my admiration."

"All right. Then take this little glass bottle. Go into the back room and order something cheap, in keeping with your looks. Then when you are all alone break the bottle. It is full of gas drippings. Your nose will dictate what to do next. Just tell the proprietor you saw the gas company's wagon on the next block and come up here and tell me."

I entered. There was a sinister-looking man, with a sort of unscrupulous intelligence, writing at a table. As he wrote and puffed at his cigar, I noticed a scar on his face, a deep furrow running from the lobe of his ear to his mouth. That, I knew, was a brand set upon him by the Camorra. I sat and smoked and sipped slowly for several minutes, cursing him inwardly more for his presence than for his evident look of the "*mala vita.*" At last he went out to ask the barkeeper for a stamp.

Quickly I tiptoed over to another corner of the room and ground the little bottle under my heel. Then I resumed my seat. The odor that pervaded the room was sickening.

The sinister-looking man with the scar came in again and sniffed. I sniffed. Then the proprietor came in and sniffed.

"Say," I said in the toughest voice I could assume, "you got a leak. Wait. I seen the gas company wagon on the next block when I came in. I'll get the man."

I dashed out and hurried up the street to the place where Kennedy was waiting impatiently. Rattling his tools, he followed me with apparent reluctance.

As he entered the wine-shop he snorted, after the manner of gasmen, "Where's de leak?"

"You find-a da leak," grunted Albano. "What-a you get-a you pay for? You want-a me do your work?"

"Well, half a dozen o' you wops get out o' here, that's all. D'youse all wanter be blown ter pieces wid dem pipes and cigarettes? Clear out," growled Kennedy.

They retreated precipitately, and Craig hastily opened his bag of tools.

"Quick, Walter, shut the door and hold it," exclaimed Craig, working rapidly. He unwrapped a little package and took out a round, flat disk-like thing of black vulcanized rubber. Jumping up on a table, he fixed it to the top of the reflector over the gas-jet.

"Can you see that from the floor, Walter?" he asked, under his breath.

"No," I replied, "not even when I know it is there."

Then he attached a couple of wires to it and led them across the ceiling toward the window, concealing them carefully by sticking them in the shadow of a beam. At the window he quickly attached the wires to the two that were dangling down from the roof and shoved them around out of sight.

"We'll have to trust that no one sees them," he said. "That's the best I can do at such short notice. I never saw a room so bare as this, anyway. There isn't another place I could put that thing without its being seen."

We gathered up the broken glass of the gas-drippings bottle, and I opened the door.

"It's all right now," said Craig, sauntering out before the bar. "Only de next time you has anyt'ing de matter call de company up. I ain't supposed to do dis wit'out orders, see?"

A moment later I followed, glad to get out of the oppressive atmosphere, and joined him in the back of Vincenzo's drug store, where he was again at work. As there was no back window there, it was quite a job to lead the wires around the outside from the back yard and in at a side window. It was at last done, however, without exciting suspicion, and Kennedy attached them to an oblong box of weathered oak and a pair of specially constructed dry batteries.

"Now," said Craig, as we washed off the stains of work and stowed the overalls back in the suitcase, "that is done to my satisfaction. I can tell Gennaro to go ahead safely now and meet the Black Handers."

From Vincenzo's we walked over toward Center Street, where Kennedy and I left Luigi to return to his restaurant, with instructions to be at Vincenzo's at half-past eleven that night.

We turned into the new police headquarters and went down the long corridor to the Italian Bureau. Kennedy sent in his card to Lieutenant Giuseppe in charge, and we were quickly admitted. The lieutenant was a short, full-faced fleshy Italian, with lightish hair and eyes that were apparently dull, until you suddenly discovered that that was merely a cover to their really restless way of taking in everything and fixing it on his mind, as if on a sensitive plate.

"I want to talk about the Gennaro case," began Craig. "I may add that I have been rather closely associated with Inspector O'Connor of the Central Office on a number of cases, so that I think we can trust each other. Would you mind telling me what you know about it if I promise you that I, too, have something to reveal?"

The lieutenant leaned back and watched Kennedy closely without seeming to do so. "When I was in Italy last year," he replied at length, "I did a good deal of work in tracing up some Camorra suspects. I had a tip about some of them to look up their records—I needn't say where it came from, but it was a good one. Much of the evidence against some of those fellows who are being tried at Viterbo was gathered by the Carabinieri as a result of hints that I was able to give them—clues that were furnished to me here in America from the source I speak of. I suppose there is really no need to conceal it, though. The original tip came from a certain banker here in New York."

"I can guess who it was," nodded Craig.

"Then, as you know, this banker is a fighter. He is the man who organized the White Hand—an organization which is trying to rid the Italian population of the Black Hand. His society had a lot of evidence regarding former members of both the Camorra in Naples and the Mafia in Sicily, as well as the Black Hand gangs in New York, Chicago, and other cities. Well, Cesare, as you know, is Gennaro's father-in-law.

"While I was in Naples looking up the record of a certain criminal I heard of a peculiar murder committed some years ago. There was an honest old music master who apparently lived the quietest and most harmless of lives. But it became known that he was supported by Cesare and had received handsome presents of money from him. The old man was, as you may have guessed, the first music teacher of Gennaro, the man who discovered him. One might have been at a loss to see how he could have an enemy, but there was one who coveted his small fortune. One day he was stabbed and robbed. His murderer ran out into the street, crying out that the poor man had been killed. Naturally a crowd rushed up in a moment, for it was in the middle of the day. Before the injured man could make it understood who had struck him the assassin was down the street and lost in the maze of old Naples where he well knew the houses of his friends who would hide him. The man who is known to have committed that crime—Francesco Paoli—escaped to New York. We are looking for him to-day. He is a clever man, far above the average—son of a doctor in a town a few miles from Naples, went to the university, was expelled for some mad prank—in short, he was the black sheep of the family. Of course over here he is too high-born to work with his hands on a railroad or in a trench, and not educated enough to work at anything else. So he has been preying on his more industrious countrymen—a typical case of a man living by his wits with no visible means of support.

"Now I don't mind telling you in strict confidence," continued the lieutenant, "that it's my theory that old Cesare had seen Paoli here, knew he was wanted for that murder of the old music master, and gave me the tip to look up his record. At any rate, Paoli disappeared right after I returned from Italy, and we haven't been able to locate him since. He must have found out in some way that the tip to look him up had been given by the White Hand. He had been a Camorrista, in Italy, and had many ways of getting information here in America."

He paused, and balanced a piece of cardboard in his hand.

"It is my theory of this case that if we could locate this Paoli we could solve the kidnapping of little Adelina Gennaro very quickly. That's his picture."

Kennedy and I bent over to look at it, and I started in surprise. It was my evil-looking friend with the scar on his cheek.

"Well," said Craig, quietly handing back the card, "whether or not he is the man, I know where we can catch the kidnappers to-night, Lieutenant."

It was Giuseppe's turn to show surprise now.

"With your assistance I'll get this man and the whole gang to-night," explained Craig, rapidly sketching over his plan and concealing just enough to make sure that no matter how anxious the lieutenant was to get the credit he could not spoil the affair by premature interference.

The final arrangement was that four of the best men of the squad were to hide in a vacant store across from Vincenzo's early in the evening, long before anyone was watching. The signal for them to appear was to be the extinguishing of the lights behind the coloured bottles in the druggist's window. A taxicab was to be kept waiting at headquarters at the same time with three other good men ready to start for a given address the moment the alarm was given over the telephone.

We found Gennaro awaiting us with the greatest anxiety at the opera house. The bomb at Cesare's had been the last straw. Gennaro had already drawn from his bank ten crisp one-thousand-dollar bills, and already he had a copy of *Il Progresso* in which he had hidden the money between the sheets.

"Mr. Kennedy," he said, "I am going to meet them to-night. They may kill me. See, I have provided myself with a pistol—I shall fight, too, if necessary for my little Adelina. But if it is only money they want, they shall have it."

"One thing I want to say," began Kennedy.

"No, no, no!" cried the tenor. "I will go—you shall not stop me."

"I don't wish to stop you," Craig reassured him. "But one thing—do exactly as I tell you, and I swear not a hair of the child's head will be injured and we will get the blackmailers, too."

"How?" eagerly asked Gennaro. "What do you want me to do?"

"All I want you to do is to go to Albano's at the appointed time. Sit down in the back room. Get into conversation with them, and, above all, Signor, as soon as you get the copy of the *Bolletino* turn to the third page, pretend not to be able to read the address. Ask the man to read it. Then repeat it after him. Pretend to be overjoyed. Offer to set up wine for the whole crowd. Just a few minutes, that is all I ask, and I will guarantee that you will be the happiest man in New York to-morrow."

Gennaro's eyes filled with tears as he grasped Kennedy's hand. "That is better than having the whole police force back of me," he said. "I shall never forget, never forget."

As we went out Kennedy remarked: "You can't blame them for keeping their troubles to themselves. Here we send a police officer over to Italy to look up the records of some of the worst suspects. He loses his life. Another takes his place. Then after he gets back he is set to work on the mere clerical routine of translating them. One of his associates is reduced in rank. And so what does it all come to? Hundreds of records have become useless because the three years within which the criminals could be deported have elapsed with nothing done. Intelligent, isn't it? I believe it has been established that all but about fifty of seven hundred known Italian suspects are still at large, mostly in this city. And the rest of the Italian population is guarded from them by a squad of police in number scarcely one-thirtieth of the number of known criminals. No, it's our fault if the Black Hand thrives."

We had been standing on the corner of Broadway, waiting for a car.

"Now, Walter, don't forget. Meet me at the Bleecker Street

station of the subway at eleven thirty. I'm off to the university. I have some very important experiments with phosphorescent salts that I want to finish to-day."

"What has that to do with the case?" I asked mystified.

"Nothing," replied Craig. "I didn't say it had. At eleven thirty, don't forget. By George, though, that Paoli must be a clever one—think of his knowing about ricinus. I only heard of it myself recently. Well, here's my car. Good-bye."

Craig swung aboard an Amsterdam Avenue car, leaving me to kill eight nervous hours of my weekly day of rest from the *Star*.

They passed at length, and at precisely the appointed time Kennedy and I met. With suppressed excitement, at least on my part, we walked over to Vincenzo's. At night this section of the city was indeed a black enigma. The lights in the shops where olive oil, fruit, and other things were sold, were winking out one by one; here and there strains of music floated out of wine-shops, and little groups lingered on corners conversing in animated sentences. We passed Albano's on the other side of the street, being careful not to look at it too closely, for several men were hanging idly about—pickets, apparently, with some secret code that would instantly have spread far and wide the news of any alarming action.

At the corner we crossed and looked in Vincenzo's window a moment, casting a furtive glance across the street at the dark empty store where the police must be hiding. Then we went in and casually sauntered back of the partition. Luigi was there already. There were several customers still in the store, however, and therefore we had to sit in silence while Vincenzo quickly finished a prescription and waited on the last one.

At last the doors were locked and the lights lowered, all except those in the windows which were to serve as signals.

"Ten minutes to twelve," said Kennedy, placing the oblong box on the table. "Gennaro will be going in soon. Let us try this machine now and see if it works. If the wires have been cut since we put them up this morning Gennaro will have to take his chances alone."

Kennedy reached over and with a light movement of his forefinger touched a switch.

Instantly a babel of voices filled the store, all talking at once, rapidly and loudly. Here and there we could distinguish a snatch of conversation, a word, a phrase, now and then even a whole sentence above the rest. There was the clink of glasses. I could hear the rattle of dice on a bare table, and an oath. A cork popped. Somebody scratched a match.

We sat bewildered, looking at Kennedy.

"Imagine that you are sitting at a table in Albano's back room," was all he said. "This is what you would be hearing. This is my 'electric ear'—in other words the dictagraph, used, I am told, by the Secret Service of the United States. Wait, in a moment you will hear Gennaro come in. Luigi and Vincenzo, translate what you hear. My knowledge of Italian is pretty rusty."

"Can they hear us?" whispered Luigi in an awestruck whisper.

Craig laughed. "No, not yet. But I have only to touch this other switch, and I could produce an effect in that room that would rival the famous writing on Belshazzar's wall—only it would be a voice from the wall instead of writing."

"They seem to be waiting for someone," said Vincenzo. "I heard somebody say: 'He will be here in a few minutes. Now get out.'"

The babel of voices seemed to calm down as men withdrew from the room. Only one or two were left.

"One of them says the child is all right. She has been left in the back yard," translated Luigi.

"What yard? Did he say?" asked Kennedy.

"No, they just speak of it as the 'yard.'"

"Jameson, go outside in the store to the telephone booth and call up headquarters. Ask them if the automobile is ready, with the men in it."

I rang up, and after a moment the police central answered that everything was right.

"Then tell central to hold the line clear—we mustn't lose a moment. Jameson, you stay in the booth. Vincenzo, you pretend to be working around your window, but not in such a way as to attract attention, for they have men watching the street very carefully. What is it, Luigi?"

"Gennaro is coming. I just heard one of them say, 'Here he comes.'"

Even from the booth I could hear the dictagraph repeating the conversation in the dingy little back room of Albano's, down the street.

"He's ordering a bottle of red wine," murmured Luigi, dancing up and down with excitement.

Vincenzo was so nervous that he knocked a bottle down in the window, and I believe that my heartbeats were almost audible over the telephone which I was holding, for the police operator called me down for asking so many times if all was ready.

"There it is—the signal," cried Craig. "'A fine opera is "I Pagliacci."' Now listen for the answer."

A moment elapsed, then, "Not without Gennaro," came a gruff voice in Italian from the dictagraph.

A silence ensued. It was tense.

"Wait, wait," said a voice which I recognized instantly as Gennaro's. "I cannot read this. What is this, 23½ Prince Street?"

"No, 33½. She has been left in the back yard."

"Jameson," called Craig, "tell them to drive straight to 33½, Prince Street. They will find the girl in the back yard—quick, before the Black-Handers have a chance to go back on their word."

I fairly shouted my orders to the police headquarters. "They're off," came back the answer, and I hung up the receiver.

"What was that?" Craig was asking of Luigi. "I didn't catch it. What did they say?"

"That other voice said to Gennaro, 'Sit down while I count this.'"

"Sh! he's talking again."

"If it is a penny less than ten thousand or I find a mark on the bills I'll call to Enrico, and your daughter will be spirited away again," translated Luigi.

"Now, Gennaro is talking," said Craig. "Good—he is gaining time. He is a trump. I can distinguish that all right. He's asking the gruff-voiced fellow if he will have another bottle of wine. He says he will. Good. They must be at Prince Street now—we'll give them a few minutes more, not too much, for word will be back to Albano's like wildfire, and they will get Gennaro after all. Ah, they are drinking again. What was that, Luigi? The money is all right, he says? Now, Vincenzo, out with the lights!"

A door banged open across the street, and four huge dark figures darted out in the direction of Albano's.

With his finger Kennedy pulled down the other switch and shouted: "Gennaro, this is Kennedy! To the street! *Polizia! Polizia!*"

A scuffle and a cry of surprise followed. A second voice, apparently from the bar, shouted, "Out with the lights, out with the lights!"

Bang! went a pistol, and another.

The dictagraph, which had been all sound a moment before, was as mute as a cigar-box.

"What's the matter?" I asked Kennedy, as he rushed past me.

"They have shot out the lights. My receiving instrument is destroyed. Come on, Jameson; Vincenzo, stay back if you don't want to appear in this."

A short figure rushed by me, faster even than I could go. It was the faithful Luigi.

In front of Albano's an exciting fight was going on. Shots were being fired wildly in the darkness, and heads were popping out of tenement windows on all sides. As Kennedy and I flung ourselves into the crowd we caught a glimpse of Gennaro, with blood streaming from a cut on his shoulder, struggling with a policeman while Luigi vainly was trying to interpose himself between them. A man, held by another policeman, was urging the first officer on. "That's the man," he was crying. "That's the kidnapper. I caught him."

In a moment Kennedy was behind him. "Paoli, you lie. You are the kidnapper. Seize him—he has the money on him. That other is Gennaro himself."

The policeman released the tenor, and both of them seized Paoli. The others were beating at the door, which was being frantically barricaded inside.

Just then a taxicab came swinging up the street. Three men jumped out and added their strength to those who were battering down Albano's barricade.

Gennaro, with a cry, leaped into the taxicab. Over his shoulder I could see a tangled mass of dark brown curls, and a childish voice lisped: "Why didn't you come for me, papa? The bad man told me if I waited in the yard you would come for me. But if I cried he said he would shoot me. And I waited, and waited—"

"There, there, 'Lina, papa's going to take you straight home to mother."

A crash followed as the door yielded, and the famous Paoli gang was in the hands of the law.